"Sweet Mollie, you ~~don't rememb~~

Remember him. As if she could forget. Even now, with him yards away, with his touch a decade past, she could feel his mouth on hers, his palms opened on her breasts.

She banked back her emotions, continuing to squint dumbly. Maybe he'd take her reaction to him as a hint and clear out. "Really, I'm sorry, I—"

"Ten years ago. Spring break. Miami Beach. Your parting words: 'I hope you rot in hell, Tabak.' Well, I expect you got your wish, sweetheart." A half beat's hesitation, a slight lessening of the good ol' boy act. "If you read the *Trib,* you know I spend a lot of time in hell."

Beneath his easy grin, she could see he was only half teasing. He wasn't unaffected by his work. Even ten years ago, objectivity hadn't come easily, a vulnerability Mollie had later tried to dismiss as a put-on for her benefit, another bit of manipulation so Jeremiah Tabak could get his first big story.

Naturally, he took advantage of her moment's puzzlement. "Mind if I come in?"

Books by Carla Neggers

White Hot
Night Scents
Just Before Sunrise
A Rare Chance
Finding You

Published by POCKET BOOKS

CARLA NEGGERS

WHITE HOT

POCKET STAR BOOKS

New York London Toronto Sydney Singapore

This book is a work of fiction. Names, characters, places and
incidents are either the product of the author's imagination or
used fictitiously. Any resemblance to actual events or locales or
persons, living or dead, is entirely coincidental.

An *Original* Publication of POCKET BOOKS

 A Pocket Star Book published by
POCKET BOOKS, a division of Simon & Schuster, Inc.
1230 Avenue of the Americas, New York, NY 10020

Copyright © 1998 by Carla Neggers

ISBN: 0-671-56770-5

First Pocket Books printing July 1998

10 9 8 7 6 5 4 3 2

POCKET STAR BOOKS and colophon are registered trademarks
of Simon & Schuster, Inc.

Front cover illustration by Melody Cassen

Printed in the U. S. A.

For information regarding special discounts for bulk purchases,
please contact Simon & Schuster Special Sales at 1-800-456-6798
or business@simonandschuster.com

This one's for my many wonderful friends in Florida,
especially Heather Graham, Joan Johnston,
Sally Schoeneweiss, Gloria Dale Skinner, Sherryl Woods,
and the members of Florida Romance Writers.
I'll see you by the pool in February!

And special thanks to Caroline Tolley, Lauren McKenna,
and Theresa Zoro of Pocket Books.
What a pleasure it's been. . . .

WHITE HOT

1

Jeremiah Tabak squinted at the scrawny kid sitting across from him at a popular South Beach sidewalk café. "You want me to check out *who?*"

"A woman up in Palm Beach. Her name's Mollie Lavender."

Croc spoke in his usual matter-of-fact, it's-nothing-to-me tone. He claimed to be twenty-four, which was a stretch, and he liked scavenging the streets for information he could bring to Jeremiah, an investigative reporter for the *Miami Tribune.* He would be the first one to admit that Croc occasionally came up with good stuff. But never in his wildest flights of fancy would Jeremiah have imagined Croc, aka Blake Wilder, would come up with Mollie Lavender, the one woman on the planet who had damned good reason to roast his balls on a spit.

Croc had to be talking about another Mollie Lavender. Or maybe he'd somehow learned of Jeremiah's week-long affair ten years ago with a college flute player named Mollie Lavender, down from Boston for spring break, and was pulling his leg.

Jeremiah shifted uncomfortably in his chair at the rickety wooden outdoor table. It was winter in south Florida, and Ocean Drive, famous for its restored Art Deco buildings and jet-setters, was crowded with scantily clad Rollerbladers, trendy Europeans, snowbirds down from Michigan, retirees in sensible shoes, and everything in between, all out to enjoy the beautiful afternoon. Water, sun, sand, pastel-colored ornate buildings. Jeremiah had first bumped into Mollie not too far from here, sitting out on her big beach towel emblazoned with musical notes. She'd had *Saturday Afternoon at the Opera* playing on her radio, and she was wearing a floppy hat and tons of sunscreen because she was fair-skinned and burned easily. She'd left her flute at her hotel. She'd said she felt lost without it, and Jeremiah had fallen for her on the spot.

Ten years was a long time, but some memories stuck. His week with Mollie was one of them.

Croc had to be talking about a different Mollie Lavender.

But he said, "She's living above the garage at some fat opera singer's place up in Palm Beach."

Pascarelli, Jeremiah thought, swearing to himself. Mollie—his Mollie—was the goddaughter of world-famous tenor Leonardo Pascarelli. He owned a house in Palm Beach. She'd declined to stay with him that week ten years ago, she'd said, because she wanted to experience an ordinary college student's spring break. She hadn't, of course. Instead she'd had a fling with a hard-news reporter out for his first front-page story, and had gotten herself burned in a way she'd never imagined.

Not that she'd have had an "ordinary" spring break even if she'd never met Jeremiah. She was not, he recalled, an ordinary twenty-year-old. When he'd ended their affair and packed her off to Boston, she'd tilted her chin, flashed those lovely blue eyes, and said philosophically, "Well, I suppose every woman must have her encounter with a dark and dangerous man."

He'd felt like a rake out of a Victorian novel. Then, less philosophically, she'd called him a lying son of a bitch, and he'd felt better. Lying sons of bitches he could understand. Apparently so could she, because he hadn't heard from her in the ten years since she and her flute and her wounded pride had boarded the plane home to Boston. He sometimes pictured her playing in an orchestra, traveling the world with other people who listened to opera on the beach, teaching young flute students, perhaps cautioning them about falling prey to men like him—but secretly pleased she'd lost her own virginity not to some washed-out tuba player but to her one and only "dark and dangerous man."

Croc slurped his chocolate shake. He'd ordered the same lunch he always ordered when Tabak was buying: chocolate shake, well-done burger with tomato, lettuce, extra pickles and mayonnaise, and well-done steak fries. Yet he remained skinny to the point of emaciation, although Jeremiah had no reason to suspect he was on drugs or even smoked cigarettes. Their only contact was always at Croc's request. He had no permanent address and no regular work, which made it impossible for Jeremiah to reach him on his own.

He did odd jobs: detailing cars, mopping floors, washing dishes, hauling boxes—anything that didn't require a long commitment or extensive contact with the public. No one wanted Croc waiting tables or standing behind a checkout counter.

He sat back in his chair, jittery, which wasn't unusual; he always had a foot or a hand moving. "She's some kind of publicist. She's on her own, not with one of the big firms."

Jeremiah frowned. "A publicist?"

"Yeah. That dog that's in the commercials is one of her clients. You know, the mutt with the attitude? And some ex-astronaut who's taken up jazz piano, and this old geezer who's written a book about his days in vaudeville. I guess he's got pictures of George Burns and guys like that, stuff nobody's ever seen before."

Maybe it was a different Mollie after all. Jeremiah said nothing, watching Croc drag a well-browned fry through a mound of ketchup. "She's got a few regular clients—a couple of upscale music shops, a Renaissance music society. Most of them have something to do with the arts." He wiped his fingers on a napkin. "I guess she's been in town five, six months."

Jeremiah kept his face expressionless. His past relationship with Mollie, he felt sure, would be news to Croc. "If you already know so much about her, why do you need me to check her out?"

Croc lowered his shoulders and glanced surreptitiously at the surrounding tables as if he expected eavesdroppers. A German couple had taken a nearby table and were having coffee, laughing, and two women with four cranky toddlers were making a big production out of dividing up three pieces of key lime pie. Two old men were eating hot dogs at another table. There was a tableful of loud teenagers, and another of a lone woman in a business suit who looked as if she'd been stood up. No one struck Jeremiah as having the least interest in what Croc might have to say.

Finally, he leaned forward and said in a dramatic, conspiratorial whisper, "I think she could be the Gold Coast cat burglar."

Jeremiah nearly spit out his coffee. "The who? Croc, for chrissake, if this is some kind of joke—"

"No, no, man. When have I ever bullshitted you about something this important?"

Jeremiah hissed through his teeth, his control shattered. Sorting out Croc's hard facts and reliable leads from his fantasies and nonsense was a constant challenge, and why Jeremiah, who'd taken off on more than one wild-goose chase at Croc's behest, put up with it was beyond him. He'd first turned up at Jeremiah's desk at the *Miami Tribune* two years ago with a tidbit about an eighteen-year-old selling stolen guns to twelve-year-olds for twenty bucks each. It proved solid, and every few weeks since, he checked in. They'd developed a rapport that Jeremiah, a seasoned journalist, found alternately mystifying and frustrating. He had other sources, but none like Croc. He wasn't a chronic liar or a hopeless paranoid so much as an imaginative kid who engaged in hyperbole and wishful thinking, sometimes blurring the line between reality and fantasy.

"You've heard about the cat burglar, right?" Croc asked.

Jeremiah gritted his teeth. "No."

"Oh." He seemed momentarily taken aback. "I figured you'd be on the story, but maybe it's too . . . I don't know, too mundane for you or something."

"Mundane? Croc, where'd you learn a word like *mundane?*"

"Television." He grinned, his teeth reasonably healthy, if in need of routine dental care. He wore baggy jeans and a threadbare T-shirt, and his scraggly hair had recently been washed. He was just, so far as Jeremiah could tell, a mixed-up kid who lived on the edge and liked to be in the know. "Come on, Tabak, you telling me you haven't heard a word about a jewel thief loose in the land of polo and croquet?"

"Not a word, Croc. So, what jewel thief, and what makes you suspect this Mollie Lavender?"

"Stay with me, okay? I'm onto something here, I can feel it. See, this guy's hit maybe a half-dozen times in the past two weeks—thirteen days, to be precise. We're not talking about your Cary Grant type who sneaks over rooftops and into people's hotel rooms. He—or she—hits right out in the open at dinner parties, charity balls—you know, your high-class gigs. Someone makes a mistake, and next thing, they're out a fifty-thousand-dollar bracelet."

"What kind of mistakes?"

"You take off a piece of expensive jewelry for any reason—it's too heavy, it's got a loose clasp, somebody else is wearing an identical piece—and drop it in a pocket, a handbag, leave it for two seconds, and our thief sees it and takes advantage."

"He's an opportunist," Jeremiah said, interested in spite of himself.

"Exactly. I figure he's netted damned close to a

half-million in jewelry so far, retail value. He's worked as far south as Fort Lauderdale and as far north as Jupiter. That's probably why the police haven't put all the pieces together and figured out they have a clever jewel thief on their hands. Too many departments involved—they just haven't compared notes yet. Once they do, the shit'll hit the fan."

"You're just one step ahead."

"Yep."

"Any evidence this stuff was stolen and not just misplaced?"

"I don't know, I haven't read the police reports. That's where you come in. I don't deal with official-dom, you know? You're between stories, right? I figure you're at a loose end, maybe you can help."

"Croc, listen to me." Jeremiah pushed aside his coffee mug and leaned over the table, the sun warm on his neck. "I find my own stories. I don't work on assignment. And I can't have you running around hunting up stories for me. I won't be responsible for you getting hurt or stepping over the line, be it ethical or legal. You got it?"

"Yeah, sure, no problem." He seemed unoffended by the lecture. "This is just off the record. Friend to friend. Okay?"

Jeremiah wasn't about to agree to any terms. And he didn't consider Croc a friend-to-friend kind of friend, not when he didn't know where he lived and wasn't even sure he knew his real name. He said it was Blake Wilder, but he could have pulled the name out of a James Bond movie for all Jeremiah knew. But he couldn't end it here and walk away, not until he'd heard Croc out. "Tell me about Mollie Lavender's connection."

"Ah." He popped another ketchup-slathered fry into his mouth, looking smug, proud of himself for having survived another Tabak firestorm and pricked Jeremiah's interest. "She's the common denominator. She's been at every gig that's been hit. Every one, from a jazz party in Fort Lauderdale to cocktails with the opera society in Jupiter."

"And how did you get this information?"

He shrugged his bony shoulders. "I have my ways."

"I suppose you've had access to all the guests lists and have checked out every hanger-on and every journalist and every guest who brought someone at the last minute or turned their invitation over to a friend and—"

"Okay." Croc was unruffled. "So she's the only common denominator I've found so far."

Jeremiah sat back, already regretting his outburst. If he thought about it, Croc might wonder why his reporter buddy was getting so upset about what was, in reality, just another weird lunch with an informant. "What's the point here, Croc? Why the interest in this story?"

"It just kind of grabbed my attention. You going to check it out or what?"

"I don't do Gold Coast jewel thieves." Especially if they involved a woman he'd once slept with, something that didn't bear thinking about with Croc's beady eyes on him.

"Then just check into it for me, Tabak. As a favor."

In two years, Jeremiah's twitchy, independent, cagey, young informant had never asked him a favor.

Money wasn't an issue because Jeremiah would never pay for information, but Croc had never so much as asked for a ride across town. Whatever satisfaction he received from providing the occasional useful tidbit to a high-profile Miami reporter was his alone to understand. Croc's main skill was to pull his tidbits, whether useful or ridiculous, seemingly out of thin air. Like Mollie Lavender as jewel thief.

"You've never asked a favor of me, Croc," Jeremiah said, calmer. "Why now?"

"There's something about this thing . . . I don't know . . ." He pushed his plate aside, his food only half eaten, another departure from the norm. "You don't have to write the story, Tabak. I don't care about that. Really. If it's not your thing, fine. Just look into it. You know, you've got sources and access that I don't. You go through the front doors. I go through the garbage."

"You don't have to." Jeremiah spoke quietly, trying to get his sincerity across to a kid who'd probably never had anyone in his life he could trust. "You've got good instincts. If you want a job at the paper, maybe there's something I can do. You'd have to start at the bottom of the ladder—"

"But seeing how I'm in the gutter now, that'd be a step or two up." He grinned suddenly, his gray eyes sparkling with self-deprecating humor. "You get used to the gutter, you know? After a while, you don't fit in anywhere else." He got to his feet, snagging two last fries. "I'll be in touch."

"You don't want to stay for dessert?"

"Nah. Mollie Lavender, Palm Beach. Cary Grant loose on the Gold Coast. You got it?"

Jeremiah might have had a hot knife twisting in his gut. "I've got it."

Eight hours later, Jeremiah sat in his beat-up, disreputable truck, his prize possession, outside the exclusive Greenaway Club in Boca Raton, just south of Palm Beach. His was the only pre-1990 vehicle—never mind the only truck—he'd seen in the last hour. This was the Florida Gold Coast, another world from the one he covered, and lived in, fifty miles to the south.

He had shocked the hell out of the *Miami Tribune*'s gossip columnist when he surfaced in her office looking for information on tonight's goings-on up the coast. A classical dessert concert at the Greenaway had struck him as the most promising for Leonardo Pascarelli's goddaughter and a flute-player-turned-publicist.

He had not explained his interest. Helen Samuel, a million-year-old chain-smoking *Trib* fixture, had winked at him and said, "You don't have to explain, Tabak. I'll find out on my own."

She would, too, which was something Jeremiah refused to think about on the trip north, 95 clogged with tourists and locals enjoying the balmy winter Wednesday evening.

He had his windows rolled down. Orchestral music floated across the manicured lawn of a pink stucco mansion designed by society architect Addison Mizner in 1920 and now the posh Greenaway Club. The soft chords mingled with the sounds of crickets, ocean, and wind, creating a sense of luxury and relaxation that he resisted. This was not the Florida Jeremiah knew. His Florida was the Everglades outpost where he'd grown up with his widowed father, and it was the diverse, pulsing, sometimes violent, sometimes sublime streets of Miami. There were days when he wondered if south Florida should have been declared a national park a hundred years ago, its land left to the birds, the alligators, the panthers, the hurricanes. The bugs.

He had tried parking inside the tall wrought-iron fence. No dice. No ticket, no membership, no tuxedo, no proper press pass. Ugly truck. So, now he was parked outside the fence, enveloped with the smells of salt off the ocean, the palms and banyans and live oak, some particularly sweet, fragrant flower.

If not for Mollie Lavender, he'd be off stalking the criminal and the corrupt or at least home with a beer and a good ball game on the tube.

A dessert concert. Hell, he'd rather watch his turtle eat lettuce.

Which led him back to the main reason he'd told his twenty-year-old flute player he was unethical and not a man she should have trusted. He'd have told her anything she needed to believe in order to go back to her life of classical music and concerts. She couldn't get sucked into his world of crime, corruption, despair, and violence. He knew it, even if she didn't, at least not consciously, not then, at twenty, on her first ordinary spring break. He remembered watching her while she was asleep in her hotel bed and knowing he had only to ask her to stay and she would.

But he hadn't, and she'd returned to Boston, where she belonged.

It hadn't been an amicable parting. He'd let her believe he had deliberately used her to get his first front-page story. It was on drug use and drug dealing among college students on spring break, and it had helped launch his career as an investigative reporter. He had fallen for Mollie accidentally, unintentionally, without motive, while covering the story, not as a way into it. Acting on a tip about where the dealers were selling their stuff, he'd spread his blanket next to hers. At first he hadn't realized she was a college student. Her poise, her intelligence, her sense of humor, and her self-awareness distinguished her from the loud, fun-loving students who'd flocked to the beaches. Lunch led to dinner, and next thing, they were in bed together.

He'd told her he was a reporter, although not any details of the story he was working on. By its conclusion, he'd realized that the drug use and dealing had occurred right in front of her, and she'd been oblivious, not because she was naive, but because she was so intensely focused. Music was her life. Nothing else could get in. He had, for that week. She'd responded hungrily, gobbling up everything she could about him, the passion of sudden romance, the excitement and energy of everything they'd been together for those seven memorable days. But when they ended and she had to go back to her conservatory in Boston, Jeremiah felt an obligation to make sure she did.

Now she'd moved to south Florida, and Croc thought she was a jewel thief.

"It's a strange world," Jeremiah muttered, and climbed out of his truck, restless and not at ease with what he was doing.

He stood on the smooth, unpocked sidewalk, debating his next move. Knee-high impatiens in a half-dozen colors and squat, well-trimmed palms softened the imposing austerity of the iron fence. Inside the fence, strategically placed ground lights illuminated the sprawling lawn with its impeccable landscaping, and royal palms lined the long driveway to the main entrance. He supposed he could find a way inside if he put his mind to it. He received invitations and complimentary tickets to benefits, parties, and every manner of south Florida do on a regular basis. Unless it was a command appearance, he tossed them. He didn't like parties. He didn't like small talk. He didn't like the encroachment of celebrity status onto his role as a serious journalist.

And he didn't know if Mollie was even at this particular party on this particular night. She could be at Leonardo Pascarelli's practicing her flute, or working up copy for her astronaut-turned-pianist client.

He shut his eyes, his gut twisting, his mind flooding with the memory of a sweet, airy tune she'd played after they'd made love their last time, when she'd had no idea what was coming, when he refused even to fathom that what they'd had that week was anything that could last.

Two more minutes, he decided, and he was heading home.

He watched a dark, gleaming Jaguar roll through the gates ahead of the crowd. No, this wasn't his territory. The car stopped, the driver checking for oncoming traffic. He caught the toss of pale blond hair of the woman behind the wheel, then, as she turned in his direction, her face. The mouth, the straight nose, the high cheekbones.

His stomach knotted.

Mollie.

So Croc hadn't been kidding. She was in south Florida.

Jeremiah remembered eyes that were a clear blue with flecks of ice white, intelligent, cool, yet sparkling when she laughed. He stiffened, willing away the sudden surge of regret. Whatever had existed between Mollie and himself had been meant to last only a week.

The Jaguar turned up the street and sped off.

Jeremiah returned to his truck and quickly checked his watch. He would stand there for five minutes before he permitted himself to leave. Otherwise he might run into the Jaguar and be tempted to follow it.

In precisely four minutes and forty-two seconds, a police car arrived with lights flashing and went through the gates of the Greenaway Club.

Jeremiah gave a low whistle. He got on his phone and called the paper, had the desk check into why the Boca Raton police had just arrived at the Greenaway Club. He would hold. He stood outside his truck and waited, impatient, phone stuck to his ear, until he got his answer.

It looked as if a jewel thief had struck a dessert concert at the Greenaway.

"Well, well, well," Jeremiah said under his breath as he tossed the phone back into his truck. "Croc, my friend, you could be on to something."

And whatever it was, Mollie Lavender just could be in the thick of it.

Mollie flung herself out of bed fifteen minutes before her alarm was set to go off at six and staggered to the bathroom in the guest quarters above Leonardo Pascarelli's garage. The master suite all by itself was bigger than her entire apartment in Boston. She splashed her face with cold water and stared at her reflection in the mirror above the sink. Dark circles, puffy eyelids, little red lines in the whites of her eyes. Nope. She wasn't in her twenties anymore.

"Hell's bells," she groaned. "What a night."

She stumbled back into the bedroom, with its warm, soothing colors, and made herself pull on shorts, a tank top, and running shoes. A run along the beach would help put her long night of tossing and turning and bad dreams—very bad dreams—behind her.

She had one nightmare about living in south Florida, even about visiting south Florida, and last night, long before she'd fallen asleep, it had come true.

15

She'd run into Jeremiah Tabak.

Taking deep breaths, she did an abbreviated series of stretches before heading into the kitchen and downing a perfunctory glass of orange juice. She was shaky and jumpy, and she tried to tell herself that Tabak hadn't necessarily seen her leaving the Greenaway or, if he had, recognized her. And it was nuts to think he'd had her staked out. That was pure paranoia, the stuff of 3 A.M. sweats. She and Jeremiah operated in completely different circles and knew virtually no one in common—and why on earth would he care about a new publicist specializing in arts and entertainment?

Damned if he'd care about an ex-lover. He'd need more reason than *that* to track her down.

The first light of morning streamed through the windows of her cheery, honey-colored kitchen, making rational thought at least slightly less elusive than it had been during the night. Then, she'd easily manufactured a dozen reasons—none of them good—why Jeremiah Tabak of the *Miami Tribune* would hunt her down.

She'd left the charity dessert concert early to make several calls to the West Coast and clean up her e-mail. After just five months in business, she had a college intern working for her ten hours a week but still couldn't afford full-time help. That meant she typed, filed, answered the phone, did all the bank and post office runs, swept the floors, and made the coffee—in addition to strategizing, brainstorming, applying her experience and energy on behalf of her clients, all of whom had made a leap of faith in hiring her.

She had, therefore, to be deliberate about her use of time. But spotting Jeremiah at the Greenaway had done her in for the evening. She'd recognized him instantly, her visceral reaction alone enough to convince her she hadn't made a mistake.

"But maybe you *did* make a mistake," she said aloud as she slipped out the kitchen door, in no mood for a run anywhere, except maybe far away. "Maybe it wasn't Tabak you saw."

It could be like her first days in Palm Beach when she'd expected alligators, lizards, and fat, hairy spiders at every turn. Once she'd mistaken the shadow of a passing seagull for a snake. Maybe it was that way with her and the man last night.

Except it wasn't, and she knew it.

She made her way along a brick path to the front of the garage. Leonardo had expected her to use the main house, but it was so big and sprawling she decided she'd feel like a pea rolling around in the bottom of a barrel. The guest quarters were just fine. She'd converted the living room into an office and still had plenty of room to stretch out and feel as if she were living in the lap of luxury, which she was.

Hard to believe, she thought as she punched in the code to open the front gates, that a year ago she was ensconced in her job with the Boston branch of an international communications firm, safe, satisfied, even a little smug. She'd planned on upgrading to a condo and taking a trip to Australia. Then two things happened that caught her by surprise and forced change upon her. First, her thirtieth birthday came and went without fanfare. A non-event. She had dinner with her parents and sister and drinks with a sometime boyfriend, a guy her age just as immersed in the status quo. There was no bow from the universe, no bolt of lightning, no tip of the hat that today she'd turned *thirty*. The next morning she got up and went to work, thirty years old instead of twenty-nine, and that was that.

Second, Leonard Pascarelli blew into town three days later, when she was still trying to sort out why she'd gone into a funk. They cooked dinner together in her apartment—the world-famous tenor, son of a Boston butcher, and his urban, upwardly mobile god-daughter—and he'd drawn her out, urged her to pour out her soul, insisted on it.

She was thirty, she'd said. She had no man in her life she gave a real damn about or who gave a real damn about her. She had a job she loved but didn't absorb her as it once had. She had a great apartment and a nice wardrobe, but so what?

"That's my life," she'd told Leonardo. "A big 'so what?'"

He was a big man, black-haired, clean-shaven, round-faced, with dark, penetrating eyes and a keen intelligence that people often underestimated because of his passionate nature. He loved to eat, drink, fall in love, sing. He seemed to fear nothing—loss, failed relationships, disease, old age, death. Yet his singing betrayed a deep, intuitive understanding of all life offered and all it demanded. He was a complex man who cared very much about other people, even as, in his late fifties, he was alone, without wife or children.

"Is this self-pity I'm hearing from you?" he'd asked without a hint of criticism.

"Just honesty. I can't delude myself anymore."

He'd removed his wooden spoon from his bubbling saucepan and pointed it at her. "What do you want from life, Mollie? Now, at this moment. Don't think, don't hesitate. Just answer."

"Adventure," she said immediately, surprising herself. "Something new and exciting and different. Something that engages my heart, my mind, my *soul*. You know, I always thought I'd be in business for myself by thirty."

"And why aren't you?"

"It's not that easy. I've got a good job. I'd have to give up the security, the benefits. If I fell flat on my face, how would I pay my rent? What would I do for health insurance? There's something to be said for a steady paycheck, you know."

"Ah. If you left this job and found that you didn't want to be out on your own after all, or you failed, you'd never find another job?"

"No, of course not. I'm good at what I do—"

"Then what's stopping you?"

She didn't know. Fear of failure? Fear of success? Inertia? In the end, Leonardo decided she just needed a kick in the pants, and so he offered her use of his Palm Beach house. He was doing a mammoth year-long tour of Europe and Russia and could get to south Florida for only brief spells. He couldn't see leaving the place closed up.

That was Leonardo. Boisterous, generous, egotistical, and unconditionally in Mollie's corner.

"You'll have your adventure and your fresh start," he'd said. "And no overhead."

Mollie had stared at him. "You're asking me to jump off a cliff."

He'd smiled, his dark eyes intense and gleaming. "Then jump."

And so she had, quitting her job, vacating her apartment, and moving south. She printed up business cards and stationery and let her contacts know she'd put up her own shingle in Palm Beach, Florida. It was slow, steady going, but she was making money and establishing a reputation for herself as a creative, inventive, ethical publicist.

Until last night, she'd even thought she might like to stay in south Florida permanently.

With a groan, she set off on her run. The air was still a bit cool and crisp, a perfect day in the making. She headed for the beach. Leonardo had refused to buy a house directly on the water out of deference, he said, to hurricanes. As if living a quarter-mile "inland" would make any difference. But Mollie had learned as a tot not to quarrel with his incomparable logic. In Leonardo's mind, he'd made a prudent decision in choosing his lovely, tasteful home tucked between, rather than on, the Intercoastal Waterway and the Atlantic Ocean. It didn't matter that he could smell salt in the air on his terrace, even hear the waves washing the nearby beaches, or that shorebirds regularly visited his yard.

Mollie jogged along A1A, past resort hotels and condominiums on the water, until her legs were screaming and her mind was clear. It was early enough that traffic was light and the only other pedestrians were fellow runners and a few bleary-eyed couples pushing very awake babies in strollers. She stifled a jolt of loneliness before turning back, jog-walking to Leonardo's, her run having had the cathartic effect she'd hoped it would.

Her shorts and top clung to her, her arms and legs glistening with sweat as she rounded the corner to her street. Leonardo's house wasn't ostentatious or even that big by Palm Beach standards, but its Spanish lines, red tile roof, and lush, tropical landscaping made her feel as if she were living somewhere exotic and deliciously different. Coral bougainvillea dripped from the balcony of the guest quarters. She couldn't begin to afford such luxury herself and meant to enjoy it while she had the chance.

She ducked through the front gates, which she'd left unlocked while out on her run. House-sitting for Leonardo involved learning to deal with his extensive security system, his housekeeper, his gardener, his poolman, his bug man, not to mention neighbors curious about the thirtyish blonde who'd taken up residence above his garage. Mollie was accustomed to managing with three locks on her door in Boston and a primitive intercom system—and no household help.

A few cool-down stretches, she thought, a shower, and breakfast on the terrace by the pool and she'd be ready for her day. If Tabak had been at the Greenaway on her account, he'd have followed her home last night. She felt quite certain he would still be a man of incredible wiles and gall.

An engine rattled on the street, and she glanced up, going still, as if she could somehow camouflage herself, when she saw a brown pick-up paused at the end of Leonardo's driveway.

It had to be the brown truck from last night. Tabak's truck.

A dark-haired man in sunglasses peered across the

seat and out the passenger window, his features not quite distinguishable from where Mollie stood. Unfortunately. No way could he miss her in her sweaty running clothes. Her heart beat wildly. She was breathing hard from her run, but she wasn't so low on blood sugar that she'd be hallucinating. No, it was eight o'clock in the morning, and Jeremiah Tabak was on her doorstep. There was no getting around it.

"Well, well, well. Mollie Lavender." It was his lazy, easy, rural Florida drawl, laid on thick and twangy. She hadn't forgotten it. She hadn't forgotten how it could melt her spine. He grinned at her. "Ain't you a sight for these poor, sore, old eyes."

"Excuse me? May I help you?"

She squinted at him, as if he were a tourist stopping to ask directions to the Breakers. Her profession often required her to think on her feet and be coherent under pressure. If he thought she didn't recognize him, maybe he'd just go on his way.

But, of course, this was Jeremiah Tabak she was dealing with. He climbed out from behind the wheel and studied her over the roof of his truck. Sexy, confident, absolutely convinced she knew who he was. He adjusted his sunglasses, his amusement easy to read even from where she was standing. "Hi, there, darlin'. It's been a while."

Mollie blinked in the bright sun. She'd shoved her own sunglasses up on her head a mile into her run, after they'd slipped down her sweaty nose. She tried to look as if she hadn't thought about him in ten years and couldn't figure out who he was. It might not be an effective strategy, but it was the only one she had. "I'm sorry, do I know you?"

He laughed. No hesitation, no doubt, no guilt. His natural cockiness had to help him do the kind of work he did, sorting through muck and crime and corruption and making people see the tragic complexity of it all, confront the unsettling, contradictory, complicated emotions that clarity brought. He was a good reporter, even if he'd stepped over the ethical line with her.

Not that it mattered. Right now, she'd have given her soul to the devil for something to hurl through his windshield.

He patted his truck roof with the palm of one hand, and she had the uncomfortable feeling he was reading her thoughts. He kept on with the exaggerated drawl. "Sweet Mollie, you're not going to pretend you don't remember me, now, are you?"

Remember him. As if she could forget. Even now, with him yards away, with his touch a decade past, she could feel his mouth on hers, his palms opened on her breasts.

She banked back her emotions, continuing to squint dumbly. Maybe he'd take her reaction to him as a hint and clear out. "Really, I'm sorry, I—"

"Ten years ago. Spring break. Miami Beach. Your parting words: 'I hope you rot in hell, Tabak.' Well, I expect you got your wish, sweetheart." A half beat's hesitation, a slight lessening of the good ol' boy act. "If you read the *Trib*, you know I spend a lot of time in hell."

Beneath his easy grin, she could see he was only half teasing. He wasn't unaffected by his work. Even ten years ago, objectivity hadn't come easily, a vulnerability Mollie had later tried to dismiss as a put-on for her benefit, another bit of manipulation so Jeremiah Tabak could get his first big story.

Naturally, he took advantage of her moment's puzzlement. "Mind if I come in?"

That snapped her back to reality. She gave up the act. "Look, Jeremiah, we haven't had any contact in ten years. Let's just leave it that way, okay?"

"But I want to hire you."

She stared at him. "You want to *what*?"

He walked around the truck, nothing in the way he moved indicating he'd changed one whit. "Hire you. I've decided I need a publicist."

"You?"

"Sure. I've become something of a star reporter these days. I'm inundated with requests for my presence at various functions, speaking engagements, interviews, appearances. It's pretty irritating."

"I would think it would be flattering," Mollie said stiffly.

"That's why you're a publicist and I'm not. I need someone to run interference for me. What do you say?"

"I say you're not serious."

He eyed her, within touching distance now. He was still trim and well-muscled, a flat six feet tall. Mollie tried to ignore the flutter in the pit of her stomach. He wore his near-black hair shorter, but he had the same blade of a nose, the same thin, hard mouth and dangerous sexiness. She didn't need him to take off his sunglasses for her to see his eyes. They, too, would be unchanged, the same mix of grays, greens, and golds that had intrigued and fascinated her right from the start.

She inhaled. "Tabak . . ."

"Ten minutes to make my case," he said.

"You have no case."

He tilted his head back, the corners of his mouth twitching. "Don't trust me, Mollie?"

"With good reason."

"Ah. Then you haven't forgotten me."

She sighed. "All right, I'll give you ten minutes, but only because you'll hound me until I hear you out. *And* I don't want anyone to see us out here arguing."

"No?"

He seemed amused. Mollie could feel her tank top clinging to her in the warm sun. "No one knows about our little week together, Jeremiah. No one. I want to keep it that way."

He wasn't chastened. Not Jeremiah. Their affair hadn't even been a blip on the horizon for him. He had gone on to become one of Miami's most respected, hardest-hitting reporters, just as he'd planned.

"That's good, Mollie." He grinned that slow, lazy, mind-bogglingly sexy grin. "I like being your deep, dark secret."

Mollie raced through her shower while her unwanted guest made himself at home in her kitchen. She quickly pulled on khaki shorts and a white shirt, unconcerned about her professional image because she and Jeremiah weren't going to have a professional relationship. Or any relationship. She was going to hear him out and get rid of him.

She slipped on sandals and pulled her damp hair

back in a clip before sucking in a breath and venturing down the hall. Jeremiah had installed himself on a stool at the breakfast bar and had a pot of coffee brewing. Mollie gave him a brief nod and fetched down two mugs from the honey-colored cabinets.

"Nice place," he said. He wore a close-fitting, dusk-colored shirt, chinos, canvas shoes. Casual, not inexpensive. Deliberate. He was, Mollie remembered with a hot jolt, a very deliberate man. "I suppose it comes in handy having a world-renowned opera singer for a godfather."

"I'm house-sitting for Leonardo."

"Of course."

She bit her lip, wondering why she'd felt the need to justify her acceptance of her godfather's generosity. She was just on edge, she decided, and bound to snap at everything. She filled the two mugs. Jeremiah, she remembered for no reason whatever, took his coffee black. She shoved the mug across the bar to him.

"Is he the reason you moved to south Florida?"

"Jeremiah—"

"I'm just curious," he said.

She sighed. He was naturally curious, and he would pounce if he believed she had anything to hide. Which she didn't. "I was looking for a change, and Leonardo's on tour this year. He offered me use of his house, I accepted, and here I am."

"Why your own business?"

She shrugged, sipping her coffee, trying not to look at his eyes long enough to see if the mix of colors was still so apparent. "I like being my own boss, doing everything from soup to nuts. It's challenging, and it's fun. I don't think I'll stay in Palm Beach after the year's up, but I like south Florida."

Jeremiah drank more of his coffee, studying her with a calm she found faintly irritating. He was an accomplished journalist, she reminded herself. He was accustomed to keeping his emotions under check. But he didn't seem to be suffering any of the shock, self-consciousness, awareness, or simple embarrassment she was at being thrown back together.

"What happened to your flute?" he asked quietly.

She stiffened, not wanting to go down that road. "Nothing. It still plays just fine."

"You didn't join an orchestra after all?"

"Nope."

"Why not?"

"Because I went into communications instead," she said briskly and changed the subject. "How did you find me?"

He didn't answer right away. She could see him calculating just how far he could push her before she chased him out. Finally, he said, "Coincidence. A colleague on the paper happened to mention you. Don't worry," he added with a quick smile, "I didn't let on about our 'past.' She said I might talk to you about publicity. Here for the past ten years I've been picturing you in a concert hall with your flute and a black dress, and it turns out you're a publicist."

Mollie wasn't sure if she detected a note of disdain for her profession or if she was simply being defensive. Jeremiah was hard news all the way. He would consider publicists roadblocks thrown between him and the truth.

"She warned me your client list is a little weird," he said.

"Weird?"

"She said unusual. Same difference."

Mollie set her mug in the sink and regarded him with a cool, measured look. He was lying. Flat out, one hundred percent, no doubt in her mind. The only question was, what was his motive? He would, she knew, have a reason. "So why would a hard-hitting, award-winning investigative journalist like yourself want to join such a list?"

His eyes narrowed on her abruptly, a shock, an almost physical reminder of this man's relentless drive and intensity. Then it was gone, and he sat back, everything about him relaxed and even somewhat amused. "Seems you doubt my sincerity, Miss Mollie."

"And why would I?"

"Because you hold a grudge against me for ten years ago," he said flatly.

"No, because you didn't come here to hire me, you came here because you couldn't stand not to. You saw me last night, and you couldn't resist. You did your reporter thing, found out I'd set up shop as a publicist, and had to see for yourself." She took a breath. "And I haven't thought about you in ten years."

"Ah. Then you don't believe a colleague put me onto you."

"Jeremiah, I want to be there the day, one, you want to hire a publicist, and, two, you find one who'd take you on as a client."

He grinned, entertained. "Think you know me pretty well, don't you?"

"Some lessons I never forget."

The phone rang, and Mollie snatched up the kitchen extension, prepared to get rid of whoever was on the other end. But it was *Boca Raton* magazine returning her call, and she knew she had to take it. She looked at Jeremiah. "This is someone I've been trying to reach for two weeks. I need about two minutes. Would you mind—"

"No problem."

He slid off the stool and headed into the den off the back of the kitchen. It was usually off-limits for business, but she didn't bother directing him to her living room–office. Instead she put him out of her mind and focused on her call. "Hi, I'm so glad you called. I've been—"

The den!

Mollie choked and gripped the phone, calling upon every ounce of professionalism and her limited experience as a performing artist. "Excuse me, something's just come up. I'll call you back in five minutes."

She hung up, steadied herself, and rushed into the den.

She was too late.

Jeremiah glanced back at her from his position in the middle of the room. His eyes gleamed with humor, and his straight mouth twitched. "Haven't thought about me in ten years, have you, Mollie?"

She stood very still. The den was small and cozy, with simple, comfortable furnishings. She'd added a few personal items brought down from Boston: two photo albums, photographs of her family and Leonardo, movie videos, her CD player and CD collection.

And her dartboard.

She'd nailed it to the wall above a rattan chair in the corner. She'd started playing darts shortly after her Miami spring break and first and only fling on the dark and dangerous side. The game relaxed her and helped her process her emotions, even think.

Two weeks ago, something had possessed her—she now couldn't imagine what—to enlarge a black-and-white photo of Jeremiah and staple it to her dartboard. It was a candid shot from a *South Florida* magazine piece on Miami's star reporters. He'd refused to pose for the story, preferring to be the one doing the interviews, not giving them. And he had no patience with celebrity.

"That was just . . . I was just amusing myself." She tried to sound as if she wasn't choking from embarrassment. If he'd changed in any significant way—gained weight, lost some of his intensity, started wearing dopey clothes, *anything*—she might not have felt so exposed. "I was bored one night, and I saw that picture, and . . ." She took a breath, summoning the last shreds of her dignity. "I have no animosity toward you."

"That why most of the darts landed between my eyes?"

She forced a laugh. "I'm a good shot."

He settled back on his heels, glanced again at the dartboard, having a hell of a good time for himself. "I guess I should consider myself lucky you aimed for my forehead." He shifted back to her. "At least most of the time."

"Look, don't go thinking that just because I threw

a few darts at your picture that I've been carrying a torch for you or plotting revenge or even *thinking* about you for the past ten years. I haven't. I saw your picture, and it amused me, and—"

"And you stuck it up on your dartboard."

"Yes. Exactly. You shouldn't feel flattered or insulted."

"What was on your dartboard before me?"

"Nothing. It was just a regular dartboard." She licked her lips, feeling somewhat less self-conscious. "No one comes in here but me. I'd never leave your picture up for company to see."

"Because I'm your deep, dark secret," he said, taking a step toward her.

Before he could come any closer, she gave up trying to explain and charged back into the kitchen. Why had she agreed to let him make his case? He'd never meant to hire her. She'd *known* that. He'd just had to see for himself if she'd gone to pieces after he'd admitted he was a heel who'd used her to get a story and then sent her home to Boston. This little visit was an exercise in male ego. Nothing more.

He rejoined her in the kitchen, and she flew around at him. But before she could get a choked word out, he picked up his sunglasses. She noticed the blunt nails, the dark hairs on his forearms, the taut muscles. And the eyes, probing, assessing. "Coming here was a bad idea, Mollie. I'm sorry if I've upset you."

Her anger went out of her even before it had a chance to take firm hold. She brushed back a strand of hair that had come loose in her mad dash from the den. "You haven't, not really. You never meant to hire me, did you? You just wanted to see what'd become of me?"

"I'm a reporter," he said dryly, heading for the door. "I have an insatiable curiosity. Good seeing you again, Mollie."

"You, too."

He winked. "Maybe I'll see you around sometime."

"Maybe."

The door shut, and he was gone.

Mollie let out a long, slow, cleansing breath and collapsed onto a bar stool. There. She'd survived. The encounter she'd dreaded since agreeing to Leonardo's proposal had come and gone, and here she was, intact, sane, her own curiosity satisfied. As she'd predicted, Jeremiah hadn't changed at all. Not in ten years, not in a million.

And he hadn't figured out the impact he'd had on her life. After their affair, she'd returned home questioning herself, her life, her commitment to music, everything. She could no longer just drift along in currents not of her own making. So she had dropped out of the conservatory and given up her dream of becoming a world-class flutist. She simply didn't have the drive, the talent, the desire. Her week with her dark and dangerous reporter, for all its drama, had forced her to look inside herself and see what was there.

For that, she thought, she couldn't hate him.

For betraying her, she could. He had used her shamelessly to get his first big story, sitting next to her on the beach, inviting her out, even going to bed with her because he thought she had something to do with the drug dealers operating practically at her toes.

She had to admit that from what she'd heard and read about him since her arrival in Florida, such unethical conduct didn't seem to be part of his current modus operandi. But that didn't mean she had to forgive him.

She returned to the den and peeled his picture off her dartboard. It had been stuck with darts so many times it didn't come easily. She crumpled it into a tight ball and charged to the kitchen to toss it immediately into the trash, hesitating at the last moment. She didn't know why.

Muttering to herself, she smoothed out the picture and shoved it into her thick Miami Yellow Pages. Later she'd burn it while she was grilling chicken or roasting marshmallows on her deck. Make a ceremony out of it. A cleansing ritual. Prove to herself that Jeremiah Tabak was well and truly out of her life.

Twenty years old, on her first trip over spring break and just so sure she was in love.

Don't think. Don't remember.

But she couldn't stop herself.

She'd spent previous spring breaks in Boston, playing flute in dingy, windowless, sound-proof practice rooms. That week, she'd indulged in Florida sun and sand . . . and a young, hungry, impossibly sexy reporter. Their relationship was improbable from the start, a future together impossible.

He'd used her to get his drug story, not realizing, until it was too late, that she didn't even smoke or drink, much less use drugs, and barely knew anyone who did. Her life was music. Hours and hours of daily practice alone and in ensembles and orchestra. Classes in music theory, music composition, music history, all in addition to her regular academic classes.

And, of course, there was her family. Her parents were violinists, her older sister a cellist, her godfather a world-famous tenor. Mollie remembered trying to explain the nuances of Lavender family life to Jeremiah in the predawn darkness after they'd made love, when he'd seemed so attentive and empathetic, so certain of himself. The rivalries, prejudices, expectations of classical musicians—their drive and ambition—mystified him. "Your family and friends back in Boston sound like a bunch of flakes to me," he'd pronounced, inoffensively.

They were. They were loving, tolerant, devoted to their work and their families and friends, but not tuned into the world in any conventional way, in the way, Mollie finally realized, that she wanted to be.

She smiled, thinking of them.

After Miami, after Jeremiah, she could no longer pretend she shared their passion for music. She was different. She'd packed up her flute, quit the conservatory, and entered the world of communications, expecting never to see her ex-lover again.

She realized she was trembling. *Damn.* Thirty years old, trembling over a man she'd known for only a week and hadn't seen in a decade. She'd convinced herself Palm Beach was well removed from the world of crime and corruption in which Jeremiah operated, that she needn't worry about running into the *Miami Tribune*'s star investigative reporter.

So why had she?

Why had he been parked outside the Greenaway Club last night?

She frowned, not liking the direction her thoughts were taking. He had to have his share of ex-lovers. Why such curiosity about her?

Jeremiah Tabak, she remembered, didn't do things for personal reasons. Not ten years ago, not now.

And that could mean only one thing: he was on a story.

3

Jeremiah arrived at his desk at the *Miami Tribune* wondering how many women had his picture on their dartboards. He supposed he should have told Mollie the truth about himself ten years ago. But she did seem to enjoy thinking of him as scum.

Which, as far as she was concerned, he was. Twenty was young, but twenty-six wasn't old, and he'd tried to do the honorable thing, even if it had, in retrospect, been awfully damned dumb. Now he had a blonde-haired publicist up in Palm Beach firing darts between his eyes.

"Son," his father liked to tell him, "remember that more than anything else, what a woman wants from a man is the truth."

In his twisted logic, Jeremiah had thought because what he'd told Mollie made him look like a snake, he was off the hook as far as telling the truth. He'd acted honorably, in his estimation, trying to soften the blow of ending their weeklong affair by telling her he'd used her to get his drug-dealing story. The truth was, he'd fallen for her just as hard and fast and incomprehensibly as she had fallen for him. Yet he'd known—and saw it before she did—that they couldn't last.

So he'd lied to her then, just as he'd lied to her two hours ago. Both lies had been expedient. The first, because he'd thought it would be easier to have her hate him than to try to explain the complexities of why they couldn't be together. The second, because he'd thought he could get out of there without a dart somewhere on his person if he let her believe simple, human curiosity had driven him to her doorstep rather than a story.

"God, what a chickenshit," he muttered, hitting the space key on his computer, just to interrupt the image of her trim legs and pale, straight hair, her natural, incongruous elegance, apparent even in her sweaty exercise clothes.

He tried to concentrate on the task at hand, namely ferreting out information on Croc's jewel thief. He was, as his skinny young friend had so accurately pointed out, between stories. In fact, his editor had been urging him to seize the moment and take a vacation, his first in two years. He'd even contemplated where he might go. But it seemed silly to leave south Florida in the dead of winter, and then Croc had approached him with tales of Mollie Lavender as a jewel thief.

Ten years ago, he recalled, trouble had swirled around her, leaving her untouched, like the lone tree standing after a hurricane. Although innocently on spring break and as committed and driven in her life as a musician as he was in his as a journalist, he'd sensed a restlessness of soul and spirit. She was more uncertain and unformed than any twenty-year-old would willingly let anyone know or see, and he'd been drawn to the secret parts of her that she hadn't yet explored or even admitted existed. Ultimately, he'd let her sort through those complexities herself, without him.

Could she have turned into a jewel thief in the meantime?

Possibly. Why the hell not?

But he could also imagine her right there in the thick of things, oblivious.

Yet the woman he'd seen that morning hadn't seemed oblivious or airheaded or anything but sharp, professional, and in control.

Except for that picture of him on her dartboard, of course.

Jeremiah grinned, feeling better. How, he wondered, had Croc landed on her as his chief suspect? There had to be more than his common denominator theory. Croc liked being mysterious and in the know. He wouldn't be above withholding vital information.

Hurling himself to his feet with sudden energy, Jeremiah made his way through the sea of desks and reporters in the big, open *Trib* newsroom and down the corridor to the separate offices of the arts and entertainment and leisure sections. Helen Samuel had her own office, one, because no one could stand her smoking, and, two, because no one could stand *her*. Her abrasiveness aside, she was an old-style gossip columnist who prided herself on knowing what was fair game and what wasn't. A jewel thief on the loose in Palm Beach was right up her alley.

"This is too good, Tabak," she said when he appeared in her doorway. She stuffed out a cigarette in an already overflowing ashtray. "You sucking up to me for information two days in a row is worth a line in my column, except you're too goddamned boring. If you kept company with something besides reptiles, I could work with it." She flashed dark, incisive eyes at him. "You don't sleep with your lizard, do you?"

"Helen, you make most of my informants seem downright respectable."

"They're cockroaches. I'm a professional. Close the door and sit down. I presume you don't want anyone listening in on our conversation?"

"I'm not hiding my interest—"

"Sure you are." She waved a tiny, bony hand. She lied about all her personal stats, but she had to be seventy, she couldn't be over five feet, she weighed at most a hundred pounds, and she prided herself on never having gone "under the knife." Jeremiah couldn't imagine what a face-lift could do for her. Rumor had it she'd looked like Loretta Young in her youth. He couldn't picture it. She pointed at the door. "Shut it. Sit."

Jeremiah shut the door and sat.

Helen tapped another cigarette out of a sequined case. If lung disease or heart disease did her in, she would only say it saved her from a lonely retirement. She'd been declaring she planned to go out of her office on a gurney long before Jeremiah had arrived at the *Trib* eighteen years ago as a college student working part-time. Most of her colleagues thought she'd simply ossify first. One of the janitors swore she didn't go home at night. "She's really a mummy," he liked to tell Jeremiah. "You just think she's alive."

Jeremiah eased back in the ratty vinyl-covered chair. The tiny office reeked of stale smoke. Helen sat with an unlit cigarette expertly tucked between callused forefinger and middle finger. "So," she said with a hint of victory in her hoarse voice, "you're on the cat burglar story."

He grimaced. "I'm just nosing around. I'm supposed to be on vacation."

"I haven't taken a vacation in ten years. Don't believe in 'em. Of course, I can plant my fanny on a cruise ship and call it work. You and me, Tabak, we're not so different." She grinned at his stricken expression. "Ha, scares the shit out of you, doesn't it? This work's either in your blood or it isn't. It's in yours."

"I have a life, Helen."

"Yep, and it's the job. Might as well make your peace with it now, save you a lot of heartache in the future. Don't worry, you won't end up like me." She grinned, a hint, indeed, of Loretta Young in the sparkle of her dark eyes. "You don't smoke."

Jeremiah reined in any impulse to argue with her. He was not like Helen Samuel. He would never be like Helen Samuel. Thirty years from now, he would not be sitting behind a crummy desk in a crummy office talking Gold Coast gossip with a young investigative reporter. He would be . . . what? He didn't know. He didn't have to know. But damned if he'd be an aging, chain-smoking, cynical gossip columnist with a warped sense of humor.

"If you don't object," he said, "I'd like to hear what you know about this jewel thief."

"Know? I don't *know* shit. But I've heard a few things."

She stuck her cigarette in her mouth and fumbled for a lighter as ancient as she was. Jeremiah waited impatiently. When she had the cigarette lit and had taken a deep drag and blown what smoke didn't get sucked into her lungs into his air space and *still* didn't go on, he groaned. "Helen, if you're going to make me beg for every word . . ."

"Beg? You, Tabak? Wait, lemme get a photographer in here. We'll print it on page one."

He glared at her.

She waved her cigarette at him, ash flicking off onto her blotter. "Oh, you love it. Playing the big, bad reporter. Anybody who hasn't been around as long as I have is scared shitless of you. Which means everyone else in the goddamned building. Okay, here's the poop." She laid her cigarette on her ashtray, getting down to business. "So this little bastard's hit eight, ten times in the last couple weeks."

"Seven times in fourteen days, including last night at the Greenaway."

"Yeah, whatever. Facts are your department." She grinned, but he didn't rise to the bait. "Okay. At first, nobody thinks anything. Maybe it's robbery, or maybe it's some daffy socialite who forgot to put on her jewels and would rather cry cat burglar than admit it, or maybe it's an insurance scam. You know, all these baubles are insured. Pretty convenient, if not suspicious, that none of the victims has been hurt or has seen a thing."

"No witnesses?"

"Nope. None that are talking, anyway. It wasn't until the fifth or sixth hit that people starting admitting they've got a problem on their hands."

"The police?"

"They're investigating. The different departments involved are coordinating. I mean, that's what I hear. I make a practice of not talking to the police if I can help it. But the modus operandi for each hit is the same—the guy strikes at parties, not sneaking into an unoccupied home or hotel room like your typical cat burglar, and takes advantage of the least little mistake. I guess people are regarding him as a cat burglar because he hasn't been seen—he's not sticking people up, just slipping into their pockets and handbags unnoticed."

"Bold," Jeremiah said.

"And observant as hell."

"So he must be in a position to watch the crowd without drawing attention."

"He or *she*," Helen amended pointedly.

"You think it's a woman?"

She shrugged, plucking her cigarette from its position on her ashtray, taking a quick drag, and replacing it again, a half-inch of ash dropping into the mound. "Something about this jewel thief's different. Maybe it's gender, I don't know. You were at the Greenaway last night?"

He nodded.

Helen rocked back in her chair, thinking. Jeremiah could imagine her applying her decades of experience with people, with the Gold Coast, with a world, he thought, with which he was largely unfamiliar. "Okay," she said. "We've got a socialite wearing a diamond-encrusted salamander brooch. She notices the clasp is loose and tucks it into the pocket of her Armani jacket and forgets about it. When it gets a little warm, she takes off the jacket and hangs it on the back of her chair. Later in the evening, she puts the jacket on, remembers the brooch, dips her hand into her pocket, and, lo and behold, it's gone. She gets security, they search everywhere, but no salamander."

"That doesn't mean it was stolen."

"Two weeks ago, probably no one would have thought a thing of it. Now, it fits the pattern."

"How much was the brooch worth?"

"Thirty grand. It's covered by insurance."

"Has anyone else come forward who lost jewelry before the last two weeks and now thinks it might have been the work of our thief?"

Helen shook her head, iron-gray wisps dripping out of the mass of bobby pins she used to keep her hair up. "Not yet."

Jeremiah ran the slim set of facts through his mind. "People scared?"

"Not enough to leave their good stuff in the vault."

"Have the police landed on any common denominators?"

"Not that they've shared with me." Her eyes narrowed suddenly, and she leaned across her cluttered desk. "Why? Have you?"

But Jeremiah was already on his feet. If he mentioned Mollie, Helen Samuel would eat him alive. Then she'd eat Mollie alive. She wasn't hard news, but she was a hell of a reporter. "Thanks, Helen. I owe you one."

She snorted. "Yeah, yeah. Put me in your will."

Now that Jeremiah was real to her and no longer a ghost of her misguided past, Mollie hoped her nightmares would subside. She buried herself in client meetings and on the phone until mid-afternoon, then headed down to Leonardo's pool for a long break before tackling another couple hours of work after dinner. Tonight she was staying home. No battered brown pickup for her.

Why, she asked herself for the hundredth time, was Tabak interested in her? What story could he possibly be tracking down that might involve her even in the remotest way? She didn't even know that many people in Palm Beach.

But two she did know called her from the front gate moments after she'd spread her towel on a lounge chair in the shade. She'd brought her portable phone down with her, just in case an important call she wasn't expecting came through. If serendipity struck, she didn't want to miss it.

"Are you lollygagging?" Griffen Welles asked, mock-horrified.

Mollie smiled. She'd met Griffen, an upscale caterer, through Leonardo on a long weekend two years ago, her first real friend in Palm Beach. "Shamelessly."

"There's hope for you yet. Your Yankee soul isn't balking at such decadence?"

"Oh, it's balking. I'm just ignoring it."

"Well, hit the gate code and let us in."

That meant Deegan Tiernay was with her. He was eleven years younger than Griffen, a college senior and the son of Michael Tiernay of Tiernay & Jones Communications in Miami. Instead of doing his internship with his father's prestigious and very large firm, he'd asked Mollie—after meeting her through Griffen—if she'd take him on. She couldn't have made as much progress as she had without his ten-hour-a-week contribution.

She punched in the gate code and settled back in her lounge chair, welcoming their company even if she wasn't entirely comfortable with Griffen and Deegan's relationship. She'd warned herself to remember that Deegan Tiernay at twenty-one was not herself at twenty. And Griffen Welles was no Jeremiah Tabak.

They joined her at the pool, a paradise of sparkling azure water, terra cotta urns of flowers, a curving terrace scattered with enough chairs and small tables for a throng, and adjoining gardens of flowers, decorative palms, citrus trees, and the biggest bird-of-paradise Mollie had ever seen. She could not even imagine taking care of such a yard by herself. That Leonardo's gardener could do it in twice-weekly visits amazed her; she never failed to compliment him, and often watched him from her deck, imagining herself with a house and a yard of her own someday.

Griffen whistled, grinning. "You've got your shoes off and everything. I'm impressed."

"I'm working tonight," Mollie said.

"Of course you are, Ms. Workaholic. I know, I know. One year is all you have before you turn into a pumpkin again."

Mollie laughed, appreciating Griffen's irreverence.

She was thirty-two, tall and lean, her body all angles and taut muscles and long, thin limbs. Her face was more striking than pretty, framed by masses of dark curls. She wore a long sundress in a deep, dark red that added to her exotic good looks. Deegan, in shorts and a polo shirt, looked eleven years younger, but hardly out of his element. He was blonde, athletic, preppy, and soon to come into a sizable trust fund. His maternal grandmother, Diantha Atwood, was a formidable force in Palm Beach society. If she or his parents disapproved of his choice of internship, they were discreet, kind, and supportive on the few occasions Mollie had encountered them. Deegan claimed he'd learn more working with a newbie publicist who had to do everything herself than with his father's firm, where he wouldn't get such diversity of experience. Of course, working with Mollie also conveniently established his own independence and no doubt raised a few eyebrows among the authority figures in his life.

"What about you?" she asked Griffen, who'd immediately kicked off her sandals. "Do you have anything on tonight?"

"A small cocktail party in Boca. Everything's supposed to be low-fat and ultra-fresh."

"Sounds like fun."

"I guess it's a challenge, if I don't dawdle here too long and have to race around like a maniac. Maybe our cat burglar will make an appearance and liven things up."

Mollie sat up straight. "Cat burglar? What cat burglar?"

Deegan squatted down beside the pool, scooping up

stray impatiens blossoms floating on the water. He cocked a grin at Mollie, his eyes a blue somewhere between that of the sky and the pool. "We've got to get you tuned in to Palm Beach gossip. You were at the Greenaway last night. You didn't know a jewel thief struck?"

She could feel the blood draining from her face and thought, *Tabak*. "No. I left early."

"It was in the morning papers," Griffen said. "It wasn't a big headline. The papers are still playing this one safe. But local gossip says we've got a serious cat burglar on the prowl."

Deegan got to his feet, flicking the dead, soaked blossoms into the grass. "He swiped a jewel-encrusted salamander out of Marcie Amerson's Armani jacket pocket last night. Supposedly her insurance company has launched an investigation."

So that was it, Mollie thought, trying to retain her composure. Jeremiah was on this cat burglar story. That explained why he was at the Greenaway last night. And he had tracked her down this morning for the same reasons he had plopped down next to her towel ten years ago: access, information, a way into a world where he didn't belong. Then, it was college students. Now, it was Palm Beach society. In both cases, Mollie was an outsider in a unique position. And oblivious.

"Any leads?" she asked.

"Not that anyone's saying publicly," Deegan said. The jewel thief, however, didn't hold his interest. "Mind if I sneak upstairs a minute? I left a few threads dangling. It'll make work tomorrow easier if I deal with them now. Door's open?"

Griffen frowned. "I've got ten minutes to spare, tops."

"No problem," he said, and blew her a kiss. "Mollie?"

"Door's open," she said, and he took off at a half-trot, his irrepressible energy making her feel enervated. What was she going to do about Tabak?

Nothing, she told herself. She'd already called his bluff. With any luck, he wouldn't be back.

"You look preoccupied," Griffen said. She was at the shallow end of the pool, dipping in her toes. "Perfect. I'm such a baby—I hate cold water. Hey, everything okay?"

"It's just been one of those days." Part of her wanted to tell worldly, savvy Griffen everything, but Mollie had become accustomed to keeping her affair with Jeremiah to herself. It wasn't an easy habit to break. Not even Leonardo, the one person in her life who would understand a mad, doomed affair, knew. Her parents would have understood intellectually, but not in their gut. "Do you really think there's a jewel thief on the loose?"

She shrugged. "Could be. I'm not worried. I only wear costume jewelry and not much of that. I hate having stuff hanging from my neck and earlobes, especially if it's heavy. Gets on my nerves."

"Then our thief's not likely to make you his next target," Mollie said, amused.

"Damned straight."

Griffen had both feet in the water now, standing on the top step with her sundress hiked up to her knees. She was born and raised in south Florida, but not of a wealthy family. Her rise as one of Palm Beach's top caterers was her own doing. She was hard-working, creative, a natural self-promoter, and fun to be around—and scrupulous about the food she served. Mollie felt they were friends as much because of their differences as in spite of them, but she and Griffen shared an entrepreneurial spirit that allowed both to understand the ups and downs of being self-employed. Griffen had simply been at it longer.

Before she aroused her friend's suspicions, Mollie changed the subject. Deegan came down, finally, and they were off.

Suddenly itching to be away herself, Mollie dove into the pool, the water the perfect temperature, enveloping her as she tried to ease an unsettling sense of loneliness and fear of the future, the optimism and daredevil energy of her first months in Palm Beach gone. Seeing Jeremiah again, she knew—stirring up the past, the confusions and hopes and terror of being twenty and not quite sure of her path—had undermined her confidence, worked on her nerves. Her affair with him had been a lesson not only in the appeal and the danger of such a man, but in her own vulnerabilities. She'd never thought herself capable of falling in love almost at first sight, of throwing caution and reason to the wind.

But of course it hadn't been love. It had been infatuation, obsession, hormones, a dip into the kind of life she didn't live. And chose not to live. She didn't do torrid affairs. She wasn't even much of a party girl, not at twenty, not at thirty. She worked hard, but she didn't play hard. Her appearance at the Greenaway last night had been for the music and her work, her need to establish a presence and a reputation in the area—the fun of it was just a pleasant by-product.

It was Jeremiah's work, too, that had led him to the Greenaway. He had staked out last night's party in case the jewel thief showed up. Which he had, the police apparently arriving not long after Mollie had headed home.

She gasped, choking on a mouthful of pool water as she shot to the surface.

Of course.

She leaped out of the pool, wrapped up in her towel, slipped on her flip-flops and stalked upstairs. Before she could think, analyze, or calm down, she'd pulled out the phone book and dialed the *Miami Tribune*'s number. The switchboard put her through to Jeremiah, and finally he answered. "Tabak."

"I don't know anything about your jewel thief," Mollie said, breathless from her swim, her mad dash upstairs, her indignation. "I didn't see anything last night, I didn't *do* anything last night, and I don't know one damned thing. I don't have access to him, I don't have any information about him, I didn't even know he was on the loose until twenty minutes ago."

"You doing anything for dinner?"

"What?"

"I'm in Palm Beach. The call got put through to my truck phone. The miracles of modern technology, eh? I'll be there in two minutes."

He hung up.

Mollie stared at her phone. How had *that* just happened? Given Leonardo's state-of-the-art security, she didn't have to let him in. But she didn't think she could explain two altercations in her driveway with a man in a beat-up brown truck to her neighbors. That left her less than two minutes to get into dry clothes before he arrived on her doorstep.

She raced down the hall, pushing back images of Jeremiah peeling off her wet bathing suit and making love to her at the same time.

"This is not good," she muttered. "Not good at all."

But like ten years ago, she couldn't seem to stop herself.

4

Mollie personally ushered Jeremiah through the gates and almost made him park in Leonardo's garage. She wasn't up to explaining him to any friends and neighbors who happened by, but decided sticking him in the garage would only encourage him to stay longer.

"Hop in," he said through his open window. "We'll walk on the beach and talk."

"You mean *you'll* talk. I have nothing to say."

He gave a curt nod. "Fine."

She eyed him suspiciously. Something had changed. The earlier cockiness and game-playing had disappeared. She wouldn't say he looked guilty, but *something* was different.

"Mollie," he said, "get in. I'd like to say what I have to say on neutral ground."

"You want witnesses?"

He wasn't wearing his sunglasses, and his eyes sparkled, sending a tremor of awareness through her. "Witnesses would be nice."

Neutral ground just might be to her advantage, too, she decided, and went around and climbed up into the passenger seat without a word. He had his phone, steno pads, maps, phone books, pencil stubs, and an array of newspapers and magazines tucked on seat and floor. A Post-it note with "lizard food" scrawled across it was stuck to the glove compartment. Jeremiah saw her staring at it and said, "It's a reminder. There's no lizard food inside."

"I see."

"You spoiled by Pascarelli's Jaguar?"

She attempted a smile, too uptight still to relax. "Not yet. I admit I'm enjoying it."

"Well, this old heap suits me. It doesn't stick out in the neighborhoods where I usually hang out, and I won't lose any sleep if it gets stripped." He backed out into the street, and Mollie pulled on her seatbelt, trying not to dwell on the play of the muscles in his arms, the shape of his hands on the gearshift. "What about the gates?"

"I'll leave them unlocked. I'm sure we won't be long."

He didn't argue, just shifted into first and rolled down the smooth, sunlit road. Mollie sat with her hands fisted on her thighs. If only he'd lost his appeal, she told herself, this wouldn't be so difficult. He wasn't handsome in any traditional sense. He was possibly more cynical, harder-edged. But he was also every bit as edgy and sexy as he'd been when she'd first realized he would be her first lover, and time hadn't tempered her reaction to him. If anything, it was more uncontrollable, more dangerous. She'd had the illusion of her safe world in Boston then. Now, no more. Nothing seemed safe or permanent, which only left her feeling more vulnerable.

"I'm going to have to put your picture back on my dartboard," she said half under her breath.

He grinned over at her, a touch of this morning's irreverence back. "And adjust your aim?"

She didn't answer, just felt herself sinking into her seat high above the road. He drove the short distance to the water and pulled into a narrow parking strip. He got out without comment, and Mollie was still fiddling with her door when he came around and opened it for her. "Watch your step," he said, staying close as she stepped down.

A stiff wind had kicked up off the water, which lay a good fifty yards down a set of wooden stairs and across the width of sandy beach. The lot was almost full, but she and Jeremiah were the only people around. She took a breath, keeping tension and frustration at bay. "We can talk here."

He looked out at the sparkling water, the beach that was only lightly dotted with bright umbrellas, sunbathers, kids running with plastic buckets. "I don't get up here that often. Let's go down by the water."

"Jeremiah—"

"I've got something I need to say, Mollie. I don't want to say it in a parking lot."

"If it's about this jewel thief, it can be said right here."

"It's not."

He walked out ahead of her, leaving her little choice but to follow. They headed down the sand-covered steps to the beach. The wind must have pushed the crowds off the water, but Jeremiah seemed undaunted as he walked across the sand to the ocean's edge. The air was cooler, the wind stiffer, penetrating the light-weight khakis and black henley Mollie had pulled on in haste. She wished she'd brought her windbreaker. She reminded herself she was with a man who'd always lived in this ecologically complex maze of water, land, wildlife, and people. She remembered walking on the beach on a late afternoon such as this, with gulls wheeling in a clear sky as he'd told her about growing up in the Everglades, an only child with a widowed father, his soul as tangled up with exotic birds and tall grasses and mysterious waters as hers was with music.

If he was to be believed. For all she really knew, he'd grown up in Buffalo.

The tide was going out, wide stretches of sand dampened and packed down from the recent influx of water. That was where they walked, leaving footprints. The wind whipped Mollie's hair into tangles, but she had to admit it felt cathartic, as if it were trying to whip some of the anger and confusion out of her.

"Here's the deal, Mollie." He walked steadily beside her, his mind clearly made up to say whatever he'd come to say. "I lied to you ten years ago."

"Yes. We've been over that ground. You wanted your story, and you used me to get it. It happened a long time ago. And I forgave you a long time ago." She smiled. "Sort of."

He didn't smile back. There was a seriousness about him, a weightiness, that hadn't been there this morning. In the harsh late afternoon light, she saw lines at the corners of his eyes she hadn't noticed, either. "I wanted the story," he said, "but I didn't lie to you or use you to get it."

Mollie kept walking, ignoring the catch in her knees. "What do you mean?"

"I mean I thought it would be easier for you if you hated me. So I made up the story about using you."

"Whoa, back up. You're saying you didn't use me for your drug-dealing story?"

"Correct."

"And you thought painting yourself as a morally corrupt journalist who'd bed a twenty-year-old flute player—i.e., me—to get a front-page story would be *easier* on me?"

He nodded, expressionless.

Mollie sputtered, nearly speechless. "Easier than *what?*"

"The truth," he said.

"You mean it gets worse?"

He squinted against the wind and sun, regarding her with infuriating calm. "I guess that depends on your point of view. The truth is I did fall in love with you that week."

"Well, hell," Mollie breathed.

A smile twitched at the corners of his mouth. "But I knew it never could have worked, and so I tried to spare you—spare myself is more like it—by making sure you went back to Boston in high dudgeon over having been used by your first—what was it you called me?"

"A son of a bitch, I believe."

"Your first 'dark and dangerous' man. That was it."

She scowled. "I was young."

"So you were."

"And you were *dumb,* Jeremiah. Good God, what were you thinking? Here you were, caught in this inconvenient, impossible relationship with a Boston flute player, trying to end it as gently as possible—and so you make sure I hate your guts. Boy. *That* makes sense."

Now that he'd said what he'd had to say, he seemed more at ease. The wind gusted, kicking up the surf. Down the beach, a middle-aged couple packed it in for the day. Jeremiah just kept walking, the water lapping almost at his toes. "I was trying to be honorable."

"The truth, Tabak, is honorable. A lie is a lie."

"What can I say? I was twenty-six, I wanted to do the right thing, and now, here we are."

"Yes. Well, no wonder you wanted witnesses."

He smiled, and she thought she saw a flicker of amusement in his eyes, half-closed as they were.

"Did you pine for me?" she asked.

"For weeks."

"Good. Would you have lied to me if I hadn't been a virgin?"

"Mollie, you weren't a virgin when I made the decision to lie—"

"That was at the end of the week. At the beginning of the week, I was a virgin. Did it matter?"

"Of course it mattered, just not in my decision."

"Well," she said, "I know how you men can get all chivalrous and protective and make perfect asses of yourselves when you've realized you're a woman's first lover."

Jeremiah stopped and stared at her. "Mollie, we men didn't sleep with you. I did."

As if she needed the reminder. But she'd brought up the subject. "All right. So I have to adjust my thinking about your journalistic ethics. I'm just not sure how that plays into your visit this morning. You are on this jewel thief story, aren't you?"

"Unofficially. I can't write it now that your name's come up."

She swallowed hard. "How in hell did my name come up?"

"It came to my attention that you've attended every event that the thief's hit so far."

"I'm sure a lot of people have—"

"I don't think so. You're the only common denominator we have right now."

"We?"

He shrugged, some of his natural cockiness returning. "Consider that an editoral *we*. In any case, hearing your name, discovering you were in Palm Beach and a publicist, piqued my curiosity."

"Jeremiah, the last thing I'd want to do is pique the curiosity of a Miami investigative reporter. That it's you just makes it worse. How can I un-pique your curiosity?"

"Tell me what you know," he said.

"I don't know a damned thing. I didn't even realize a jewel thief was on the loose until a few minutes before I called you."

"Oblivious as ever, eh, Mollie?"

"I just don't have a suspicious mind. Plus I've got a lot of work to do," she added, "and I'm new in town. I'm not tapped in."

"You're still an outsider."

"I guess you could say that."

"But because of Leonardo and your work, you have an insider's access. You didn't see or hear anything—you have no reason to believe your name came up as a common denominator except by coincidence?"

She shook her head. She was feeling chilled now, the sand shifting around at the bottoms of her shoes, grinding in between her toes. "None. I'm not a witness, and I'm not a credible suspect. If you want to go back right now and search Leonardo's place from top to bottom for jewels, clues—"

"Mollie, it's way too early to consider you a suspect."

"It's more than too early, Jeremiah, it's nuts."

He paused. "You could be right."

She tightened her hands into fists. "I *am* right!"

"I'm just trying to remain objective." He turned to her, the wind at his back, his mouth a hard line. "Which isn't easy."

Her breath caught at what she saw in his eyes. "Jeremiah . . ."

He took another step closer, and he brought his mouth to hers, said, "In fact, objectivity where you're concerned is downright impossible," and kissed her lightly, softly, as if he'd appeared in one of the countless dreams she'd had about him over the past ten years, elusive, there but not there. He straightened, becoming real, yet somehow also more distant. "We should go."

"I should . . ." She cleared her throat, her insides quivering, burning. "I should take some time to digest what you've told me. I can walk back to Leonardo's."

"You're sure?"

She nodded.

He fished a dog-eared card out of a pocket. "Here's my number at work and at home. If you want to call for any reason, don't hesitate."

She took the card and tucked it into a pocket without looking at it, and he headed off across the sand. She continued along the beach, watching seagulls and children and waves, hearing laughter carried on the wind, and remembering herself at twenty, in love with a man she wanted to believe she knew.

Two hours of four constant, humming lanes of traffic had a strangely calming effect on Jeremiah, and he felt pretty good when he took the causeway to South Beach, a barrier island of eighty blocks, with much more than just the expensive, trendy stretch of renovated Art Deco buildings along the water. His street was a few blocks inland, untouched by celebrities, speculators, and tourists. He found a space in front of his building, which did not have security gates, fancy landscaping, or a pool, and said hello to the handful of bony old retirees sitting out front on lounge chairs, enjoying the warm evening.

He turned down their offers of beer and a whittling knife and took the stairs up to his fourth-floor apartment. One bedroom, one bathroom, a living room, an eat-in kitchen. No maid, no gardener, no high-tech security. The upkeep was minimal, his neighbors were all so deaf they didn't object to his state-of-the-art sound system, and his landlord didn't come by often enough to know about his snake, turtle, and lizard, castoffs from a friend's pet shop. He kept their cages on his kitchen table. He'd found that lizards in the bedroom were a deterrent to romance. He didn't eat in much himself, and only his snake ate the occasional live animal, so it wasn't as if his critters were disgusting on a regular basis. Nevertheless, when he had company, he removed their cages from the table.

It was not the sort of lifestyle he expected the goddaughter of Leonardo Pascarelli to appreciate. Then again, her parents were flakes. Who knew? Maybe all Mollie needed was a place to hang her dartboard.

He checked his voice mail, his eyes glazing over at the polite requests for his presence and expertise at three different functions. Maybe four. He wasn't paying close attention. His had been an unintentional leap to celebrity status, not a calculated one. He'd erase these messages without answering them. He knew it was rude. But rude didn't worry him.

The last message was from Croc. "Tabak? You there or did your lizard eat you for an afternoon snack? I'll call back at eight."

It was quarter of now. Jeremiah got a beer and some spinach from the refrigerator and waited for Croc to call. He sipped the beer, fed his turtle the spinach, and thought about Mollie walking on the beach with the wind in her hair and the sand in her shoes. She hadn't gone to pieces. She hadn't tried to drown him. And when he'd kissed her, she hadn't smacked him one. All in all, things could have gone worse.

He just wished he knew how she'd come to Croc's attention.

When the phone rang, he picked it up on the first ring. "Croc?"

"None other," he said.

"I need a way to reach you." Jeremiah suddenly

felt grouchy. "I can't just sit around waiting for you to call. You have a phone number, an address?"

"I'm calling from a pay phone up in Broward. It's costing me. You got anything?"

"No."

"Shit. I know this Mollie Lavender's hooked into this thing somehow."

"Why her, Croc? Tell me the rest. You've got more, and I know it. Is it something to do with Leonardo Pascarelli, a client, the gardener, someone she pals around with? I'm not playing games with you. I need everything you've got."

"I gave you my best lead."

Best didn't mean only. Jeremiah gripped the phone. "Croc, you'd better not be this damned thief yourself. If you are, I swear to you I'll find out and I'll nail your hide to the wall one inch at a time."

Croc took no offense. "What, you think I wouldn't stick out in Palm Beach? I'm insulted. Keep digging, Tabak. I'll dig on my end. Anything comes up, I'll let you know. Right now, I'm hearing stirrings. I don't like it."

"What kind of stirrings?"

"Just talk. I think this thing could get dangerous."

"Croc, goddamnit—"

"I don't have shit, Tabak. Just feelings. One thing I know for sure is, none of the hot ice has been fenced locally. Not one rock. So our thief's either sending it out or holding on to it." He paused, and Jeremiah pictured him at some rat-hole pay phone, resisted a surge of sympathy for a wasted life. "Any chance you can search Pascarelli's place?"

"Jesus Christ, Croc. No, I can't search Pascarelli's

place. I'm a reporter, not a goddamned burglar. And I'm not a lunatic." Jeremiah went still, eyeing his turtle, thinking. "Croc . . . don't you go trying to search Pascarelli's place yourself. I don't need a loose cannon on my hands."

"Hey, I was just kidding. I know you play by the rules."

"You'd best play by those same rules. You break the law, don't expect me to be landing at your jail cell with bail money."

"A cheap bastard like you? Nah. I wouldn't expect that. Whoops, I'm running out of time. Hate to spend another quarter listening to you spout off. Keep digging, okay?"

"How can I reach you?"

But Croc had hung up, and Jeremiah growled at the phone and hurled it into the kitchen. He went through a lot of phones that way. His lizard stared at him, motionless. His snake slept. His turtle continued to eat his spinach. Jeremiah swore viciously. His gut burned. His head pounded. Whatever calm he'd managed to find en route south had deserted him. Things didn't feel right. He couldn't pinpoint what, or why it was getting to him. Rich people were losing a few baubles to a clever, nonviolent thief. It wasn't dangerous, it wasn't sick, it wasn't controversial or depressing, and he probably shouldn't trust his instincts to work right up in Palm Beach.

He should find a real story or go fishing with his father for a week. He had no business chasing down a jewel thief, especially not on behalf of a street creep who wasn't being straight with him.

But Croc wasn't the problem. Mollie, Jeremiah

knew, was the problem. He'd picked her off a beach filled with college students ten years ago because something about her had grabbed at his soul.

He groaned at his own romantic idiocy. A decade hadn't made him any smarter about her. He grabbed his own whittling knife and went down to join the boys on the porch. Four eighty-plus-year-olds and him. They passed him a cigar and a hunk of wood, and Jeremiah figured it beat driving back up to Palm Beach and sneaking around Leonardo Pascarelli's house just in case his big-eyed ex–flute player ventured out tonight. He could follow her, search her house, or just sit out on the street talking to himself like a damned fool. Best he just sit out with the guys instead and let the night sort itself out.

It wasn't until after eleven that Mollie got the brush of Jeremiah's lips off her mind. She couldn't even characterize it as a real kiss, and yet she'd obsessed on it for *hours*. Work had not served as a distraction. She made her West Coast calls, brainstormed with pad and pen, and spent thirty minutes updating her contacts database. Then she threw darts and, finally, sank into a hot, scented bath. As a means of restoring her universe to some semblance of order, she projected herself five years into the future. She'd have a cute little house, an office, a small staff, talented clients, and a fun man in her life. It wouldn't be Jeremiah. It *couldn't* be Jeremiah, no matter how dark and sexy she still found him.

Jeremiah, she reminded herself, wasn't fun.

When she bundled up in her bathrobe and slid into bed to watch a late-night rerun of *I Love Lucy*, she found herself almost wishing for a Boston winter. Winds howling. Radiators hissing and knocking. Thermometer plummeting. Instead a cool breeze filled the room with the scents of the tropical night and the sounds of the ocean not far off, and crickets chirping madly, dozens of them, as if to remind her she was up above Leonardo's garage, all alone.

The telephone rang, jolting her upright, sending the remote flying out of her hand. She picked up, heart racing wildly.

"Mollie, sweet Mollie," Leonardo Pascarelli crooned.

"Leonardo! Good heavens, you almost gave me a heart attack! Isn't it the crack of dawn or something in Italy?"

"Or something. I've been wandering and pacing in my suite for hours. I sang *La Bohème* tonight." He hummed a few bars of the overture. "Now I'm having a drink on my balcony and unwinding. Did I wake you?"

"No, I'm in my room watching *I Love Lucy*. It's the episode with Lucy and Desi in London and she wants to meet the queen."

"Yes! I remember! And she makes Desi let her perform with him. Ah, those were the days of the great shows. Sometimes," he went on in his wonderful voice that even when not performing resonated in the listener's soul, "I wish I'd stuck to singing in the shower and worked in my father's butcher shop."

"Your father's butcher shop went out of business twenty years ago."

"I could have sold lamb chops in Haymarket Square and sung Desi Arnaz songs to snotty young conservatory students." Mollie could hear him gulping his drink, his melancholy palpable. He had always wanted more—more love, more romance, more acclaim, more everything—and yet wished he didn't, wished the abyss inside him, that he could neither define nor ever fill, would just vanish, even if it took his drive and ambition with it. He sighed heavily. "If Papa could see me now . . ."

"He'd be proud of you, Leonardo."

"I don't know. No wife, no children. I forget even where I am. Florence, Venice?"

"Leonardo, this isn't your first drink, is it?"

"It is. I'm just being mournful because I haven't been to bed yet and I'm alone in the country of my ancestors, and I've just sung Puccini." He cleared his throat, pushing through his dark mood. "But never mind me. Tell me about you, sweet Mollie. How are you? How's your business? How's your life?"

She sank back against the pillows, the room suddenly feeling strange with its warm colors and sprawling bed, its tasteful paintings of flowers and its beautiful blown-glass lamps. Everything in the guest quarters was chosen by an interior decorator because Leonardo had used up his limited patience for decorating in the main house. He didn't care, didn't have time. His world—his abyss—lay inside him, not outside, as much as he tried to find it there. He enjoyed the material success his talent brought him, but ultimately it didn't matter, couldn't help quiet his demons. Mollie smiled, remembering Leonardo and her parents engaging in a loud discussion of a new conductor's interpretation of Mozart as they drank tea from a chipped teapot. It could have been Austrian china or a Kmart special, and none of them would even have noticed.

Mollie knew she could tell Leonardo about Jeremiah and his jewel thief. Her godfather didn't know about her affair and its role in her decision to drop out of the conservatory, but he was no stranger himself to the dark places of the soul found after succumbing to the whims of passion. He sang opera, after all. And he could draw upon personal experience, decades of his own love affairs gone wrong.

But to say out loud to anyone, even this godfather she adored, what had happened between Jeremiah and her ten years ago—what had happened today—was just too risky, too daunting. Once she started, where would she stop? Where would the words take her? She'd practiced self-containment for so long. It was like coming upon long-buried nuclear waste, wondering if it had been down there for enough half-lives to be safe.

So she told Leonardo about business and how Deegan Tiernay was working out, and that she and Griffen were becoming even better friends, and just kept Jeremiah and his jewel thief to herself.

"Oh," she added, "I almost forgot. I'm going to the children's hospital charity ball tomorrow night. Don't you have an ex-girlfriend or someone who left a nice dress in a closet?"

He paused, obviously taking her question seriously. "Upstairs. The pink bedroom. There should be several dresses in your size or close to it. Pick any you want."

"Leonardo, I was just kidding."

"Well, I'm not. What do I need with dresses? There's

jewelry, too. A lovely diamond-and-ruby necklace. Come, Mollie, I can't believe you haven't snooped."

"I'd never search your closets!"

He laughed, his melancholy dissipating. "You're your parents' daughter after all. No curiosity."

"I'm as curious as the next person, just not about what's in your closets. Your mind, yes. Your closets, no."

"I rest my case," he said, and added dryly, "But I'd rather you invaded my closets than my mind."

"I'm not planning to invade either one. Thanks, Leonardo. I don't know, living at your house—" She grinned, feeling better. "I can see myself in diamonds and rubies."

"Then wear them. And enjoy your ball, Cinderella."

5

Jeremiah dug through the rubble on his desk for an invitation to a private party before the children's hospital charity ball that evening. He knew he'd received one. He wasn't organized, but he had a good memory. He picked through scraps of paper, steno pads started and abandoned, computer diskettes, articles ripped from newspapers and magazines, printouts off the Internet, unread memos from the *Trib* brass. He had a tendency to let things that didn't interest him pile up. Periodically he'd decide everything was out of date and sweep it all into his trash can.

Croc's jewel thief just might consider a private party and one of the big charity balls of the season prime targets. Then again, he hadn't hit anything that high-profile. Even if the thief didn't show, Jeremiah figured he could get a sense of how a jewel thief was being received among his potential victims. The papers and police might not be calling the string of stolen and possibly misplaced jewels the work of one thief, but he'd be willing to bet that speculation and rumors were running rampant sixty-five miles to the north.

He wasn't ready to back out totally and abandon Mollie to Croc's devices. He wouldn't write the story, but he damned well wasn't going to leave it to Croc, aka Blake Wilder, aka an elusive pain.

Since he was already invited, he could show up in Palm Beach, in his own truck, without calling attention to himself.

If he could find the goddamned invitation.

Helen Samuel edged up to his desk. He could see the shocked look on the faces of his fellow reporters. Helen made a practice of avoiding the newsroom and disdained the idea of "investigative" reporters. To her, news was news, and a reporter reported it. She was sipping a watermelon-colored health drink with green flecks, the smell of rancid smoke emanating from her bright orange knit suit. Without so much as a good morning, she said, "My spies tell me you're on this jewel thief story for personal reasons."

"Such as?"

"Such as a pretty young publicist from Boston."

Jeremiah tilted back in his chair and regarded her with an equanimity he didn't feel. "You mean Mollie Lavender."

Helen sipped her drink. "I like it when people don't try to bullshit me. You're not going to ask how I got her name?"

"Helen, you own every fly from Cocoa Beach to Key West. I'm surprised I had twenty-four hours before you found out." He paused, considering his options. "Off the record?"

"Sure. What the hell."

Jeremiah debated how much to tell her; there were a lot of things he'd rather have buzzing around him besides Helen Samuel. If he told too much, she'd buzz. If he told too little, she'd really buzz. "I knew Mollie briefly about ten years ago. A source said she's one of the common denominators in this jewel thief story."

"Meaning she was at every party hit," Helen said, staying with him.

"Right. I checked her out, just in case she'd stumbled into something. She's only been in town a few months."

"Five. She set up shop in Leonardo Pascarelli's guest quarters. He dotes on her."

Jeremiah had to allow that Helen Samuel was a formidable force in south Florida. She knew everything about everybody and made up none of it. She just didn't keep much of it secret, either. "I don't think she knows anything about our jewel thief."

"You haven't kept up with her in the past ten years, I take it?"

He didn't avert his gaze. "No."

"Part on good terms?"

"No."

She grinned, leaning toward him. "One day, Tabak, you're going to bump up against a woman who'll like nothing better than to hand you your balls on tongs, and you're going to want her so bad—" She laughed hoarsely. "And when she won't have you, you'll hear half the women in Miami let out a cheer at you finally meeting your match."

"You're assuming I'm the one who did Mollie wrong. Maybe it was the other way around."

She shook her head, confident. "It wasn't."

Jeremiah decided a change of subject was in order. "Well, that's all I've got. You going to this children's hospital ball tonight?"

"I'll pop in. Why? You want to sit at the table with the bigwigs from the paper?"

"I was invited," he said.

She snorted. "Star reporters. Christ, what a business. In the old days—"

He couldn't let her get started on the old days. "I'm more interested in the pre-ball private cocktail party. Our thief hasn't hit any of the big galas. I'm not expecting anything, I'd just like to see what's what at this kind of event."

"A party's a party. You're just angling to see this Mollie Lavender."

"Helen—"

She waved a hand. "Forget it, I'm just jerking your chain. If you can't find your invitation, I wouldn't worry. I expect our illustrious publisher will pull up an extra chair for his star reporter if you show up."

Under ordinary circumstances, it would have to be a command performance before he'd sit at a *Miami Tribune* table at a Palm Beach charity ball, even one benefiting a children's hospital. Even then, he'd shoot himself in the foot first.

"Be tacky to show up at the pre-ball private party and skip the main event," Helen said.

He gave her a deadpan look. "I wouldn't want to do anything tacky."

"You're so full of shit, Tabak. Keep me posted on Mollie Lavender."

She withdrew with her green-flecked pink drink.

Jeremiah debated calling to see about putting a billboard up on 95 saying he'd slept with Mollie, just to get it over with. Or sending an e-mail around the *Trib* staff. *Yes, it's true. I slept with Leonardo Pascarelli's flute-playing goddaughter ten years ago.*

But, in a strange way, he trusted Helen to keep her mouth shut, at least for now.

So he focused on the task at hand, which was finding the damned invitation. He dragged his wastebasket over and dug in with both hands. Because he tended to throw things away prematurely, he didn't deposit organic matter, or allow anyone else to deposit organic matter, in his wastebasket.

Gold lettering? Cream-colored paper?

This story was getting complicated, not from a professional standpoint—he wasn't writing it—but from a social one. One way or the other, by the time his little jewel thief mystery was solved or he gave it up, he figured he was going to end up having to buy a suit.

He spotted the invitation six inches from the bottom. Holding back the rest of the trash with one arm, he fished it out and dropped it onto his desk. Yes, he had one hell of a memory. Cocktails at six in the Starlight Room of the Palm Beach Sands Hotel, then on to the ball.

He sat back, pleased with himself. Then he noticed the fine print.

The gig was black-tie.

There was no way out of it. He was going to have to buy that damned suit. It was two o'clock. That gave him two hours, no more, before he had to hit the interstate north.

"Hell," he said through clenched teeth, and lurched

to his feet. He rushed out in such a way that eyes widened, and he knew his compatriots at the *Trib* thought that Jeremiah Tabak, star investigative reporter, was following up a hot lead, not heading out in search of a suit.

The pink bedroom was where Mollie always stayed when she visited Leonardo, and she knew exactly which dress she wanted to wear. The champagne silk. She'd tried it on two years ago on a visit and already knew it fit. She brought over shoes, stockings, makeup, hairpins, and three possible pairs of earrings and necklaces and spread them out on the big, canopied bed. Dressing in Leonardo's house was almost as good as having him with her. His gaudy, eclectic taste permeated every room, making his presence almost palpable. She knew he would try to get her to wear the fiery red dress. She'd feel like a hooker, or a doomed heroine from one of his favorite operas.

The champagne dress was perfect. Simple lines, a not-too-low neck. And she had shoes to go with it.

She admired herself in a gilt-edged three-way mirror in the huge, spotless pink bathroom. Yep. Perfect. A pity she had to do her own makeup and hair.

It took three tries with her hair, but finally she had it up and staying put. The makeup was easier. With such a pale dress, a soft touch worked fine.

But none of her earrings and necklaces worked at all.

She frowned, already knowing she was tempted. She'd been tempted the second Leonardo had made his offer.

She didn't quite remember the story of the diamond-

and-ruby necklace. It was dramatic, wrenching, and involved at least two women, both of whom still claimed to love and adore Leonardo. He had two locked, alarm-equipped closets for his valuables, but he left the necklace in a velvet box in the top drawer of the tall dresser in the pink bedroom, exactly where a cat burglar would look, as if he were setting up the fitting end to its story of woe.

"Only you, Leonardo," Mollie muttered, and dug out the velvet box.

The necklace was even prettier than she remembered. A cluster of diamonds and rubies on a mid-length, thin gold chain. Not as ostentatious as it could have been, true, but nothing she'd ever buy for herself. She tried it on. The pendant licked the top edge of her bodice. It was irresistible.

And if Leonardo had one role in her life, it was to tell her not to resist.

She wouldn't even bother with earrings. The necklace was enough. Feeling decadent, glamorous, a little like Cinderella off to her ball, Mollie locked up and headed out to Leonardo's Jaguar. Chet Farnsworth, her astronaut-turned-jazz-pianist client, and his wife had invited her to sit with them at their table at the ball. Diantha Atwood, Deegan's grandmother, had invited her to her annual pre-ball cocktail party. Actually, Mollie assumed Deegan had put her up to it.

The Palm Beach Sands Hotel was, appropriately, on the water, a sprawling resort of beach, tennis courts, pools, golf course, glittering elegance, and everything else anyone weary of a northern winter could want in a Florida vacation. Mollie left her car with a valet and found her way to the mezzanine level and the Starlight

Room. As princess-like as she felt, she realized she wouldn't have cared if she'd shown up in the reliable, classic black dress she'd worn to formals for the past five years. Her parents' influence, she supposed.

"Well, well." Jeremiah's voice, low, deliberate, and close. "Tempting our jewel thief, I see."

She spun around, almost landing on top of him. He was as dark and devastating in black-tie as he was in chinos, and it was all she could do to keep herself from gasping. "You mean this?" She fingered the teardrop-shaped cluster of diamond and rubies. "I borrowed it from Leonardo on a whim. I don't even know if it's real."

"Uh-huh." He laid on the drawl, and out of the corner of her eye, she could see guests coming up the escalators, recognizing him, raising eyebrows. Jeremiah, however, had his own gaze pinned on her. "But you knew it'd be a temptation."

"That's silly. It has a firm clasp, and I assure you, it's not leaving my neck until I put it back in its little velvet box." She tried to ignore the flicker of awareness in his eyes, the hot jolt of the memory of him removing a necklace from her neck one warm winter night. "I didn't realize you'd be here tonight."

"Neither did I." He relaxed only slightly. "I've owned this suit for three whole hours. Bennie hemmed it for me. He's a retired tailor in my building, claims he hemmed suits for every mayor of New York from the Depression through the opening of the new Yankee Stadium. But," he added, "don't let me keep you if you're meeting someone."

Her only someone was a retired astronaut with a crew cut and a special talent for jazz, and not until the ball.

She wished, suddenly and fervently, that she'd scrounged up a date for the evening, just to throw Tabak off. Because he knew damned well there was no man in her life.

"You're not keeping me," she said tightly. "But perhaps we should go in and mingle before people start wondering if there's more between us than meets the eye."

He leaned toward her, half-whispered, "There is, darlin'. Lots more."

"There was. There isn't anymore. And you, Jeremiah, have more outright audacity than anyone I've ever known. Now, if you'll excuse me." She started off, stopped, and turned back. "Oh, and enjoy hunting your thief tonight. I know that's why you're here."

He withdrew a gold-on-cream invitation from his dinner jacket. "I was invited."

With an unprincess-like snort, Mollie whirled back around and gave her own invitation to a man posted at the door to the Starlight Room. Inside, Diantha Atwood's party was in full swing. Guests wandered among a dozen small hors d'oeuvres tables and an open bar, waiters carried trays of champagne, and a harpist plucked out a pretty, soothing melody. Huge windows overlooked an ocean so calm as to be lakelike, mirroring the cloudless sky and drawing strollers to its beaches.

Mollie swept a glass of champagne from a tray and smiled pleasantly at people she didn't know. Her parents would have found somewhere to sit and listen to the harpist, dissecting the music, unaware that anyone might consider them rude or eccentric. As she sipped her champagne, Mollie suddenly felt as if she were caught between two identities, each vying for her submission. The musicians' daughter who hovered on the fringes of a world she'd given up, and the successful young Palm Beach entrepreneur who couldn't afford her own designer dresses and expensive jewelry.

Except she was neither, and Jeremiah's presence seemed to accentuate that awareness of who she was, and wasn't, and didn't want to be.

She could sense his eyes on her. She resisted the urge to guzzle her champagne. She already felt a little dizzy, a little out of control, a little too aware of the hard, impossible man across the room, watching her, not giving a damn that he was distracting her and making her drink her champagne too fast.

Finally, she couldn't stand it any longer and marched over to him. "You've your nerve, you know, Tabak?"

He laughed, unembarrassed. "A necessary evil of the profession. No nerve, no story. Enjoying yourself?"

"Not with you watching me like a hawk."

"You noticed? I thought I was being subtle." Even he didn't believe subtlety was in his bag of tricks. "Planning on getting used to Leonardo Pascarelli's lifestyle? Borrowing his ex-girlfriend's jewelry, driving his car, living in his house, getting invited to his parties."

"Leonardo didn't get me invited tonight. I happen to know Mrs. Atwood myself. And I wouldn't care if I weren't invited." She swallowed more champagne, a mistake. "And if you must know, I'd prefer to have my own little car and my own little house somewhere. Just because I'm Leonardo Pascarelli's goddaughter doesn't mean—" She stopped abruptly, fingers tensing on her glass as she digested Jeremiah's real meaning. "You think I could be the jewel thief!"

"Do I?"

She kept her voice to a low hiss, out of range of any of Palm Beach's notorious gossipmongers. "I won't be able to afford my current lifestyle in another seven months. Ergo, I could lower myself to stealing. *That's* what you think."

He shrugged, calm, unrepentant. "Interesting theory."

"It's not interesting, it's ridiculous. Damn you, Jeremiah, I'm no jewel thief!"

"If you are," he said in that deep, rough, exaggerated drawl, "it sure will be fun catching you."

Before she could respond, Griffen and Deegan cruised up. Mollie hadn't seen them arrive and wondered how much of her exchange with Jeremiah they'd witnessed. She saw amusement dance in his eyes, the light of the chandeliers bringing out the flecks of gold. She turned to her intern and friend. "My, don't you both look dashing tonight."

They did, Griffen in a sparkling white dress that accentuated her dark curls and angular figure, Deegan in black-tie, looking not older than twenty-one, but, somehow, younger. Mollie quickly introduced them to Jeremiah, trying to sound as if she'd just met the Miami reporter herself. "We were just chatting," she added inadequately when she noticed the spark of curiosity in Griffen's dark eyes. "Are you two staying for the ball?"

"Oh, no," Griffen said. "We're just making an appearance to please Granny."

Deegan grinned at her irreverence, and Mollie explained to Jeremiah that Diantha Atwood, Palm Beach widow and hostess *extraordinaire*, was Deegan's grandmother. "His parents," she added, "are Michael and Bobbi Tiernay who are . . . where?"

"Right behind you," Griffen whispered, nudging her with her elbow.

And Deegan's grandmother with them. Just what I need, Mollie thought, noticing that Jeremiah was showing no sign of removing himself to the bar or anywhere else. Michael Tiernay, a trim, gray-haired, pleasant man, was drinking a martini, his wife hanging on his arm. Her son had inherited his looks from her. She was a striking, golden-eyed woman, wearing a tasteful dress and spectacular jewelry. Diantha Atwood, Bobbi's mother, was even smaller and thinner, her blondish hair swept into an elegant, timeless style. She'd had various lifts and tucks and wore understated cosmetics, but there was no mistaking the high price and authenticity of the jewelry she wore. Setting the tone, no doubt, for others not to be intimidated by a potential cat burglar in their midst.

"Jeremiah Tabak," Diantha Atwood said, sparing Mollie the need to make introductions. She smiled, playing the hostess game to the hilt. "What a coup to have you here tonight."

"Sorry I didn't RSVP."

It was a crack, and Diantha knew it. "I'd never expect a reporter to let me know anything, Mr. Tabak. I see you've met my daughter and her husband, and my grandson, Deegan. Deegan, darling, how are you?" She offered her cheek, and he gave her a quick peck, squeezing her hand. "And Griffen. How nice to see you. I'm surprised you have an evening free at this time of year."

"I kept it free," Griffen replied, no hint of sarcasm in her tone. She believed—and Mollie suspected she was right—that neither Deegan's parents nor his grandmother approved of her relationship with their son and grandson. But they'd never openly voice such disapproval.

Bobbi Tiernay turned to Jeremiah, whose eyes looked about to glaze over. "Griffen is a caterer much in demand."

"Mollie," Diantha Atwood continued smoothly, "I didn't see you. Don't you look lovely tonight."

Mollie was half-tempted to tell her where she'd gotten her outfit; from the sudden humor in Jeremiah's expression, she guessed he knew what she was thinking. She smiled politely. "Thank you."

"How's business?" Michael Tiernay asked cheerfully, apparently oblivious, or simply choosing to ignore, the frosty undertones of the conversation.

Relieved to have the distraction, Mollie engaged him in a pleasant conversation about business. That he conducted his from a glass building in Boca Raton and she conducted hers from the living room of Leonardo's guest quarters made no difference to her, nor, it seemed, to him. They dragged Deegan into the conversation, but he wasn't the least bit awkward talking shop with his father. Mollie was well aware that Michael Tiernay considered his son's choice of internship something of a rebellion, and maybe it was. Maybe, when he finished his semester with her, Deegan would return to the fold and take his place at Tiernay & Jones. But that didn't mean either Tiernay disrespected the work she did. She might be a small fish, but they swam in the same pond.

And Jeremiah, she noticed, drifted to the bar with Griffen on his heels. She would seize any excuse to make her exit from her boyfriend's family, not to mention check out a man she'd caught talking to her friend, the new girl in town. Mollie felt a faint stab of uneasiness. It wasn't beyond Tabak to grill Griffen about her friend the publicist, who wore borrowed dresses to attend fancy parties and just might be bored or desperate enough to help herself to other people's jewels.

Damn him, she thought. He didn't really believe she was his jewel thief. He was just throwing her off—or letting her throw herself off—for the hell of it, in case she started encroaching on his turf.

She remembered their tantalizing kiss yesterday on the beach. He wouldn't want her getting too close, either. She'd proved a near-fatal distraction once. He wouldn't want that to happen again.

Nothing would be allowed to come between him and his work.

Griffen caught her eye from the bar, registering her suspicion that there was more to Mollie's relationship with the *Trib* reporter than a chance meeting at Granny Atwood's party.

Which meant Tabak was, indeed, grilling her.

"Relentless bastard," she muttered under her breath, and excused herself.

Griffen slid in beside her, martini in hand. "Okay, you and Tabak. Tell me all."

"Oh, I knew him a million years ago. I just ran into him. Why?"

"I know sparks flying when I see sparks flying. Comes from too much time at a stove, I suppose. I don't know as I've seen him at any parties like this. I wonder why tonight."

"The *Tribune* has a table at the ball."

"And that old prune Atwood invited him because she'd love to have a respected journalist to show off. Especially one as sexy as Tabak is." Griffen eyed her friend, her mass of curls gleaming, softening the angles of her face. "You sure there's nothing between you two?"

"I'm positive."

Griffen grinned suddenly, a devilish glint in her dark eyes. "Mm, well, I'd say *he's* not. I think the man has the hots for you. Who can blame him with you in a getup like that. It's not Leonardo's. He wouldn't fit."

"You are so bad, Griffen. It was left by an old girlfriend."

"The necklace, too?"

"I guess so. I feel weird wearing it."

"You would, but keep it on. You take anything off for half a second, and our cat burglar pounces. Crafty bastard, isn't he? Think he's around tonight?" She paused, then realization dawned, and she clapped her hands together. "That's it. Tabak's here because of the robberies."

"Griffen, shh. Maybe not everyone's heard about the thief."

"Are you kidding? This is Palm Beach. Everybody knows what I served at last night's party down to the fresh raspberries. They're going to know about a jewel thief on the prowl. I wouldn't have thought that was Tabak's kind of story, but you never know." She frowned, considering. "But don't worry. I still think he has the hots for you."

Deegan joined them, sparing Mollie an answer. He said, "I'd hate to go through a hurricane with you two. You'd abandon me in a flash to save your own skins. I just managed to escape with Mother hounding me about pacing myself so I don't come down with mono." He grinned, unperturbed by anything his mother might say to him. "Gran's invited me to lunch. I expect I'm going to get the lecture about sowing my wild oats and then settling down."

"They hate me," Griffen said, matter of fact.

"They don't hate you," Deegan said, "they just find you 'unsuitable.' "

"Well, we've made our appearance. Another pass at the hors d'ouevres and we're out of here. Mollie?"

But suddenly eager to be alone, she wished them well and slipped off to the ladies' room to see if she still recognized herself in the mirror and regroup. If Jeremiah stayed through the entire ball, she was going to have to figure out a way to cope—or an excuse to leave early.

The ladies' lounge was down the hall and then off to the left, down another hall with stairs, two elevators, and another smaller function room. Mollie sank into a brocade chair in the sitting room of the lounge, with its fresh flowers in a tall Delft-style urn and scented potpourri in heart-shaped china bowls. She avoided her reflection in the mirror on the opposite wall. A borrowed dress, a borrowed necklace, a borrowed house. Even a bit of a borrowed life. *Was* she getting sucked into Leonardo's posh lifestyle?

No. She wasn't trying to impress anyone with her

choice of outfit. She was having fun, exercising a little Yankee frugality, being expedient. Leonardo would be pleased she was enjoying his necklace with its tortured history.

Jeremiah had unsettled her, eroded her confidence about the choices she'd made. He probed, dug, threw people off balance, ever in anticipation of anyone and everyone betraying their sorriest side. No rose-colored glasses for Jeremiah Tabak. He saw people right on, undiluted. And he'd learned to expect the worst.

But Mollie knew she was drawn to that intensity and clarity. If he had no illusions about the human flaws in others, he had none, either, about those in himself. With him, even a decade ago, she'd felt no need to apologize for her own doubts and weaknesses, but simply to be herself, which had—she hated to admit it—also allowed her to really see herself for the first time.

Of course, now he wouldn't put it past her to swipe other people's jewelry.

An open mind. Right.

"He's an exhausting man," she said half-aloud, the lounge empty as she got to her feet. She washed her hands and dried them on an individual finger towel, the light reflecting off every gem in her necklace. Crazy to wear it. But fun. She smiled at herself in the mirror. Yes, she could handle Tabak, and Diantha Atwood, and the Tiernays.

She headed back out into the corridor. It was quiet. Guests would be starting to make their way to the ballroom one level up. She could hang in for the evening, Mollie told herself. In for a penny, in for a pound.

The elevator dinged behind her, but she didn't bother to look around.

As she made the turn down the hall to the Atwood party, she heard a footstep behind her, assumed someone had gotten off the elevator. She started to glance around, but felt something at her neck, a feathery touch. Creepy. A fly, something. She went to brush it off, but felt something pulling at the loose hairs at the back of her neck, then her necklace yanked up hard against her throat.

A gloved hand.

The thief. He was *there,* just behind her.

In a single, vicious yank, he snapped the thin gold chain of her necklace.

Choking, a fiery pain at her throat, Mollie sank to her knees. She could hear the thief running back toward the elevators and stairs, hardly making a sound.

Her stomach lurched, and she screamed.

6

A woman's scream silenced Diantha Atwood's party.

Mollie.

Jeremiah knew it in his gut. A collective gasp went through the party. Guests looked around, momentarily paralyzed. Jeremiah cast aside his drink and ran out into the hall ahead of anyone else.

Up to his left, a gleam of champagne silk and pale hair. He swore under his breath, realized she'd sunk to the floor, collapsed against the wall. She held a hand to her neck, trembling.

In two seconds he was there, kneeling beside her. "Mollie—honey, are you all right? Let me see."

"He's gone." Her voice was shaky, her skin ghostly. "Down the stairs, I think. I tried to chase him . . ."

"Sweetheart, let me see your neck."

"The bastard," she said, squeezing back tears.

Jeremiah touched her hand gently, and she lifted it from her neck. Blood. Not a lot. Her diamond and

87

ruby necklace was gone. The thief must have ripped it right off her neck, leaving a fiery, stinging rope burn where the gold chain had cut into her skin.

She attempted a smile. "I'm okay. He just grabbed the necklace and ran. It happened so fast . . ."

"Don't try to talk now."

"Bastard," she whispered, and Jeremiah knew she meant the thief. Her neck must hurt like hell, and there'd be a bruise. But he hadn't strangled her, knifed her, shot her, carried her off into the night.

Still, Jeremiah could feel the blackness coming into his eyes. She removed her hand from the raw streak along her neck. Her palm was smeared with blood. Another weak attempt at a smile. She would, he knew, be embarrassed at making a scene. This wasn't her turf, her people. With a bunch of crazy musicians, she'd have felt free to scream, curse, cry, go after the guy, do whatever she damned pleased.

She sank her head back against the wall, thick locks of hair dislodging from their pins. "Really. It's just a scratch."

She shut her eyes, and Jeremiah could see her willing control over herself, fighting back nausea, shock, fear. People were rushing up the corridor. Someone was yelling for security, the manager, the police.

And Jeremiah remembered Croc's words. *I think this thing could get dangerous.*

A warning? Or a threat?

And here was Mollie, their only common denominator, Croc's only lead, once again in the thick of things.

"The thief," he said. "Did you see him?"

She shook her head, wincing. "He grabbed the necklace from behind. He just snapped it and ran off."

She gulped in air, her face, if possible, even paler. "I felt the brush of his hand. I think he was wearing gloves."

She shivered, visibly steeling herself against shaking as more people gathered round. Jeremiah stayed close to her. "It's over now, Mollie. You can explain later."

Her eyes, clear and so blue, focused on him, reminded him that he needed to take great care not to underestimate her. "Am I looking a bit green at the gills?"

He smiled. "More than a bit."

"I'd hate to throw up," she said dryly. "Then I'd feel like a *real* idiot. It's bad enough as it is. No one else who was robbed screamed bloody murder."

"No one else was physically attacked."

A thickset hotel security man in a nondescript navy suit materialized at Jeremiah's side, two doormen and the hotel manager coming up fast behind him. The manager—in his mid-forties, good-looking, well-dressed—calmly urged guests to return to the Starlight Room or move on to the ball. The security man spoke into a walkie-talkie, supervising a thorough search of the hotel and grounds, the protocol of handling a robbery on the premises quickly and efficiently kicking into gear.

Tiny Diantha Atwood inserted herself into the discussion. She spoke firmly, graciously to the manager, requesting to be kept advised of all developments. Despite her pleasant tone, Jeremiah detected a hint of disapproval directed at Mollie. He wasn't sure which was her greater social error: screaming, or getting robbed in the first place.

The walkie-talkie crackled with news that the search had so far turned up nothing.

"This thief seems to disappear with ease," Jeremiah said, and added, just to be provocative, to separate himself from the rest of the crowd, "Maybe you should consider searching the guests."

The hotel manager blanched. Diantha Atwood inhaled sharply, lips thinning as she glared at Jeremiah, as if she'd forgotten he really was a reporter, not just a coup for her party. "That's out of the question."

Of course it was. But Jeremiah didn't regret his comment. He'd served notice that the hotel, and the police when they arrived, ought to consider that they might have a thief among the black-tie crowd, not just some thug scampering through the shrubbery to make good his escape. He figured part of his job was to probe, push, goad. Do what had to be done, short of breaking the law and violating journalistic ethics, to get to the truth.

But Mollie was frowning at him, and he expected she knew what he was up to. This new-found ability she had to guess what was on his mind was a little disconcerting, but also quite intriguing. No gullible twenty-year-old was she.

The police arrived, and Jeremiah withdrew to let them take Mollie's statement. He had no intention of discussing his interest in the jewel thief, or how it had come about, with them. First chance he got, he'd check his police sources for what they had. He noticed that Mollie had perked up. She was still pale and shaky, but she was on her feet and spoke in a clear, calm voice to the detective. Jeremiah wasn't planning to go far. He wondered if she knew that.

A few stragglers remained at the Atwood party, the indomitable hostess and her daughter and son-in-law reassuring them that Mollie was just fine. "She was startled," Bobbi Tiernay said, "that's why she screamed."

Startled? She was attacked from behind. She'd had her damned necklace yanked off her. Who the hell wouldn't have screamed bloody murder? Mollie, however, was the new publicist in town and therefore vulnerable to taking the blame for ruining a pleasant evening of drinks and small talk.

Jeremiah reminded himself that no one there was accustomed to what amounted to a mugging occurring under their noses. Bobbi Tiernay, like most of the others, would want some way to make herself feel less vulnerable. So, blame the victim. A Cary Grant–type jewel thief on the loose was one thing. They could all have fun with that. But Cary Grant never drew blood.

"You're going to be late for the ball," Diantha Atwood told him.

Jeremiah decided he'd rather be boiled in oil, staked to an ant hill, and shot in the ass than sit through a Palm Beach charity ball, even one for a good cause. He'd start to twitch even before the salads were served.

"Or are you going to play reporter?" she asked coolly. "I noticed you were the first to reach Mollie. You have excellent reflexes."

Play reporter. As if he could click his instincts on and off again. As if he had no idea of the responsibility to the community his role as a journalist entailed. He didn't like the attack on Mollie, its daring nature or its violence. He especially didn't like the fact that its victim was Mollie. But to Diantha Atwood, it was a black mark on her party, a social awkwardness to be smoothed over and forgotten.

Don't get ahead of the facts, he warned himself. The woman could be as shaken as anyone else by the sour turn of events and was just acting out of her own shock and fear.

"I've offended you," she said, her eyes steady on him. "Please, forgive me."

"Not to worry." He gave her a wink. "I've been accused of worse than playing at my job. Thanks for the party."

"Are you going to write this for the *Tribune?*"

"Conflict of interest," he said, and headed out, hoping she believed his conflict arose from having been a guest at her party and wasn't guessing at his relationship with her grandson's boss.

The police and hotel people were still gathered around Mollie in the hall. Jeremiah walked the other way and looked over the balcony down at the main lobby. Lots of flowers and polished brass, a fountain, soft chairs and couches, marbled floors and thick carpets, men in tuxedos and women in long dresses arriving for the charity ball. Even Jeremiah, who was looking, couldn't tell a hunt for a jewel thief was taking place.

He stiffened, all but fell off the damned balcony. There, planted on a cushiony loveseat like he owned the place, was Croc. He had his skinny legs stretched out, his ankles crossed, and his hands clasped behind his head as he watched an elegant couple pass in front of him.

If Jeremiah had had a rock, he might have dropped it on Croc's head.

As if reading his mind, Croc glanced up at the balcony, grinned, and waved. Jeremiah's grip tightened on the polished brass rail. He pried his fingers loose and took the escalator two steps at a time down to the lobby. He'd probably have jumped over the rail except he didn't want to draw the cops' attention.

"Yo, Tabak," Croc said when Jeremiah dropped onto the loveseat next to him. "Cozy, huh? Nice place, although I'm not crazy about the flower arrangement over by the fountain. Too New England. You know? This is Palm Beach. People want glitter and ostentation."

Ostentation? "Croc, what the hell are you doing here?"

"Watching the festivities." He folded his hands on his middle; he had not one ounce of fat to spare. He wore black jeans, a black T-shirt, and black sneakers, and his hair was pulled back in a ponytail, but clean. If he had a diamond-and-ruby necklace on him, it would have to cause a noticeable bulge somewhere. "You should have seen them shuffling to get the cops in here without a lot of fanfare. Very discreet. I was impressed."

"Then you know about the attack on Mollie Lavender?"

"Yep."

"You're lucky the cops haven't hauled you in as a suspect."

"That's not luck, Tabak, that's skill. How's she doing?"

Jeremiah glanced up at the mezzanine. All he

needed was an enterprising police officer to take a peek down into the lobby and see a *Miami Tribune* reporter talking to an obvious informant. The cops would pounce. "She's shaken up, but not seriously hurt. You want to tell me what the hell you're doing here?"

Croc shrugged. "I'm just sitting here, minding my own business, hearing what I hear."

"You arrive before or after Mollie was attacked?"

"Ah." His clear gaze settled on Jeremiah. "You're making sure I didn't swipe the necklace. Well, I didn't. Too much effort involved."

"You still haven't answered my question," Jeremiah pointed out.

"True."

Stonewalled. Croc didn't like to divulge his tactics. Jeremiah gave up for the moment. "I suppose now you can eliminate Mollie Lavender as a suspect."

"How do you figure?"

"Because she's up there bleeding, Croc—"

"Yeah, so? Why did she wear an expensive necklace? Why didn't anyone see anything? Why no trail? You got no clues, no suspects, no witnesses, no evidence. You can't eliminate her or anyone else yet."

Jeremiah checked a hiss of impatience. "You think she ripped the necklace off her own neck?"

"Why not?"

"The question is *why?*"

"How the hell should I know? Okay, here's one. Insurance."

"It's Pascarelli's necklace. The money would go to him."

Croc was unchagrined. "Then she wanted to inspire

fear in potential victims—make them nervous so they won't put up a fight next time she gets light fingers."

"That doesn't wash, either. If there's a threat of violence, people will leave the real stuff in the vault. It'd dry up business."

Croc frowned. "Okay. I'll give that one some thought." A foot started going, then a hand, fingers drumming. "She could also want the thrills, the attention. High-profile party, daring thief. Makes good drama, Tabak." He paused, a half-second halt in his fidgeting as he eyed Jeremiah. "So what's the story between you two?"

"Between Mollie and me?"

"No, between Diantha Atwood and you. Come on, Tabak. Don't bullshit. You're no good at it."

Jeremiah balled his hands into fists. Tension. Irritation. Frustration. He felt them all. Sitting there and trying to appear calm required every scrap of self-control he had. "Mollie and I had a brief relationship about a million years ago. It ended badly."

"How brief?"

"A week."

"When?"

"Ten years ago. She was a music student on spring break."

Croc was silent a moment. Then he sighed. *"Now* you tell me."

"It has no bearing on your jewel thief."

"Bullshit. It explains why you're not seeing this thing with your normal cold, clear, cynical eye. Jeez, I can't believe I missed this one. You and our Miss Mollie. I tell you, Tabak, she's involved. You mark my words. I'm checking into her clients—and that caterer friend and her boy-toy, Miss Mollie's intern. Look like a couple of nitwits to me."

Jeremiah gave him a steady look. "Croc, if you're not careful and keep landing yourself in the wrong place at the wrong time, people are going to start suspecting you."

He went still, a rarity for him. "Do you? Come on, seriously. Do you suspect me?"

"Not yet," Jeremiah said.

He couldn't tell if Croc was insulted or not. "I guess that'll have to do."

"Maybe if you quit holding back—"

But Croc hurtled to his feet, suddenly looking as if he wanted to jump out of his skin. "Listen, I need to get out of here. Atmosphere's getting to me. I might be barking up the wrong tree with this Mollie Lavender character, but I don't think so. I think she's right up there on a high branch, laughing at the rest of us while we scurry around in the muck."

"Your instincts about people aren't reliable, Croc."

"Maybe not, but you put Miss Mollie up on a bulletin board, and all roads lead to her."

Croc wasn't known for his felicitous metaphors, but Jeremiah got his point. Mollie as common denominator. Mollie screaming. Mollie bleeding. Mollie up there with the police and hotel security even as he and Croc sat there discussing her.

What did Jeremiah know about her anymore?

But it was nuts. She was the goddaughter of a world-famous tenor, the daughter of flaky musicians, a publicist for flaky clients. Considering her as their jewel thief was just silliness. A diversion. A way of *not* thinking about her in other terms, such as in danger, in despair . . . or, Jeremiah thought grimly, in his bed, which maybe was scariest of all.

"Hey, Tabak, you're lucky I'm on your side." Croc grinned, somehow looking even bonier, out of place yet not the least bit awkward in the elegant surroundings. "I'm the one here who's clear-eyed and without prejudice."

"There's nothing between Mollie and me."

Croc just laughed, and Jeremiah watched him saunter over to the revolving doors and walk out of the hotel without anyone giving him so much as a second glance.

Mollie stumbled onto the escalator with the hotel manager hovering behind her. She felt unsteady and vaguely embarrassed, but the nausea had abated. Her neck stung. It was like a nasty rope burn, one of those short, intense bursts of pain that would subside quickly, the worst probably over by morning. Or so she kept telling herself as she clung to the escalator rail.

The police were still up with hotel security, searching for clues. She didn't expect they'd find anything useful. The thief had been quick, deft, clever, and daring. He wouldn't leave a trail. She knew nothing about crime and criminals—mercifully, she thought—but what she knew about *this* crime and *this* criminal told her the police weren't going to find him. Not tonight.

She gave an involuntary shudder. "Are you all right?" the manager asked, worried. His concern seemed genuine, not simply strategic.

"I'll be fine, thanks." She smiled, trying to encourage herself as much as him.

He held out a hand, ready to catch her if she passed out as the escalator came to the lobby and she slid off. She must look even worse than she felt. Neck bloody, face pale, dress askew. And she couldn't seem to stop shaking. Her eyelids were heavy, and even as she shivered and shook, she felt as if she could drop off to sleep. The aftermath of her ordeal, she knew. The excess of adrenaline, the drop in blood sugar, plain old nerves. Her entire system was out of whack.

"Are you sure you don't want a ride home?" the manager asked. "I can have someone drive your own car back at the same time."

Her own car. It wasn't hers any more than the necklace or the dress. Or her "home."

He'd made the same offer twice on the mezzanine. Mollie understood. He thought she was being needlessly, even recklessly, stubborn about driving herself back to Leonardo's. Certainly she needed to reassert normalcy into her life, but she could do it tomorrow, after she'd had a chance to rest from her ordeal. But she wanted to do it now.

Out of the corner of her eye, she saw Jeremiah making his way across the lobby. If possible, he looked even more devastating, more darkly unpredictable than he had upstairs. It was the combination of elegance and irreverence, she decided, feeling giddy from champagne and adrenaline. He moved with such ease no matter where he was—or with whom. He wasn't fazed by the Atwood and Tiernay crowd, and he'd seemed right in his element with a crime committed, a woman crumpled at his feet, police and security people swarming.

"I'm a friend," he told the manager with unsurpassed gall. "I'll drive Mollie home."

The manager looked relieved. "Wonderful. Ms. Lavender, if there's anything else I can do, please don't hesitate. You can reach me anytime, night or day."

She mumbled her thanks, and he retreated back up the escalator, leaving her alone with Jeremiah. "The hotel can send your car," he said, taking charge.

"I'm fine. There's no need for you to drive me home—"

"Mollie, you're not getting behind a wheel."

"I look worse than I feel." She knew she was white-faced, her eyes sunken, her mascara smudged. With her low-cut dress, there was no hiding the marks on her neck. Why couldn't the thief have stolen her handbag? She could feel rage roaring to the surface, but banked it back down.

"This isn't about you, it's about me and everyone else who doesn't want you on the road right now. Indulge us."

"You just want to grill me about the thief," she said, not willing to give in no matter how much she knew he and the manager both made sense.

"Believe whatever you need to believe. It just doesn't make sense to drive, not when there's an alternative."

"I know," she said reluctantly. "But I'll be back up to snuff in the morning."

"Of course you will."

She shot him a look, but immediately saw he wasn't being patronizing, just simply stating his belief. She'd be okay in the morning. She could drive, she could make her own decisions without the influence of adrenaline, a touch of alcohol, not enough food. To her surprise, Jeremiah's quiet confidence helped ease some of the tension that still had her in its grip.

They went outside—the air warm, cooler gusts coming in off the water. Limousines and expensive cars rolled up in long lines, depositing ball-goers in their elegant clothes and glittering jewels. Mollie didn't regret her decision not to stay. She wanted to be alone, sitting out on her deck listening to the crickets and the palm trees in the evening breeze.

They spoke little on the short drive to Leonardo's house. Mollie just sank into the ratty truck seat, staring at the lizard food Post-it on the glove compartment. She really knew nothing about this man. Nothing at all. Except she was glad he was driving her home, not some nameless security guard from the hotel.

"I'll wait until you're inside," he said, stopping at her driveway. "Griffen left before you were attacked. If you know where she and Deegan are, maybe she can come stay with you."

She nodded, suddenly exhausted, and climbed down out of the truck, her legs wobbly. She tapped in the code on the keypad outside the gates, grateful for Leonardo's elaborate security system. It was dark now, the truck headlights on. As the gates opened, she went to Jeremiah's open window. Her throat was tight, her head spinning. "It was no accident I was the victim tonight, was it? Even if I hadn't been wearing that necklace, the thief was gunning for me. I think—" She swallowed, trying to make sense out of the flashes of memory, the bits and pieces of information all vying for attention. "I think the thief was lying in wait. The dinging of the elevator . . . that was just to throw off the police."

The truck's interior lights and the angle of the streetlight cast Jeremiah's face into shifting, eerie shadows, his eyes darkened, his straight, hard mouth unyielding. "Mollie—"

She didn't let him finish. She was too keyed up with her own theories. "But I don't *know* that. I just—" She exhaled. "Why me? Especially when I'm the only 'common denominator' you have."

"Don't try to make sense of it tonight," he said. "Look at it in the morning."

"He could have been at the party and seen me in the necklace, then slipped out after I went to the ladies' room and waited for me . . ."

"Mollie, at this point anything's possible."

Her head shot up. "Including that I'm the thief? That I did this to myself?"

He sighed. "No. I really don't believe that's possible."

"But you considered it," she said.

"I consider everything."

His matter-of-factness, his truthfulness, had a calming effect on her. In her frazzled state, she would have reacted strongly to even a hint of condescension or lying. "Fair enough. I should go on up now."

"The hotel will be here any minute with Leonardo's car. Why don't I stay and handle that for you?"

"Thanks." She smiled. "I'd appreciate that. And— well, you might as well come upstairs when you're finished. We both missed dinner. I'll fix us a couple of sandwiches."

"Mollie—"

She glanced back at him as she headed inside the gates. "You're not hungry?"

The truck hadn't moved. "You don't have to fix me a sandwich, Mollie."

"It'll give me something to do. I'm ready to jump out of my skin as it is. It's just as easy to make two sandwiches as one." She smiled, already feeling better. "And I'm more likely to throw up if I *don't* eat something."

"Well, then," he drawled, and she heard his beat-up old truck grind into gear, "by all means, fix us a couple of sandwiches."

7

They ate sandwiches at the kitchen table. Turkey and lettuce on sourdough with pickles on the side. Although she knew she needed to eat, Mollie's stomach had turned midway through fixing them. "I wonder what they're having at the ball," she said. She'd thrown a sweatshirt over her dress to ease a sudden chill; she'd deal with her bruised, raw neck later, after Jeremiah left. "I could have made it through dinner if they were having something good."

But she could only get halfway through her sandwich. Her stomach clamped down. Nerves. Jeremiah finished off her second half while he stood up and rummaged in her freezer. Without a word, he got out a tray of ice, set it on the counter, found a dish towel, dumped most of the ice in it, tied it up, and handed it over to Mollie. "Put this on your neck. First aid stuff in the bathroom?"

"The hall bathroom," she said, pointing.

He withdrew down the hall. She could hear him rattling around in the medicine cabinet. She didn't have much by way of first-aid necessities. A box of Band-Aids, antibiotic ointment, aspirin, a thermometer. She'd been blissfully healthy since her arrival in south Florida.

Jeremiah returned with a tube of antibiotic ointment and a dampened face cloth. "You want to do this or shall I? I've had basic first aid, but I haven't had to use it since I dropped my turtle in the kitchen sink while I was cleaning his cage."

"I'll do it."

She took the face cloth first and gently wiped off her neck, which didn't sting when she touched it nearly as much as she'd anticipated. That finished, Jeremiah squeezed out some of the ointment on her finger, and she dabbed it on.

"You need a mirror—you've missed a couple of spots," he said, and proceeded to squeeze goo on his own finger, then dab it onto her neck. His touch was gentle, functional, but still sent warm, welcome tremors through her. "I'd leave it uncovered."

"I'll do that. Thanks. I guess I know a little of what it feels like to be garroted."

"Nasty business," he said.

"Yes, it is." She narrowed her gaze on him. He was still standing, not pacing, but not at ease, either. "You're not going to tell me how you got involved in this story, are you? How you found out I was your 'common denominator'?"

He didn't hesitate. "I can't."

"You're protecting a source?" But he didn't answer—didn't need to answer—and she said hotly, "But if you have a conflict of interest because of me and can't do the story, why do you need to protect this source?"

"Because that's how I operate."

And because he didn't owe her an explanation, she thought.

"Mollie, pour yourself a glass of wine, keep the ice on your neck for as long as you can stand it, and try to put tonight out of your mind and get some sleep." He walked over to her, tucked a fat lock of hair behind her ear. "If you want, you can call me tomorrow."

"Will you tell me anything then that you won't tell me now?"

"Probably not. But you'll take it better after you've rested." He touched her cheek with the back of his hand. "Now, I'd better get out of here while I still can."

"Wait."

She placed her towel of ice on the table and took his hand, pulling herself to her feet. She brushed his mouth with the tips of her fingers, cold from the ice, and then followed with her lips, kissing him softly, sinking against his chest just for a moment. His arms went around her, and she could have stood there all night.

He kissed the top of her head, said, "Mollie, you need that glass of wine."

"And the good night's sleep." She smiled, pulling back. "I know. Thanks for your help tonight."

"We'll talk soon."

She nodded, and he left. She wondered if his sense of honor was at work again—she was in pain, in shock, out of balance, and he wasn't going to take advantage—or if he simply wanted to make sure she hadn't ripped a necklace off her own neck before he got into bed with her. The Tabak-as-rogue of her imagination would have capitalized on her trauma and stayed the night, eliciting every bit of information he could in the process.

This complicated, honorable Jeremiah Tabak had her mystified. And frustrated. How much easier to get her addled brain around a driven, unethical skunk of a reporter than the man she'd encountered tonight. Irreverent, suspicious, intriguing.

She returned to the kitchen and added more ice to her sopping towel before wandering into the den, not sure what to do with herself. She put on the fourth movement of Beethoven's Ninth Symphony with Leonardo as the tenor soloist. She turned up the volume, the entire apartment pulsating with the rich, swelling sounds of orchestra and chorus, the emotion and passion and wonder of a piece written more than two hundred and fifty years ago by a dead man.

Tears streamed down her face.

She collected up her darts and threw them one by one, hard, her aim off, but she gathered them up and threw them again, harder this time, her aim truer. It was the aftereffects of the shock of the attack, the confusion of dealing with Jeremiah and his jewel thief, the realization that she was alone, alone, alone.

At the end of the symphony, she was singing along like a maniac, and it was just as well her godfather was on another continent.

But she felt better. This, she thought, was what she'd needed. And maybe Jeremiah knew it.

She aimed a final dart, threw it, and stuck out her tongue in defiance when it went wild and hit a lamp. She returned to the kitchen, poured herself a glass of wine, and sat out on her deck, letting the sounds of the Palm Beach night soothe her tattered nerves and absorb her soul.

When she finally ventured to bed, she had it solid in her head once more: It would be stupid to fall for Jeremiah Tabak all over again.

Griffen and Deegan stopped by first thing Saturday morning with muffins, coffee, and the *Palm Beach Daily News*, or the Shiny Sheet, as the locals called it. They dragged Mollie out to the pool and made her sit in the sun. She noticed how the morning light intensified the yellows, pinks, oranges, and reds of the impatiens, hibiscus, begonias, and bougainvillea and brought out the nuances in all the different shades of green of the palms and live oak and shrubs, even the grass. She seemed hyper-aware of everything, and the smell of fresh, warm blueberry muffins struck her as perfection.

Griffen spread the muffins and coffee on a small table and mock-slapped Mollie's hand when she started to serve herself. "You are going to sit back and be pampered—at least for ten minutes. Let's see this neck," she said, and winced when Mollie peeled back her polo shirt. "Ouch."

"It only hurts when I touch it."

Deegan made a face. "Nice color, anyway."

"I consider myself lucky," Mollie said. "He could have slit my throat."

Griffen shuddered. "Don't even think about it. I'm

sorry we weren't there to provide moral support, but we'd already made our exit. I've had my fill of Granny Atwood, that's it, I'm on the move." She handed Mollie a generously buttered muffin, coffee, and a napkin. "Sorry the napkin's not cloth, but we have to work with what we've got."

Deegan helped himself to a muffin. "You must have been scared shitless, Mollie. I can't imagine. I've never been attacked like that."

"It was pretty scary, but I'm feeling much better now."

"Here we were thinking we had kind of a fun jewel thief on our hands—daring but nonviolent. Nobody sees him, nobody gets hurt. Now . . ." He shrugged, tearing open his muffin. "I don't know."

"Yeah," Griffen said, "last night changes everything. I don't think this guy's in it for the money. It's not greed with him, it's the thrills. Maybe he changed his MO to get a bigger thrill. You know, go extreme."

"What's the Shiny Sheet say?" Mollie asked, biting into her muffin, trying to stay focused on the present, not relive last night.

Griffen showed her the article, which was short, stuck to the facts, and had nothing to report that Mollie didn't already know. "It was silly of me to wear that necklace," she said.

Griffen didn't argue. "Have you told Leonardo?"

"Not yet. He'll be very understanding—this'll just confirm his suspicion that that necklace was jinxed. Deegan, how's your grandmother? The attack really ended her party on a sour note."

"I haven't talked to her, but she's an old pro. She'll find a way to work it all to her advantage. My bet is she'll throw it off onto the hotel. You'll notice the article says you were attacked at the hotel, not at Gran's pre-ball cocktail party. It doesn't even mention the party, just says you were at the Sands for the charity ball."

"I keep thinking if I'd been more alert . . ." Mollie sighed, sinking back into her chair with her muffin and coffee, the warmth of the sun on her. "If I'd at least gotten a good look at him."

"Did you see him at all?" Griffen asked.

Mollie shook her head. "There wasn't enough time. I tried to get back up on my feet—" She stopped, her stomach lurching at the memory. "I guess I didn't really know if he was finished with me."

Griffen shuddered, plopping down on a chair next to her. "Jesus, Mollie."

"Well. It all worked out in the end."

"I heard Jeremiah Tabak got to you first." She angled Mollie a look. "You sure there's nothing between the two of you?"

"Yes, I'm sure there's nothing between us, but I guess—well, we did meet before, when I was in Miami on spring break in college. It was pure happenstance that we ran into each other again."

"You're kidding." Instantly intrigued, Griffen sat up straight, muffin crumbs falling on her lap; she had on one of her many sundresses, looking exotic and beautiful even on a Saturday morning. "Must have been a hell of a spring break for you to remember each other."

Mollie ate more muffin, welcoming the sweetness of the blueberries, noticing everything about this moment. The flowers, the sun, the slight breeze, the birds.

If she could stay in the moment, she could keep herself from spinning totally out of control. She debated how much to tell Griffen about her past relationship with one of Miami's more famous reporters. "I sort of got caught up in a drug-dealing story he was working on. I wasn't involved or anything. Anyway, it ended up on the front page after I headed back to Boston."

"I see," Griffen said, dubious.

"It's true."

"I'm sure it is, as far as it goes." She reached for another still-warm blueberry muffin and placed it on Mollie's lap. "You need to eat. You're still pale as a damned ghost. I wished I'd run into that thief last night." She squinted up at Deegan, who was eating his muffins and drinking coffee on his feet. "We'd have nailed his ass, wouldn't we, Deeg?"

He grinned at her. "I'd have let you have first crack at him."

"And relax, Mollie," Griffen said, giving her a friendly pat on the knee, "I'm not getting out the thumbscrews to find out the rest about you and Tabak, although, I don't know . . . I think I can see you two together . . ."

"Griffen!"

She laughed. "You can be such a Boston prude, you know that? Honestly. However, we didn't come here to harangue you. The police will step up their investigation now that this guy's shown a capacity for violence. The Palm Beach crowd won't stand for a cocky thief waltzing into their parties and ripping necklaces off their throats. I expect they'll beef up security, too. In fact, I'm catering a luncheon on Tuesday on that

110

very subject. One of the women's societies is sponsoring it. You should come."

"I might," Mollie said.

They finished the muffins and coffee, chatting about the weather and the weekend goings-on and a little bit about work. Griffen and Deegan were off to the beach for a couple of hours before she had to pull together a small dinner party up in West Palm that evening.

After they left, Mollie found herself wandering around on the terrace and in the yard, smelling flowers, trying to stop herself from shaking. She'd thought she'd be fine this morning. And she wasn't. She kept thinking of the gloved hand on her neck, of her relief when Jeremiah came to her side, of his questions and suspicions and his damned open mind.

"Damn it," she said aloud, charging across the lawn. She didn't stop at the pool's edge. She just thought, *to hell with it*, and jumped in, clothes and bruises, cut neck and all. The muffins and coffee churned in her stomach, but the water was just cool enough, refreshing, swirling around her and slowly, inexorably easing out the accumulated tension in her mind and body. She swam until her muscles cried out in protest, then crawled out of the pool and lay on her stomach on the warm terrace, letting the sun dry her, telling herself if Jeremiah had stayed last night, they'd both be regretting it now.

Finally, she headed upstairs with a vague plan for the rest of her Saturday. First, she would report the stolen necklace to Leonardo's financial manager and let him deal with the insurance company and the hotel. Second, she would grit her teeth and call Leonardo and talk him out of taking the next plane out of Florence—she thought he was still in Florence—to see her through this crisis.

If her conversation with Leonardo didn't totally exhaust her, she would do a little work before lunch. Then she'd go for a long walk on the beach, take a nap, and afterwards see which of her new friends were around for dinner.

With any luck, the police wouldn't call, and Jeremiah wouldn't show up at her door.

Or, she thought, she at his.

Jeremiah knew this whole damned jewel thief nonsense, and maybe his life as a reporter, was really falling apart when he found himself back in Helen Samuel's office. It was Saturday, and he ought to be cleaning his apartment, listening to tunes, and whittling with the boys—and if he was going to work, find a damned story he could actually write.

Helen was hammering out her column a half-hour before the midnight deadline for the Sunday paper. "Goddamned computers," she said, cigarette hanging from her lower lip as she pecked on the keyboard. "No satisfaction hitting a 'delete' button. Give me a bottle of Wite-Out any day." She glanced up at him with a skeletal grin. "I miss the fumes."

"Why not do your column from home? You could just—"

"Modem it in?" She snorted, setting her cigarette on her overflowing ashtray. "Modems scare the shit out of me. Trust me, Tabak. I was right about television. I'm right about modems."

Jeremiah didn't ask her to elaborate. Her predictions on televisions or modems no doubt included the end of civilization as she knew it. Helen was even more doomsday about human nature and the future of mankind than the average reporter—which in Jeremiah's experience was saying something.

"You want to know what I keep deleting?" She didn't wait for his answer, her beady eyes boring into him. "Your name. I type, 'The *Tribune*'s own Jeremiah Tabak was the first to rush to Mollie Lavender's aid,' and I delete it. Then I hit 'redo' and stare at it awhile, and delete it again." She picked up her cigarette, inhaled, set it back down. "I kind of like that 'redo' button."

"I've never known you to be indecisive, Helen."

She squinted at him. "What have you gotten yourself into, Tabak? I can sit on this for a while, but you're up to your nose in stink."

He sat on the edge of a ratty chair. Fatigue gnawed at every muscle. He hadn't slept last night. He doubted he'd sleep tonight. He'd spent the day plumbing every source he had. Police, lawyers, street informants, fellow reporters. He'd lost hours wandering around on the Internet for anything on Mollie, Leonardo Pascarelli, Blake Wilder, recent jewel heists, cat burglars. Helen would tell him he'd have been better off hitting the streets himself. She might be right. At least he would have been physically as well as mentally exhausted. Now every nerve ending seemed to twitch.

"That's one way of putting it," he said. "I wish I knew what I've gotten myself into."

"Brass find out you were at the Sands last night and didn't report the story?"

He shook his head. "No."

"They won't like being scooped by the freaking *Palm Beach Daily News*." She grabbed her cigarette case and tapped out a long, slim cigarette, the other one still burning in her ashtray, smoke curling up from its inch of ash. "I don't like it, either."

"You had the story last night?"

"Of course. Just think, Tabak, you and I could have written the same story at the same time." She gave a hoarse laugh. "Scares the shit out of you, doesn't it?"

"We'd have come at this thing from different angles," he said.

"I'm not so sure about that. You think Mollie Lavender is in the thick of this cat burglar/jewel thief business, and so do I." She settled back in her chair, her coral lipstick bleeding into the tiny vertical lines in her upper lip; she wasn't beautiful or young, and her chain-smoking had taken its toll in wrinkles and skin texture, but she was, Jeremiah thought, a handsome and complex woman, and more astute than he'd ever realized. She said calmly, "How hard have you fallen for her?"

He bit off a sigh. "Helen, Jesus."

"Okay. Here's the way it is, Tabak. We're living in a celebrity culture. You're damned near a celebrity reporter, which should be an oxymoron, but isn't. So. That means if you get involved with a flaky arts and entertainment publicist who also happens to be the only goddaughter of a world-famous opera singer, people are going to notice, and they're going to want to know more."

"It's none of anyone's damned business."

"Doesn't matter. And if she turns out to be a jewel

thief, you're in the middle of a scandal. If you withheld information from the public, your goose as a credible reporter is, as we say, cooked."

"For one thing, not that I need to explain to you or anyone else, what I have isn't solid—"

"You were *there* last night, Tabak."

He ignored her. "For another, I'm not in a position to withhold anything from the public. It would be a conflict of interest for me to write this story."

"That's what I was going to say in my column." She held the fresh cigarette tight in one hand. "But that's too damned subtle. I've been at this job a long time, and I'm smelling a scandal. My advice—not that you're asking—is to pass the baton and bow out."

"Let someone else do the story," Jeremiah said.

"That's right."

He sighed.

"I know, I know." She tucked the unlit cigarette on her lower lip. "You're not *on* the freaking story. This is personal, between you and Mollie Lavender. Well, keep in mind it could cost you your credibility. And that's your stock in trade, my boy."

"Thanks for the lecture."

"You're welcome." She dragged out a lighter and fired it up, her moves almost ritualistic as she lit her cigarette, inhaled, and blew out a cloud of smoke. "You didn't risk coming down here and getting tongues wagging just to hear me lecture you on maintaining your reputation. What's up?"

"You've followed this jewel thief probably even more closely than I have."

"Right from the beginning. I'm not a Johnny Come Lately."

"Okay. Last night's attack—" Jeremiah paused, past knowing if he was making any sense. He studied Helen, the cursor blinking obnoxiously on her monitor, her old cigarette burned out, her new one angled rakishly between her middle finger and forefinger. "It's either our thief getting violent and even more daring—"

"Or it's someone else. A copycat of sorts."

"What are your sources telling you?"

She tilted her head back, eyeing him through lowered, blackened eyelashes, debating whether she needed to tell him, a colleague who for eighteen years had hardly given her the time of day, anything. Finally, she said, "Nothing. Not one damn thing. And I'm only telling you because you're not doing this story. Silence," she added, raising her cigarette to her lips, "can be very intriguing."

"Helen—"

"I've got a deadline, Tabak, and an empty paragraph to fill where I should be telling my readers that you and Leonardo Pascarelli's goddaughter are the talk of the town."

Jeremiah glared at her. "We're not."

"You will be," she said, and swiveled around to her monitor.

Dismissed, he headed out of her office and kept walking until he reached the parking garage. He sat in his truck. There were times he wondered why he hadn't just stayed in the Everglades with his father. This was one of them. He could have been a guide, a loner like his father, except by choice rather than by the cruelty of fate. His mother had been snatched from husband and young son by a deadly cancer that had moved fast and furiously. In Jeremiah's experience, true love—the kind of love his parents had had for each other—couldn't last, was doomed by its own perfection.

He remembered sitting out on the still, shallow water not far from home, swatting mosquitoes, thinking that if his parents had loved each other less, his mother might have been allowed to live. The tortured logic of a twelve-year-old. But it had stuck, and on nights such as this, when sleep had eluded him for too long and answers lay outside his grasp, he couldn't escape that one great fear of loving someone so much that it simply couldn't last.

He started up his truck and drove back to his building. The old guys had all gone in for the night, no eighty-year-old insomniac up whittling. Jeremiah went upstairs, got his knife, and came back down. He found a small piece of discarded wood and sat on one of the cheap lounge chairs, imagining his father alone at his isolated outpost, listening to the Everglades night as he smoked his pipe and whittled until the wee hours, perhaps thinking of the woman he'd loved and lost, perhaps not.

Mollie slid into a booth in a corner of the posh Fort Lauderdale jazz club where Chet Farnsworth, her astronaut-turned-pianist client, was playing for a late Sunday afternoon crowd. Not much of a crowd, actually. And those who were there were mostly elderly, not that Chet, a true pro, would care. He was grateful for the opportunity to play and an audience who connected with his music. Mollie had promised to attend as a show of support and for her own research, to help her better understand his particular needs as a client and how she could best address them as his publicist.

She'd already offered an apology for not making the charity ball, which Chet had received with a complete lack of grace, barking at her for even thinking she needed to explain.

Appreciating the quiet atmosphere of the club, Mollie ordered a non-alcoholic margarita. No one could rip any jewelry off her this evening because she wasn't wearing any. She'd slipped on a simple navy silk dress and inexpensive silver earrings. When she'd finally caught up with Leonardo, he had, of course, offered to fly immediately to Miami to be with her. And he'd given her until tonight to call her parents. As for the necklace—"good riddance," he said.

Chet gave her a quick wave from the baby grand piano. He was as at home there, she thought, as aboard a spacecraft. An astronaut taking up jazz piano as a second career would be a challenge for any publicist, but one with Chet's curt personality made it that much more interesting. He wasn't unfriendly, she'd learned, so much as self-contained and disciplined—a man who didn't suffer fools gladly. Her personal experience with eccentric musicians gave her insight and credibility that another publicist might have lacked.

But ultimately, Chet Farnsworth had to be good. And he was. His outward self-control and rigidity, his crew cut and ubiquitous coat and tie, made his audience expect the precision of his playing, but not the heart. At the piano, he allowed people a peek into the soul of a man who'd been to the moon and back, whose unique view of himself and his place in the world his music somehow communicated. Mollie listened from her dark corner, mesmerized.

When she finally became aware of her surroundings again, she noticed the crowd had picked up. Chet seemed to be having a good time, although it was hard to tell with a man of his control. He was the consummate professional, impossible to rattle. He caught her eye, and she smiled her approval, but he frowned and pointed.

She turned in her chair, and there was Jeremiah at the bar.

Chet had taken it upon himself to warn her about Tabak, having heard, of course, that Jeremiah had run to her side after the attack. He knew about single-minded, driven men, he said. He'd been one himself. "You should have no illusions about Jeremiah Tabak, Mollie."

He was sipping a martini, and he wasn't watching Chet at the piano. He was watching her. Her reaction was immediate and intense, and so unexpected she couldn't stop it before it took on a momentum of its own. Her body turned liquid. It was as if she were melting into the floor. Chet's music, the dark, sexy atmosphere of the jazz club in contrast to the bright, sunny day, and Jeremiah—his unsettling mix of hard edges and casual ease—all came together to assault her senses, her nerves. If she had even guessed he might be here, she could have prepared herself, steeled herself against just such a reaction. As it was, there could be no more denying that he had the same effect on her now as he'd had when she was twenty, that nothing had changed.

He knew she'd spotted him. He tilted his glass to her in a mock salute and drank. She attempted a cool smile. He climbed off the bar stool and walked toward her. He wore a black canvas shirt and pants, and the dim light reflected every color in his eyes. She noticed the few flecks of gray in his close-cropped black hair as he slid into the booth opposite her. He'd been only twenty-six himself ten years ago. Not so old.

"Afternoon," he said.

"I take it this isn't a coincidence."

He sipped his martini, smiled over the rim of the glass. "You don't think I'm out on a Sunday afternoon to hear an astronaut play jazz?"

"Did you follow me here?"

"No need. I saw Chet in the *Trib*'s listing of weekend events and figured you'd be here, good publicist that you are. Also, you're too stubborn to stay home."

"I stayed home yesterday," she said.

He smiled. "I rest my case. I see you skipped the fancy jewelry. How's your neck?"

Mollie ran one finger along the rim of her empty glass. "Healing nicely, thank you. It only hurts when I touch it. All considered, I was lucky."

His gaze settled on her. In the background, Chet segued into a mournful piece. "Mollie, I need to be straight with you and very clear about why I'm here."

She nodded. "Okay."

"I spent all day yesterday and most of today pulling together every fact I could find on this jewel thief story. There's not much, you know. The police are stymied. The rumors are all over the place, nothing I can grab hold of. The jewelry hasn't shown up for sale in any of the expected places."

"Must be frustrating for you," she said, willing herself back into solid form. He was here on business. The man breathed, ate, drank, lived the next story, whether it was one he could write or not. And she didn't even have the satisfaction any longer of knowing he could make a serious ethical mistake. As far as she knew, Jeremiah was exactly the reporter his reputation said he was. Tough, honest, ethical, probing, and determined not just to get the story, but to get it right.

"Yes, it's frustrating, but probably not for the reasons you imagine." He swallowed more of his martini, seemed to hate saying what he'd come here to say. "Mollie, I'm on this thing because of you and I'll see it through because of you."

"Wait just a minute—"

He held up a hand. Now that he'd started, he wasn't going to let her stop him. "I wouldn't have touched this thing if your name hadn't come up as the only person my source could find who'd attended every event the thief's hit. He—my source—thinks you're involved somehow."

"Involved? Involved how? Who is this guy?"

"Mollie, I didn't come here to upset you or to divulge information I'm not in a position to divulge. I just think you should know why I'm on this thing."

"Because of me," she said.

"Yes. Because of you."

His voice was deep and low and could liquefy her bones if she let down her guard. It seemed to blend with Chet's music, seeping into her soul, lulling her into a state of tranquillity she hadn't felt in days.

Then his words penetrated the fog and registered in all their starkness, and her chin shot up.

Jeremiah was already on his feet. Smiling, he touched her cheek, then bent down and kissed her lightly, his lips soft, tasting of martini. "I'm relentless when I'm focused on something," he half-whispered into her mouth, "and right now, I'm focused on you and this jewel thief. If you're involved, think about telling me how, and why, and what you plan to do about it. Because I'll find out, one way or the other."

She pushed him away and shot to her feet, her pulse racing, every nerve ending in her aching to smack him, even as the rest of her reeled at his kiss, wanted more, wanted all of him. "You are off base, Tabak, and way ahead of your precious facts. I'm not involved. And if I were, damned if I'd tell you."

He frowned. "You know, darlin'," he said in his twangy, exaggerated drawl, "you don't make it easy for somebody to care about you."

"Accusing me of being involved with a jewel thief is *caring* about me?"

"I'm not accusing you of anything. I'm just letting you know where I stand."

As he hadn't, not with any honesty, ten years ago. He'd let her believe the worst about him. Now, he was getting it all up front and center. "You'd better leave now, Tabak, before I . . ." Too incensed to think clearly, she didn't know what she'd do. "Well, you can imagine."

"I sure can, sweet pea." He smiled sexily, knowingly, incensing her even more. He touched her cheek with the back of a knuckle. "If you're in trouble, you have my number. You have my address. Call me, find me. I'm after the truth, and if it hurts you, it hurts you. But I'll still be there for you."

"Lucky me," she said bitterly.

A glint of humor sparked in his eyes. "You're right on there, darlin'. Right on. I owe you for lying to you ten years ago. It's a debt I aim to pay."

He blew her a kiss, and Chet's fingers stumbled on the keyboard. He recovered quickly, and again the room filled with his music. But Mollie was still reeling.

Jeremiah, in total control, left.

After a few seconds, Mollie was able to return to her booth. *Well,* she thought. Didn't that serve her right? She'd been starting to think of Jeremiah with a soft and tender side, and he'd just shown her. Probably acted out of a sense of honor. Had to let her know up front what was what. If she was guilty, she'd hang. But he'd feel bad about it.

During his break, Chet beelined for his publicist's table. "What the hell was that all about?"

"I don't know." She'd ordered another margarita, this one with alcohol. "I'm as taken aback as you are."

"Should have slapped the son of a bitch."

"I thought about it."

His eyes narrowed on her. He was stocky, fit, in his late fifties. "There's a history between you two."

Mollie felt her shoulders sagging. A history. She'd talked herself out of believing a weeklong affair was any kind of history. But there was something about Jeremiah, something about their *history,* that still ate at her, still intrigued and agonized her.

"It's none of my business," Chet went on, "but guys like that, they feed on vulnerability. They can't help it. They sense it, they swoop in for the kill. It's just the way they're made. Tabak knows every button to push to get the information he wants. He's on this jewel thief story, isn't he?"

"It's not his sort of story—"

"He'll make it his sort of story. Mark my words, he'll find an angle that's pure Jeremiah Tabak." Something caught his eye, and his face lit up. "Ah, here's my bride. Excuse me, Mollie, won't you?"

"Sure, Chet."

She watched him greet his wife, who sat with Mollie and didn't ask about Jeremiah or Friday night. But after Chet had played the first piece of his second set, Mollie gave up on returning to solid form and just went home.

Driving north on 95, she played Leonardo's collection of his favorite tragic, romantic arias and turned up the volume high. At first she blinked back the tears, then she just let them flow as her godfather's incredible voice filled her soul and forced out all the emotions she'd bottled up since first spotting Jeremiah at the Greenaway. Frustration, loss, fear, anticipation. She even cried for the young woman she'd been at twenty, the path not taken, the dreams not realized. Her week with Jeremiah had slammed her up hard against reality. She didn't want a career in music. She didn't have good judgment in men. She wasn't as worldly and sophisticated as she'd thought.

Now here she was, ready to make the same mistake all over again. Wanting a man she was crazy to want. Desperate to trust him, even when he suspected her of knowing something about a jewel thief, even when he promised if the truth led him where she didn't want him to go, so be it.

She reminded herself that love and romance and physical attraction didn't necessarily respond to logic and will. If she'd once loved Jeremiah, if a part of her loved him still, there was nothing to be done about it beyond accepting it and moving on.

And not giving in, she thought.

Never giving in. She was thirty, and she liked her life, and she wasn't in the mood to let falling for the wrong man turn it upside down all over again.

8

The telephone didn't stop ringing in Mollie's living room office all Monday morning, but most of the calls were about business, none were about Jeremiah, only two were from friends about her Friday-night attack—and Deegan was there to answer them all.

"You are a godsend," Mollie told him as he left with a stack of stuff for the printer.

He laughed. "Nice to be appreciated. You'll manage without me the rest of the day? I don't mind coming back this afternoon."

"Thanks, but I'll manage. I've got to write those press releases for the Renaissance Music Society. I'll probably just hang in here the rest of the afternoon. I've got a dinner tonight."

"Not another one—"

"It's not business. Some friends of Leonardo's invited me over. Anyway, if the phone doesn't let up, I'll just let voice mail handle it." She smiled. "And if you see your grandmother before I do, please thank her for the flowers."

A big bouquet had arrived first thing that morning, with a charming card from Diantha Atwood, wishing Mollie a speedy return to normal. Her thank you card was already in the mail. Deegan said, "I'll do that," and headed out, leaving Mollie to the phone, a stack of mail, and tons of work.

Her own parents had called last night after Leonardo, as promised, had ratted her out. They'd listened carefully to the details of the attack and offered to fly down at once—and said if she wanted to return to Boston, they'd clear out her old room, which they'd converted into a music library, and she could stay there until she got settled. Mollie had to fight back tears at their unconditional support. Unanchored in the real world as she knew them to be, she never doubted their love and affection for her, nor their total, if sometimes irrational, belief in her. But she'd assured them that the worst was over—and for a moment, she almost believed it herself—and when she'd hung up, she had to admit she felt better.

After Deegan left, she sat at the computer. The weather was as unsettled as she felt, with dark clouds, intermittent showers, and a breeze that was downright chilly. At least she wasn't tempted to go sit out by the pool. She could just stay in and work.

The phone rang, and she briefly considered leaving it to her voice mail, but picked up. "Mollie Lavender."

"I know."

She sat up straight at the tinny, obviously altered voice on the other end. "Who is this?"

"Miami's a dangerous place, Miss Lavender. Perhaps you should consider going back to Boston."

A click, and then silence. Her hand shaking, Mollie quickly got a dial tone and hit the code for a playback of the most recent number called. But the disembodied voice said that the number wasn't available.

She laid the portable phone on her computer desk.

"Oh my God."

Her voice was a panicked mumble, and she thought she would throw up. Holding her stomach, she jumped to her feet and raced into the kitchen, not thinking, just reacting to the urge to get out, away from her office, her phone, her life. She grabbed keys and handbag and tore outside, not knowing where she was going, only that she had to get out of there.

"Shoes," she said, stopping midway down the steps.

She ran back inside, still shaking, still nauseous, and pulled on a pair of old sandals she kept by the door.

Two minutes later, she was in Leonardo's Jaguar, chewing on a knuckle as she beat back panic, not thinking, not planning, just driving. She hit winding A1A and cursed the tourists going too slow, gawking at the beautiful houses, the beautiful beaches. She spun off onto a street that connected with 95. She took the south on-ramp. A truck honked furiously when she wove into the middle lane too close in front of him.

She gripped the wheel with both hands and tried to calm herself. Concentrate on the present, she told herself, the moment. Early Monday afternoon, I-95 South, drizzle. She flicked on her wipers. She lifted her foot off the gas. She breathed.

There, she thought.

The call didn't have to be from the man who'd attacked her on Friday night. Perhaps she'd made a business enemy who was capitalizing on her experience, which was no secret, and trying to tip the scales into having her leave town. Go home to her family and friends and old life in Boston. That scenario was bad enough, but not as bad as having whoever had attacked her in the Palm Beach Sands Hotel take another crack at her.

But she couldn't imagine how she, with her short list of fun but not exactly wealthy clients, could be a business threat to anyone.

The rain picked up as she headed south, became briefly torrential, a perfect distraction. She turned her wipers on high and had to concentrate to negotiate the slowing, half-blinded traffic. Then the shower was over, and the sun was shining, and traffic speeded up—and her mind again raced, replaying the call, running down all the possibilities.

She spotted the *Miami Tribune* building up ahead, just off 95. She took the exit and found her way to the visitors' section in the parking garage. She still wasn't thinking, just acting on instinct. She locked up and headed for the elevator before rational thought could assert itself.

Jeremiah, she told herself, had just the kind of bulldog tenacity—the arrogance, the skill, the connections—to help her find out who was responsible for Friday's attack and this afternoon's call. Whether two different people or one, he could help her get to the truth. Unwittingly, against her will, she was involved, if not in the thick of things, as his source apparently believed, at least on the periphery. And she didn't like it.

And if she didn't get Jeremiah's help, she at least wanted everything he had, and she wanted it now.

Which sounded pretty much like a plan to her.

She signed in with a security guard in the lobby and provided the name of a contact in arts and entertainment. Best to give herself an out in case she got cold feet before she reached Jeremiah's desk. Since the guard didn't give her a second glance, she assumed she didn't look any more frazzled than the average *Trib* reporter. She'd worn a white linen shirt with a collar to hide her bruised neck.

She found her way to the newsroom and stood at the entrance, surveying the rows of desks, the flickering computers, the humming fax machines, the ringing telephones. A trio of men were arguing in front of a glassed-in corner office. No one seemed to be paying attention to them. Reporters went about their business, displaying an enviable ability to concentrate amidst the noise and general chaos.

"Looking for someone?" a young woman with a mug of coffee asked mid-stride.

Mollie took a breath. "Jeremiah Tabak."

"His desk's over on the wall." She motioned with her cup, carefully matter-of-fact. "Doesn't look like he's in. Lucky for you. He's in a bitch of a mood."

She went on her way, and Mollie, sucking in a breath, plunged on across the room to a cubicle on the far wall. She was aware of eyes on her. Strangers in a newsroom wouldn't go unnoticed. Someone looking for Jeremiah Tabak definitely wouldn't go unnoticed. If she left now, she had no doubt his colleagues would be able to provide him with a detailed description of her. Blonde hair. White shirt, little tan skirt. Shaking like hell.

He wasn't at his desk. His monitor was stuck with Post-it notes and clippings of cartoons, its screensaver of fish swimming across the screen on. The keyboard needed cleaning. His desk was cluttered with magazines, newspapers, notebooks, letters, scraps of paper, cheap pens, Star Wars pencils that might have belonged to a ten-year-old. An alligator paperweight held down one eight-inch stack of letters, many still in unopened envelopes. His ancient swivel chair looked as if he'd banged it against the wall a few too many times.

This wasn't where Jeremiah lived, Mollie thought. The man was no more interested in his surroundings than her parents and sister were in theirs. They lived in their music. He lived in whatever story gripped him.

Her pulse drummed in her ear as she debated taking a quick cruise through his desk for anything related to a certain jewel thief plaguing the Florida Gold Coast.

"You looking for Tabak?"

Mollie jumped, startled. A small, handsome older woman approached Jeremiah's desk, an unlit cigarette dangling from her fingers. Mollie reminded herself that she hadn't done anything wrong, just had considered it. "Yes. Is he in?"

"Unfortunately, yes. He took off upstairs for coffee. I tried to follow, but he growled at me. Figure I'll catch him when he's caffeined up. Me," she said, waving her cigarette, "I just smoke. I'd light up now but the freaking Nazis around here would have me shot. What we're getting in for reporters today, you just wouldn't believe." She paused, scrutinizing Mollie with a clarity that reminded her of Jeremiah. "You're Mollie Lavender, aren't you?"

"I am, but how . . . who . . ."

She grinned, pleased with herself. "I'm Helen Samuel, dear. I'm paid to know these things. Leonardo Pascarelli's goddaughter, attacked coming out of the ladies' room at Diantha Atwood's party Friday night. That must have been terrible. Are you all right now?" Mollie must have looked suspicious, because Helen Samuel, the legendary gossip columnist, grinned at her. "Relax, we're off the record."

"I'm fine," Mollie said. "I just had business in the building and thought I'd stop and thank Jeremiah for his help."

The old reporter's dark eyes registered interest and a level of suspicion that, Mollie decided, was probably natural to her. Finally, she pointed her cigarette across the open newsroom. "Check the cafeteria. One floor up." Then came a quick, compassionate smile that caught Mollie totally off guard. "I won't tell him you were snooping."

"I wasn't—"

"Dear, what do you think *I'm* doing here?"

Mollie couldn't resist a smile at the woman's cheekiness. "You're going to snoop in Tabak's desk? What if he catches you?"

"He'll be pissed as hell. What do I care? It's not as if he'll have left out a damned thing of use to me. If Tabak knows anything, he keeps it to himself. And believe me," she added with a wink, "he doesn't trust any of the rest of us."

With good reason, apparently.

Before she could change her mind, Mollie found her way up to the cafeteria, a large, almost empty room that smelled of stale coffee. Jeremiah was at a table in a corner of windows, staring out on the interstate and the now glorious Miami afternoon, a mug of coffee in front of him.

If she had made her peace with the Jeremiah of the past, Mollie thought, she'd done nothing of the kind with the Jeremiah of the present. He attracted her, unnerved her, and preoccupied her in ways she never could have anticipated. It wasn't just the jewel thief, his stubborn refusal to eliminate her as a suspect. It was his physical presence, his alertness to every nuance of his surroundings, to every nuance of *her*. He had an ability to make her rethink everything—her priorities, her life, herself. It was unsettling, but also irresistible.

She slid onto the chair opposite him and tried to look calm, in control, not as if she'd raced down here on impulse after receiving a nasty phone call—just in case she decided not to tell him about it. Because if he sensed she was holding back, he'd pounce. She smiled. "You look as if you're waiting for your coffee to say something profound."

He glanced up, squinted at her as if he had been so lost in thought he'd forgotten where he was. But the remoteness quickly vanished, and he grinned. "Nah. There's no hope for a higher life form in there. I don't know, either this stuff is getting worse or my tastebuds are finally improving."

He paused, and his eyes, with all their golds and greens and grays, took her in, seemed to drink in her very soul. Mollie forced herself not to look away. No wonder he was so good at what he did. Nothing escaped him. Nothing was beneath his probing interest. Yet, she thought, it couldn't be an easy way to live. Sometimes he had to wish he could just climb out of his own skin for a while and be as oblivious as most of the rest of the world.

"Helen send you up here?" he asked.

Mollie nodded. "She said you were in a bad mood."

"I am. She was angling to get me away from my desk so she could rummage through it. Drives her crazy thinking I know something she doesn't."

"Do you?"

"Yep."

"She won't actually go through your desk, will she?"

"Probably not. But she had to play it out. I can just see her standing there, itching to see what I've got, then congratulating herself when she doesn't go through with it."

"She knows you wouldn't leave anything out in the open."

"Even if I did, she'd stop herself. I've known Helen since I landed at the *Trib* as a know-it-all eighteen-year-old. She knows what lines she can cross and what lines she can't, not just with me. Part of the reason she's lasted as long as she has is she knows the First Amendment protects what we say, not what we do."

"Such as fraud, breaking and entering, harassment, trespassing."

He shrugged. "Such as." He eyed his coffee. "I used to pride myself on drinking swill. Times change. So, Miss Mollie," he said, shifting his gaze to her, "what brings you to Miami looking as if you've had another good scare?"

"I have." She sat on a chair at the end of the table, feeling formal, even awkward. "Had another good scare, that is."

His eyes bored into her, darkening. "Tell me."

"A phone call. It came on my business line, about ninety minutes ago. The voice was obviously altered, like those unnamed whistle-blowers on *60 Minutes*. It suggested I go back to Boston because Miami's dangerous."

"Did you report it to the police?"

She shook her head.

"Why not?"

"There's only my word that the call happened or that the caller said what he said. I don't want the police getting the wrong idea about me."

"You don't want to become a suspect."

"Or the crazy woman looking for attention."

Jeremiah pushed back his chair. "But the call happened."

She nodded.

He rose, grabbed her wrist, and pulled her to her feet. "Let's go," he said. "I've got a friend on the Palm Beach police you can talk to. It'll only take a minute. You can call from my desk." He grinned at her, an obvious attempt at levity. "Helen's had long enough to pull herself back from the precipice, wouldn't you say?"

"Jeremiah—"

"It'll take two minutes tops. You'll see."

They took the stairs back down to the newsroom, no sign of Helen Samuel at his desk. Jeremiah pulled out his chair and made Mollie sit. Then he flipped through a dog-eared Rolodex, dialed a number, got through to some guy named Frank, and handed the phone to her. She told him what had happened, the time, the altered voice, its exact words. Jeremiah made no pretense of not listening in. He sat on the corner of his desk, taking in every word. "I don't know that this is connected to the robbery on Friday," she said. "It could just be a nut who saw my name in the paper."

"Could be," Frank said. "I'll write this up. Give me your number in case I have any questions."

Mollie gave it to him. As she reached over to hang up the phone, her shoulder brushed Jeremiah's arm, immediately sending warm shivers through her. To be this close to him when she was this vulnerable wasn't too smart.

"There," he said. "Duty done. Feel better?"

"Marginally."

He slid off the desk. "It's a start."

She remained seated, blood rushing to her head as another impulsive plan took vague shape. "I have a dinner tonight in Boca Raton. Friends of Leonardo's invited me. It's at a private home on the water, probably about thirty guests."

"Our thief hasn't hit anything that small. Smallest was seventy-five."

"I know, but if I'm . . ." She inhaled, hating the word. "If I'm involved in any way, perhaps we should look at my pattern of activity, too, and not just the thief's."

Jeremiah went still. "We?"

She got to her feet, took a breath, and felt more

certain about her still-in-progress plan. "I leave Leonardo's at six-thirty. I intend to keep my eyes open. If anything strikes me as suspicious, I will do what I have to do."

"Nancy Drew strikes." But there was no humor in his voice.

"Don't patronize me, Jeremiah. I'm your 'common denominator.' I was attacked. I received that nasty phone call."

"Precisely why you should skip the dinner tonight and stay home and watch TV. Throw darts. Drag out your flute and play some tunes."

She raised her chin to him, aware of his penetrating gaze, unintimidated by his relentless intensity—or the sense he was making. "That would be giving in."

"That would be making an intelligent decision."

"Maybe, but you do what you have to do, and I'll do the same. Thank you for your time," she said, and started briskly across the newsroom.

"When you said we," he called quietly to her, "did that mean I'm invited tonight?"

She ignored him and kept on marching, and if he was frustrated and even a little irritated with her, so be it. She had come to him in the misguided hope he could be a friend, and he'd gone dictatorial and protective on her. Call the police. Stay home and throw darts.

Damn it, she thought, she half-hoped the thief would show up tonight and she could catch him herself.

"Nancy Drew," she muttered, and exited the newsroom, aware of every eye in the place on her.

But when she got to her car, Jeremiah was already

there, slouched up against its gleaming hood as if he owned it. Mollie sputtered. "How did you get here ahead of me? How did you know where I was parked—"

"I know all the shortcuts, and you'll notice there are no other black Jaguars in the visitors' lot." He eased off the hood. "You're on my turf now, sweet pea."

"So?"

"So I want to know why you drove all the way down here to tell me about this nasty little phone call. I want to know," he said, moving closer, "why you told me about your dinner tonight and said *we* should look at your pattern of activity and not just the thief's."

"The *we* was just a slip of the tongue. As for the call—" She met his gaze, ignored the flutter in the pit of her stomach, the deep, unfathomable, undeniable yearning she had to connect with this man. "I just wanted to make sure you didn't already know about it."

He had no visible reaction. "Why would I know about it?"

"Or the guy who tipped you off about me. Maybe he knows about it."

"You mean maybe he's the one who made the call," Jeremiah said, his tone steady, neutral. "And I knew about it."

"It's possible, isn't it? And if you have to keep an open mind, so do I."

"It's not possible I knew about it. If I had, I'd be throttling him right now. Is it possible he made the call? Theoretically, I suppose so, but my gut says no."

He considered a moment. The line of his jaw seemed harder, the muscles in his arms and shoulders leaner, tougher. Ten years of digging into crime and corruption seemed to have affected him physically, not just mentally. "But it's good you're keeping an open mind. Now. I'll be at your place no later than six-twenty-five."

"What? Why—"

"That's why you told me about your dinner tonight, isn't it?" His voice softened. "So I'd be there."

"I don't know. I wasn't thinking—"

"Think now."

She sighed. "I can't stand not knowing what's going on. I can't stand sitting around waiting for the next phone call. I guess I wanted to find a way to help you—or for you to help me—"

But he was shaking his head. "Mollie, we can't be a team, if that's what you're suggesting. I don't work that way."

"I know. You don't need to remind me." She hoisted her handbag onto her shoulder, tried to ease the lingering effects of the eerie call. "I understand. Really. Thanks for putting me in touch with Frank. Maybe the police will find this guy."

He touched the collar of her linen shirt, just a flick of the finger that nonetheless sent shock waves through her. "You're trying to tell yourself it's strictly business between us, Mollie, but it's not. It can't be."

"That's ridiculous." She sounded prim and unconvincing even to herself. She imagined he could see through the facade, straight into all the parts of her that still wanted him. "Of course it can."

"You're remembering. Right now, you're remembering."

Her knees quavered. "Remembering what?"

"I was your first lover." His voice was low, not much above a whisper, a caress. "You remember."

"Jeremiah . . ." She swallowed, telling herself this was a test, a way for him to establish terms. He liked making the rules. It was why he worked alone, it was why he stayed alone. She steeled herself against the onslaught of desire, the knot of confused emotions. "Jeremiah, I assure you, I'm long over you. I put your photo on my dartboard for my amusement, nothing more. It could have been a picture of Darth Vader."

He seemed amused. "And yesterday when I kissed you, could I have been Darth Vader then, too?"

"The Emperor," she said, unable to stop a smile.

"And if I kissed you right here, right now, what would I be?"

"Very forward." But her head spun, her body burned at the thought of his mouth on hers.

"I like being forward."

And his mouth descended to hers, his hand drifting to the back of her neck, where she wasn't injured. She threw a hand back on the hood of her car, steadying herself as his tongue slid between her lips, tasted, probed, her entire body responding.

He drew back slightly, his eyes dark, his own arousal evident. "That wasn't too forward, was it?"

Mollie straightened, tried to ignore the strain of her breasts against her linen top, the agony of wanting him. She was shaking with it, unsteady, her mind flooded with memories of him slowly, erotically exploring her body with his hands, then his mouth, teeth, and tongue, until, finally, when she was hot and quivering, taking her with hard, deep thrusts.

His dusky gaze told her that he, too, was remembering.

She willed coherency upon her thoughts. "Look, Jeremiah—" She swallowed, adjusting her shirt so her pebbled nipples wouldn't show. "I know what you're doing, but you don't have to worry. I'm not going to fall for you. It was my choice to drive down here. And I take full responsibility for the consequences of that choice."

"Hell, it sounds as if you decided to climb Mount Everest."

She smiled. "You just concentrate on doing your job, okay?"

He dragged one finger along the line of her jaw, sending a stream of liquid heat straight into her bloodstream. "I always do." He winked. "See you at six-twenty-five."

Jeremiah went back to his desk feeling grumpy, out of sorts, and way too damned much as if he should have taken Mollie back to his apartment for the rest of the afternoon. He checked his messages. Nothing. He plopped into his chair and stared at his blank computer screen. Neutrality and objectivity had gone straight to hell with the appearance of Mollie and her bottomless eyes, bruised neck, and tale of a nasty phone call.

Helen Samuel couldn't wait to accost him. "Okay. Tell me what Mollie Lavender was doing here."

Jeremiah swung around in his chair. Bad coffee and frustration burned in his stomach. Fatigue pounded behind his eyes. "You know why you've lasted as long as you have, Helen? You're by nature a very nosy woman."

She grinned at him, unoffended. "Yeah, yeah. You're just in a bad mood because you wanted to write the story about Friday night and couldn't. You're feeling conflicted."

"Conflicted? Jesus, Helen. A reporter has to make these kinds of calls all the time."

"Bullshit. You've got a woman wearing a necklace owned by one of the most famous tenors in the world. You've got the necklace ripped off at a fancy private party. You've got a gloved hand. You've got a daring, clever cat burglar. And you were *right there*. Jesus. It has to kill you. No wonder you're a grouch."

He shoved back his chair and stood up. "That's right, Helen. I was right there. I was a part of the goddamned story. No way could I write it. I did the right thing. So I'm not conflicted. "

"Yeah, well, you're a grump. You're still on this thing, aren't you?"

He sighed. "Damned lot of good it's doing me. I don't have a clue who's behind the robberies, or why, or how he's getting into exclusive parties without being noticed. I don't know if it's a man or a woman. I don't know if it's someone acting alone or a group. You know, even if the *Trib* had reported that Mollie Lavender, Palm Beach publicist, was robbed at Diantha Atwood's party Friday night, it would only have filled two inches on page thirty-seven."

"All right, all right." Helen studied him with an air of superior knowledge and experience that quickly got on his nerves. "You sure you're not in over your head, Tabak?"

"If I were," he said irritably, "I wouldn't tell the *Trib*'s goddamned gossip columnist. I'm going home and feeding my lizard. He's better company than what I get around here."

Helen grunted, unintimidated. "Your lizard have any say about what kind of company he has to put up with?"

Traffic on the causeway out to South Beach was miserable, the lousy weather bringing the tourists off the water and into the shops and restaurants. Although he groused and grumbled, Jeremiah supposed if he were a tourist, he'd be here, too.

He had to hunt a parking space, which didn't improve his mood, and when he got to his building, he found Croc out front with Bennie, the ex-tailor, and Albert, the ex-mobster. Not once in two years had Croc shown up at Jeremiah's home, always preferring to meet at public places on Ocean Drive. He looked like a street bum with his scraggly hair and clothes. Bennie pointed at him with his whittling knife. "This guy says he's a friend of yours. We were letting him hang around for a while, see if you showed up."

"I called the paper," Croc said, "and some woman picked up your phone and barked into it, said you'd gone home."

Helen. After his low blow, she might feel fewer compunctions about picking through his desk—and about telling an unknown on the phone where to find him. On the other hand, Croc could be very charming. Jeremiah figured Bennie and Albert had let him stick around because they had knives. A little adrenaline rush, wondering if Croc was legit or if they'd have to take him down. They seemed almost disappointed when he followed Jeremiah inside.

"I don't know why those old geezers haven't cut their hands off yet," Croc said on his way up the stairs. "Whittling's hard. You ever try it?"

"I grew up in the Everglades, Croc. I can whittle just fine."

When they reached his floor, Jeremiah unlocked his door, pushed it open, and motioned for Croc to enter first, noticed he was even more jittery than usual. "You smell my animals?" Jeremiah asked, trying to be conversational, get Croc to relax.

He paused, inhaled deeply, shook his head. "No, why?"

"In case I have anyone over, I like to know the place doesn't smell like a zoo. It's like people with cat boxes. They get used to the smell, don't realize the place stinks."

"Smells okay to me."

Not that Croc had an acute sense of smell. Jeremiah offered him a can of iced tea, all he had in the refrigerator. Croc took it, popped the top, and drank long and hard, as if he hadn't had anything to drink in days. A strange all-or-nothing kind of guy. He checked out the cages on the table and made noises at the animals, who each ignored him in turn. "I had fish once when I was a kid. I didn't take to them and they all went belly up. Then I had a dog, and he was all right. I guess he's dead by now."

"You don't know?"

"Nope. He was still alive when I left home."

Pushing Croc about his past was a guaranteed way

to shut him down. Jeremiah nibbled on the occasional crumbs Croc dropped—dead fish, a dog—and figured one of these days he might put together the whole cookie of just who Blake Wilder was, how he'd ended up on the streets at twenty-something. He sensed he was an odd stabilizing force in Croc's life, someone who took him on his own terms.

When he didn't go on, Jeremiah figured Croc had said all he planned to say about his childhood pets. He popped the top on his own can of iced tea. "So, what's up?"

"I've been doing a little legwork." Still more fidgety than usual, he paced in front of the table, polishing off his iced tea in a few big, crude gulps. He crushed the can with one hand, then dropped it on the floor and squished it down to pancake size. "Some of the rich crowd have been kind of excited about the robberies, you know, sort of getting off on the thrill."

"What're you doing, sneaking around Palm Beach and talking to rich people?"

"Hey, I never give away my methods. From what I'm hearing, the Mollie attack changed some minds. I mean, the scream, the bloody neck. Spooked some folks."

"Well it should." Jeremiah took a swallow of tea, which tasted mediocre at best, nothing like the sun tea he and his father used to make. They'd leave the jug out on the dock all morning long. He pulled his mind back to the task at hand. Croc in his kitchen, pacing, angling for something. "Look, Croc, I don't want you asking questions on my behalf. If you stick your nose in a hornet's nest, it's your doing. It's not going to be on my conscience."

" 'Course. That goes without saying." Croc frowned, studying Jeremiah as if he were seeing him for the first time since he'd gotten back. "You okay?"

"No. I'm in a lousy mood. What else have you heard?"

Croc didn't answer immediately.

Jeremiah inhaled, not wanting to take his mood out on his young friend—cohort, source, whatever Croc was these days. Kissing Mollie in a damned parking garage had used up what little patience he'd gotten up with that morning. "Croc—"

"Well, if you're crabby and I say something that pisses you off, I don't want you feeding me to your lizard here."

"My lizard's a vegetarian."

"Oh. Okay." He glanced over at the sleeping creature. "Ugly bastard, isn't he?"

Jeremiah set his can down on the counter with a bang that he didn't intend. No muscle control. He needed a run, an hour in the weight room, something to burn off the tension that had gripped him the moment he'd spotted Mollie walking across the *Trib* cafeteria.

"Heck, you are cranky." Croc grinned, highly entertained; but at Jeremiah's dark look, he got serious. "Okay, I know this isn't much, but some people in high places think Friday's attack definitely wasn't the work of our jewel thief. Could be a copycat, someone squeezing in on our guy's territory, or it could be a deliberate attempt to throw the police off the trail."

"Then you're off Mollie? You don't think she could have ripped the necklace from her own neck?"

"I didn't say that. Let's say she's our thief. She

knows she's the only common denominator we've got. So to throw us off, she fakes an attack on herself. Or let's say she's in with whoever the thief is and wants to throw us off *his* trail."

"This is getting convoluted, Croc."

"It's Palm Beach. You've got to think convoluted or you can miss the boat. These people know how to cover their tracks."

Jeremiah tried to figure out what Croc was saying. "You're mixing your metaphors."

"All I'm saying is, anything's possible when that much money and those kinds of reputations are at stake. My usual haunts, it's usually more straightforward." He leaned back on his chair, his feet going, one hand drumming the table; the critters didn't seem to mind, just slept in their cages. "So how come you're in such a foul mood? I mean, this is bad even for you."

"Mollie came to see me," Jeremiah told him, a quick tactical decision. "She had a threatening phone call this afternoon."

"Whoa," Croc said, still drumming his fingers.

"Yeah. The caller said Miami's a dangerous town and suggested she go back to Boston."

"Which says he knows she's from Boston." Croc jumped up, paced, if possible even more restless and jittery. "Wow, this is interesting. I've got to put this one into the old mental slow-cooker and let it simmer."

"Croc, if you know anything you haven't told me, you need to part with it now." Jeremiah kept his tone calm, steady, serious. "A woman's been hurt and threatened."

Croc went momentarily still. "You're either going to trust me, Tabak, or you're not."

"That's a two-way street."

"Yep. Sure is." He grinned. "Thanks for the iced tea."

"That's it? You're out of here?"

"That's it, I'm out of here." He started for the door. "See you around."

Two seconds later, Croc was gone. Jeremiah felt like kicking things, but his critters were still sleeping. With a growl, he grabbed his jackknife and headed downstairs. Bennie and Albert handed him a chunk of wood, and he whittled until it was time to head north to Palm Beach and his six-twenty-five rendezvous at Pascarelli's house. Whether she wanted to admit it or not, Mollie would be expecting him.

9

Whittling, traffic, and an attack of common sense almost kept Jeremiah from making it to Leonardo Pascarelli's by six-twenty-five. As it was, he arrived in Palm Beach with only two minutes to spare. Griffen Welles, not Mollie, opened the front gates for him and met him in the driveway. She had on a short, sleek white cover-up over a bright pink bathing suit, her long, golden legs just the right side of too thin. She tossed back her dark curls, eyeing him with frank curiosity and maybe a little suspicion. "Mollie's around back at the pool. I assume you're looking for her?"

"I am."

If Griffen were looking for a more complete explanation, she didn't say as she led him along a beautifully landscaped walk back to the pool. He had his share of rich friends. He could certainly afford a higher lifestyle than he was living, although nothing approaching that of Leonardo Pascarelli, which was still relatively modest by Palm Beach standards. He had no interest in maintaining and protecting an expensive piece of property, never mind living in it. If Croc were there, he'd be buzzing in Jeremiah's ear about whether Mollie had grown accustomed to her godfather's standard of living and didn't want to give it up.

Still, Jeremiah had to admit it was a hell of a nice backyard. The pool sparkled in the fading sun, and Deegan Tiernay was doing a deep dive off the board. He looked very young and energetic. Jeremiah watched him breaststroke underwater. It was a coolish evening, the rain at bay for now, the air laden with the smells of lush flowers and vegetation, the light shifting with the swaying of palms and oaks. There was none of the rawness and pungency of the wild swamp grasses of the Everglades to the west, a different world from Palm Beach, more Jeremiah's kind of paradise.

Deegan surfaced at Jeremiah's toes. "Mollie's gone upstairs. She'll be back down in a minute."

He went back under, and Griffen, watching him, said to Jeremiah, "We've got a pitcher of margaritas. Interested?"

"No, thanks."

She eased onto a lounge in the sun and slipped her sunglasses down over her eyes. "I haven't been into the pool yet. I'm not hot enough yet. Mollie's sweet to let us hang out here for the evening. It looks as if we'll get more rain. I have a pool at my condo, but it's not as big or as private. And needless to say, we aren't going to hang out at Deegan's house." She bent a long, tanned leg. "I'm glad I wasn't born rich. I'd hate to have the pressures on me he has on him. My folks do all right, but they're hardly in the Atwood-Tiernay league."

Jeremiah shrugged, remaining on his feet. After whittling, he had showered and dressed in dark trousers and dark shirt, allowing him to play either spy or dinner guest, depending on Mollie's state of mind. He went back and forth on which he'd prefer. A couple of hours with Leonardo Pascarelli's friends? Or a couple of hours sneaking around in the rain?

"I suppose you don't have a lot of sympathy for that sort of pressure," Griffen went on, her attention focused on him now, not her boyfriend in the pool.

Jeremiah shrugged. "A big trust fund and a snotty grandmother aren't the worst life can throw at you. Deegan will figure that out pretty quick. He's no dope."

"That he isn't."

Deegan jumped out of the pool and, bypassing his towel, splashed water on her, laughing when she squealed and leaped to her feet. He grabbed her by the elbows like the kid he was and heaved her into the pool. She went in fanny first, all the way under. She bobbed up instantly, laughing, splashing, pretending she was going to kill him. Deegan sat on her chair. "Ten laps before you're allowed out!"

She stuck her tongue out at him, looking more like a teenager herself, but eased off into the water, doing a slow backstroke. Deegan didn't take his eyes off her. And she knew it. Jeremiah observed the proceedings with mild interest. His lifestyle did not include many twenty-one-year-old rich kids dunking their older girlfriends in a pool owned by a world-famous opera singer. He was, he thought dryly, out of his element.

"So," Deegan said, eyes still on Griffen, "Mollie didn't seem surprised to have you show up. I didn't ask why not, because it's none of my business."

A smart lad indeed. Mollie didn't respond too well to overprotective males, as Jeremiah himself had discovered. He supposed it came from having a flaky family. He figured she'd been left to her own devices from the time she was a tot and had learned early on how to take care of herself, responding to a sort of benign, even healthy, neglect on the part of her parents. He'd had the run of the Everglades from the time he could walk and understood that defiant gene, if not the Lavenders particularly.

"I wouldn't underestimate her if I were you," Deegan went on seriously. "She tends to take people at face value more readily than I would, but she's not naive." He talked as if he were sitting in a sociology class. He peered over at Jeremiah. "She knows you're probably on this jewel thief story."

This, Jeremiah thought, was true. However, he had no intention of discussing his relationship with Mollie—or his work—with her college intern. "I'd say she knows a lot."

Deegan didn't take the hint. "I've been around reporters since I could walk. You live and breathe the next story. You're never off." He reached for the margarita pitcher. "Mollie's new in town, but she's got people looking out for her. Her clients are all loyal."

"Including Ash, the dog."

Deegan didn't like that one. He almost came up off

his chair, but instead just angled a nasty look at Jeremiah. "You're a real asshole, aren't you?"

"I have my moments," Jeremiah said mildly.

But the kid wasn't finished. "She's been straight with me right from the start, no BS, no coddling or hand-holding. Not just anyone would let Michael Tiernay's son intern for them, you know. Anything goes wrong, he could ruin them. But if everything goes *too* well, then they look like a toady."

"Tough balancing act."

"It's not one thirteen-year-old shooting another in the back, but, yeah, it's tough." His tone wasn't as defensive as it could have been given the sentiment beneath his words. "I'm also known as a spoiled pain in the ass. That doesn't help."

"Are you?"

Deegan paused, looked back at Griffen's long, slim, tanned body as she swam back toward their end of the pool. His mouth was grim, and he said with unexpected self-awareness, "I'm trying not to be."

Jeremiah breathed in the fragrant air, wishing he'd had more sleep last night. He was missing something. Some connection, some fragment of insight, information, truth. Here he was, sitting by a pool in Palm Beach chatting with a rich kid who was neck deep in trying to establish his own identity. It was as if someone had transported him, Jeremiah Tabak, hard-hitting *Miami Tribune* investigative reporter, out of his real life and dropped him on the damned moon. This was Helen Samuel's territory, not his.

A fragment floated by, and he grabbed it, turning to Deegan. "Your parents gave you the green light to intern with Mollie because of her relationship with Leonardo Pascarelli, didn't they?"

Deegan seemed surprised at his insight, and admitted grudgingly, "That's right. It allowed them to save face. They let me intern with Mollie or they'd have had to start talking cutting off the trust fund, and they don't want to do that. Too complicated and time-consuming, too messy. So, the Leonardo connection gave them an out." He poured himself a margarita, shrugging, distancing himself from his own emotions about his parents. He was twenty-one, the legal drinking age. What did he care? "It allowed them to postpone our day of reckoning another few months."

"I see. Does Mollie know or does she actually think she's getting to teach you something?"

He went momentarily sullen as he replaced the pitcher and sat back with his margarita glass. "She's doing right by me. I'm trying to do right by her."

"You learning anything?"

"I do my job."

In other words, up yours, Tabak. Deegan Tiernay not only was spoiled, Jeremiah decided, but an arrogant little shit. Of course, the kid was twenty-one. He was trying to sort out his identity and responsibilities and probably had no idea, really, how goddamned good he had it. He was rich, he was Michael and Bobbi Tiernay's only son, Diantha Atwood's only grandson, and he had a pretty, older, successful girlfriend. Why not be full of himself?

"I don't think Mollie realizes the extent her relationship with Leonardo colors how people around here think about her," Deegan went on. "She doesn't flaunt it or use it to her advantage—she doesn't think that way—

but other people do. Other people," he said, sipping his margarita, "meaning most everyone around here."

"Her clients?"

He shook his head. "The Leonardo connection might get them at first, but it wouldn't keep them—and once they get to know her, they forget about him. It's just going to be hard for her to figure out who her real friends are and who's just pretending because of her godfather." Deegan studied Jeremiah a moment, his damp skin drying quickly in the last of the day's sun. "I know you think I'm a jerk. No, no, it's okay, you're not the first. I just . . . well, I do respect Mollie."

"That's good," Jeremiah said.

Griffen scrambled out of the pool and snatched a towel out from under Deegan, tossing it over her shoulders as she pulled up another lounge chair and poured herself a margarita. "Are you two talking about Mollie while she's up trying to figure out what to wear? Shame on you." She smiled, sliding onto her chair. "Men."

Mollie emerged from the brick walk and joined them on the terrace. She wore a little black dinner dress with a jacket that hid her bruised neck. Simple earrings, no rings, no bracelets, no necklace. Hair brushed out, pale and shimmery in the fading light. She was, Jeremiah thought as she gave him a curt nod, more stunning than she realized.

Also not sure about having him behind her gates. "As you can see, I'm running late." Without waiting for a reply, she turned to Deegan. "Stay as long as you like. You remember how to lock up?"

"Yep. Have a good time. Griffen and I will make sure the silver stays safe."

Mollie gave a mock shudder. "I'm beginning to understand why my parents don't own anything. It's too complicated."

"What's so complicated about locking the door and turning on the alarm system?" Deegan was highly amused. "Ah, the different worlds we live in. See you in the morning, Mollie."

"Thanks for letting us hang out here," Griffen said.

"No problem."

"If the phone rings, do you want us to answer it?"

Mollie hesitated, then shook her head. "Let voice mail take it."

Griffen nodded, and from the seriousness of her expression, Jeremiah assumed Mollie had told her about the threatening call earlier that afternoon. But she started out briskly on the walk, and he followed. "They're madly curious about us."

"I didn't expect them to be here when you arrived."

"I'll bet. They're going to grill you tomorrow. They might even stick around until you come home tonight. Doesn't help that you look as if you're going off with the devil himself."

She cocked her head at him. "Who knows? Maybe I am."

"Ah," he said, "this must mean I'm not getting dinner."

"Explaining you to my intern and my best friend is one thing." The garage door was already open, and she unlocked the passenger door to the Jag. "Explaining you to Leonardo's friends is quite another. And I don't want to be duplicitous and let them believe you're someone you're not."

Presumably that would be someone she'd kiss on

the hood of a car in a Miami parking garage. "Then why am I going?"

"Because the dinner party is in a large house with extensive grounds. I can drop you off at the end of the driveway, and you can skulk." She smiled at him, coolly, and Jeremiah realized on some level she was enjoying herself. "I imagine you're good at skulking."

He climbed into the passenger seat. "Save me a doggy bag?"

The smile wanted to become genuine, but she'd had a hard day. "I'll slip an éclair in my handbag." She went around and climbed in behind the wheel. "Shall we?"

"I'm game."

She turned the key in the ignition and backed out, reshutting and locking the gates with a flick of a button. She sighed, her grip visibly loosening on the wheel. "This is crazy. You and I both know the thief isn't going to strike tonight, not at a small dinner party in a private home, even if I am *the* common denominator. It's not as if he's struck every time I've gone anywhere."

"True." Jeremiah watched her gnaw on a corner of her lower lip, imagined himself doing much the same. It could be a long night.

"Which means you're here on my account." She glanced over at him, her eyes clear and focused. "You don't want me out alone. Am I right?"

"You're right."

"And?"

"And what?"

"Aren't you going to elaborate?"

"Elaborating," he said, "would only make you nervous, and I don't want to ruin your dinner."

Her eyes, lightly made up in a way that emphasized their blueness, narrowed on him as she slowed for a stop sign. "What's that supposed to mean?"

Jeremiah settled back in the comfortable, expensive seat. "It means I think you wanted me here tonight because you don't want to be out alone, and I happen to agree."

"Oh. You're still being protective."

He bit back his amusement. "And you, Mollie, are being deliberately dense. If I were just being protective, you wouldn't give a damn. You'd dismiss it as Tabak-the-SOB-reporter. What gets you is that I care."

"About your work," she said stubbornly.

"About *you*." At her flush and abrupt pull-out from the stop, Jeremiah laughed outright. "You see? Bad enough you'll have to eat dinner with me hovering in the bushes. Now you'll have to fret about someone caring enough about you to risk Dobermans and electric fences."

She frowned. "I have a lot of friends who care about me."

"Trust me, darlin'," he said, laying on the accent, "I'm different."

Leonardo's friends lived in a pale coral stucco house on the water. Mollie dropped Jeremiah off at the end of their winding, narrow driveway, where the grounds were thick with palms, vines, banyans, and live oaks. The property was unfenced. He could go unnoticed for days, never mind an evening.

She buzzed down the passenger window and said across the seat, "By the way, there are no electric fences. And no need to worry about the Dobermans."

He frowned at her. "What Dobermans?"

"Mozart, Ludwig, Cosima."

"Cosima," Jeremiah repeated.

"Wagner's wife."

"Mollie, that's three Dobermans."

"Yes, and they're all sweethearts. They'll probably be inside tonight," she added, "because of the rain. So, not to worry."

He looked at her darkly, no doubt reconsidering his role as her musketeer, but she resumed her trip up the driveway, leaving him to whatever he planned to do with himself for the next two to three hours.

Within five minutes of her arrival, Mollie knew she wasn't going to relax and forget about Jeremiah outside, listening to the crickets and on the alert for Dobermans and God only knew what as he kept her—and by extension Leonardo's friends—from the clutches of a jewel thief. A jewel thief, she reminded herself, who had never, once, broken into one of the parties he'd robbed. What he was doing was making sure he hadn't made a mistake about her after all and she *wasn't* the thief herself.

She was absolutely sure of it, no matter how convincing he was about caring about her.

No matter how much a part of her wanted to be convinced.

If his peculiar sense of honor had misled her into believing the worst about him ten years ago, it could just as easily compel him to keep an open mind about discovering the worst about her now.

Fortunately, Leonardo's friends were so boisterous and fun, so much like him, that she had a hard time sulking about Jeremiah's motives. She did feel an occasional pang of guilt at having dropped him off on their property, but she knew, too, that they would understand. She was blessed, she thought, with indulgent family and friends.

And she was proud of herself for resisting a giggle of pure delight when it started to drizzle, and another when they let out the three Dobermans. They were well-trained, beautiful dogs who wouldn't hurt an intruder, although they might converge on him if they found him, which could be scary. Apparently they didn't, because after a few minutes, they bounded back to the roofed terrace overlooking the water, where their masters' guests had gathered for dessert and after-dinner drinks.

It wasn't until Mollie was halfway through her chocolate mousse cake that the subject of her Friday evening attack came up. One woman, a tireless volunteer for virtually every arts organization in Palm Beach, said Diantha Atwood was still upset about what had happened. "You can imagine how personally she would take having one of her guests *attacked*. It must have been horrible for you, Mollie."

"And I understand Jeremiah Tabak was the first on the scene," the woman's husband said. He was a high-profile attorney, and he spoke of Jeremiah with a measure of grudging respect.

As subtly as she could, Mollie encouraged her fellow diners to tell her what they knew about him—which, she quickly discovered, was a fair amount, certainly more than she did. They said he kept reptiles and lived beneath his means. He was a frequent, popular guest on national television news shows, especially when a Miami story broke, but had no interest in television work on a full-time basis. He was known as an opinionated, irascible speaker on the rare occasions anyone got him to speak in public. He'd been linked with a number of women, but had never married. His lifetime commitment, it seemed, was to his work. He was doing what he wanted to do, and he did it well.

This was not a man who wanted the same things out of life that she did, Mollie thought. She enjoyed her work, too, but it wasn't her life. Starting her own business had taken up much of her time in recent months, but she wanted balance in her life. Family, friends, vacations, afternoons with her feet up.

She considered herself forewarned. Or *re*warned. Jeremiah was a formidable journalist, and although he hadn't behaved unethically ten years ago, he hadn't permitted her inside his world. Ultimately, perhaps that was why he'd lied—not for her sake, but for his own, to make sure she went back to Boston and out of his life. Loving someone scared the hell out of him.

She'd worked up a good head of steam by the time she bid her hosts good evening and started down the long, dark driveway. To hell with Tabak. She didn't know why she'd wanted him around tonight. He was just keeping his options open. Damn him, anyway.

"Oh, shit!"

She was twenty yards up the main road before she realized she'd forgotten him. She turned around and went back, this time keeping an eye out for him and going slow enough that he'd have a chance to flag her down.

As she started around a curve, her headlights caught him.

No, not him. Another man. Thin, young, wearing dark clothes.

She stomped on the brake and held her breath, her window open to the sounds of the wind and the ocean, the pungent-sweet smells of the brush and trees. The man darted back behind a banyan tree. With a shaking hand, Mollie hit the lock on her door. She would drive up to the house and have her hosts call the police. Even if he was just a transient, he had no business on their property.

A tap came at the passenger window, and she nearly jumped out of her skin.

Jeremiah.

She rolled down the window. "You almost gave me a heart attack. Did you see that man? Where did he go?"

"He's right behind me. His name's Croc, and he's a friend of mine."

She blinked dumbly. "Croc?"

The skinny man poked his head out from behind Jeremiah and grinned. "Hey, Miss Mollie, how you doing?"

"I'm not doing very well at all at the moment. Who are you?"

"Jeremiah's friend."

Jeremiah grimaced. "That's stretching it right now, Croc."

Croc laughed. "He's ready to string me up because I followed you two out here." He cuffed Jeremiah on the shoulder. "But you spotted me, man. You're not bad at this cloak and dagger shit."

"Wait just a minute," Mollie said. "Jeremiah, would you mind explaining to me what in hell's going on here?"

"On our way back to your place—"

"Uh-uh. Now."

He sighed, his patience obviously stretched beyond its meager limits. "I noticed Croc in a car behind us on our way over. I didn't mention it because I wasn't positive who it was, and because Croc's not the easiest person to explain."

"He's your informant." Mollie suddenly felt a chill. "He's the one who discovered I was a common denominator."

"*The* common denominator," Croc corrected proudly.

Jeremiah shot him a look that would have silenced half of south Florida. His expression softened when he shifted back to Mollie. "I'm sorry if he scared you. He's having trouble sorting out what's his business and what's not."

"Boundary problems," Croc said. "They go way back with me. Tabak's been working on getting me on the straight and narrow."

"I've known Croc about two years," he said.

Mollie took in his words, trying to remain as cool as he was, as calmly professional. "And you couldn't have told me about him."

"Under the circumstances, no."

"Until I meet him on a dark road in the middle of the night. *Then* you can tell me."

Croc frowned. "It's what, ten o'clock? That's not the middle of the night."

Mollie directed herself to him. "I could have run you over."

"Not me. I've got quick reflexes." He patted her rooftop. "Even a Jag I could dodge."

"Croc," Jeremiah said darkly, "if you don't want Mollie to back up and try again, I'd shut the hell up."

"Right," Croc said.

Mollie felt like rolling her window up on both of them. "If anyone turns out to be missing so much as a dime-store ring tonight, I'll have the police pay you two a visit. Consider yourselves lucky I don't call them right now." She gave them a fake smile. "Good night."

And that was that. Croc started to argue, but Jeremiah grabbed him by the shirt, yanked him out of the way, and let Mollie pass. She did a neat three-point turn and continued on to the main road and out to Leonardo's house, trying not to think about anything except the traffic, her speed, the turns she needed to make. Jeremiah had known this Croc had followed them to dinner. He hadn't said anything. He'd been out there for the past three hours doing God only knew what, and she'd known it and had let it happen, had even *made* it happen. This wasn't her property, these weren't even her friends, not yet. They were Leonardo's friends, and she had used them badly.

There were no two-way streets where Jeremiah Tabak was concerned.

It was something she desperately needed to remember.

"Guess you lost your ride home," Croc said after Mollie had abandoned them.

Jeremiah gritted his teeth. It was pitch-dark, cool, raining again. "Croc, why I don't hang you from this banyan, I don't know."

"What'd I do?"

"I have half a mind to drag your ass down to the police station."

"What for?"

"Personal satisfaction."

"Hey, I'm not your thief. For all we know, your tootsie there waltzed off with a trunkload of jewels."

Jeremiah stopped in his tracks. He glared at Croc in the dark. With the clouds and the rain, it was not a pleasant night to be out. Croc's shape was visible, just not any of his features. Which was just as well. The wrong look, the wrong glint in his eye, and Jeremiah didn't know what he'd do. "Mollie is not your thief. Will you get that out of your head?"

"Okay. She's not the thief."

There was no conviction in his tone. Jeremiah sighed. "What's your interest in this thing, Croc? Just explain that to me."

"Keeps me off the streets."

"I hadn't noticed."

What Jeremiah calculated was the last of the guests drove past, making it relatively safe for him and Croc to walk out on the driveway instead of in the wet brush. He didn't mind, but Croc kept expecting alligators and snakes. "I'm probably full of spiders," he grumbled when they hit smooth pavement.

"Good," Jeremiah said.

"You're a heartless bastard, you know?"

"I haven't strangled you yet."

"Yeah, yeah, so I should be grateful. You want a ride home?"

"My truck's at Mollie's. It's not that far. I can walk."

"What, and give her time to have your truck towed? That'll cost you a mint. You know, she's pissed because you didn't tell her she was being followed."

"If you will recall, I didn't know for sure it was you."

"Yep," Croc said, "I recall."

After he'd slipped from Mollie's car, Jeremiah had hidden in the brush and waited for whoever had followed her to make an appearance. It was Croc's good fortune that Jeremiah had recognized him before he'd decked him. As it was, he'd scared the daylights out of one twenty-something informant.

"My car's down the road about a quarter-mile," Croc said.

Jeremiah relented. "All right. You can drive me back to Mollie's. But I suggest you crawl back into whatever hole you crawled out of and leave her the hell alone. Understood?"

"Aye-aye, *mon capitaine*."

Jeremiah charged down the driveway, Croc on his heels, unruffled. That they'd managed to avoid being spotted by any of tonight's dinner guests suggested Croc had deliberately let Mollie see him. He'd wanted to find out what she would do, and he'd wanted to meet her.

"Think about it, Tabak." Croc was having to move fast to keep up. "If you were an innocent dinner guest and came upon a strange man in the dark, would you have rolled down your window and chatted with him?

I mean, it would have made more sense if she'd tried to run me over or drove back up to the house and called the police."

"Croc, for God's sake. She saw me half a second after she saw you."

"I don't know." They came to the end of the driveway and turned up the road. Streetlights and passing cars provided some illumination. "I think she *knows* I wasn't the jewel thief. Which means she must know who it really is."

"That's a huge leap in logic."

"So? Logic's your department." He grinned over at Jeremiah. "I consider myself a visionary."

"Yeah, well, visionary me back to my truck."

Croc's car was a little red Volkswagen Rabbit that fit in Palm Beach even less well than Jeremiah's truck. A truck was an essential piece of equipment. Gardeners could have beat-up trucks. Rich men who drove Lincolns and Mercedes during the day liked to rough it with a beat-up truck. But a rusted, ancient Rabbit with bald tires didn't make the grade. Croc didn't seem to care. "I'm telling you, this baby costs *nothing* to keep on the road."

Jeremiah wondered who paid the insurance. And whose name it was in. He could run the license plate, but that seemed premature, a violation of the fragile trust he and Croc, aka Blake Wilder, had established. Not that the little bastard was holding up his end. He was damned lucky Jeremiah still didn't throttle him for following Mollie.

When they arrived at Pascarelli's, she was backing Jeremiah's truck onto the street. It was bucking wildly. "I don't think she's so good with a clutch," Croc said.

"That clutch is balky."

Jeremiah winced at the squeal of tires and sudden silence as the engine choked. The truck was still crooked, its front tires well out into the street, but Mollie apparently had had enough. The door opened, and she climbed out.

Croc gave a low whistle. "Guess that's a hint, huh?"

"Go home, Croc." Jeremiah pushed open the rusting passenger door and got out. "Call me tomorrow. We'll talk."

This time not arguing, Croc did a quick turnaround and sped off. Jeremiah approached his truck, and Mollie, with a certain prudent wariness. "I'm surprised you didn't let the air out of my tires."

She turned to him, dusting off her hands as if there'd been something nasty on his steering wheel, and tossed her head back, the streetlight catching the ends of her pale hair. She still had on her little black dinner dress. "That would only encourage you to stay longer."

He moved closer. "Mad, huh?"

"Very."

"You deserve to be."

She narrowed her eyes on him. "Is that an apology?"

"Mollie, I wasn't a hundred percent sure it was Croc. I wasn't even a hundred percent sure we'd been followed. I didn't want to ruin your evening if I was wrong. When I tracked him down on your friends' grounds, I could hardly waltz up to the house and come clean to you."

She didn't soften. "Would you have told me if I hadn't spotted him?"

Jeremiah moved even closer, aware of the cool evening air, the shape of her under her dress, of his own ragged muscles, his hair and clothes damp from the intermittent rain, the crazy trek through underbrush. "I don't know. I hadn't thought that far ahead."

"I see. Well, fair enough. Here are your keys." She dangled them from two fingers. Jeremiah held out his palm, and she dropped them in. "Good night."

She started back toward her open gates, casting a long shadow on the elegant brick driveway.

Jeremiah stayed where he was. "What would you do if you were trapped in there with a pack of wild dogs and your gates didn't work?"

She arched him a mystified look. "I'd just have to get out my tranquilizer gun and tranquilize them."

"You don't have a tranquilizer gun."

"You don't have a pack of wild dogs, and my gates work fine."

He settled back on his heels, studying her.

She couldn't stand the scrutiny for long. "What is it?"

"How come there's no man in your life?"

She swiveled around at him, obviously taken aback by his question. "Should there be? A woman can't be happy and fulfilled without a man in her life?" She thrust her hands on her hips. "Why isn't there a woman in *your* life?"

"Who says there isn't?"

"You don't have a committed relationship, a partnership, with a woman, Jeremiah. It's not in your nature."

He frowned. "It's not?"

"No. Your only committed relationship is with your work."

"Which isn't going too well right now. I'm spending most of my time chasing a story I can't write."

"Because it would be unethical," she said, with just a hint of sarcasm.

Jeremiah grinned at her. "You're not as hard as you think you are, Mollie. You know you've forgiven me for ten years ago." He moved toward her, enough of a saunter in his gait to aggravate her. He was having fun all of a sudden. And so, he was confident, was she. "It's just killing you to admit it."

"You changed my life. All my plans, all my expectations—everything changed after our week together."

"Maybe it needed changing."

"That's not the point."

"What's the point?" He caught up her fingers into his, drew her just a little closer. "That I hurt you?" She blinked rapidly, not answering, and he pressed her fingers to his mouth. "I never meant to hurt you, Mollie. If I could go back and unhurt you, I would."

He could see her throat tighten, her lips part, a spark of desire in her eyes. When he curved an arm around her back and she said nothing, didn't pull away, he knew she was going to let the kiss happen. His mouth on hers, the taste of her, the feel of her body pressed up against his. It was the stuff of his dreams for the past decade.

And yet when his mouth did find hers, he couldn't pretend this was anything but real. Every fiber of him flared, set afire by the taste of her, the feel of her as she wrapped her arms around him, splaying both hands on his back as if to take in as much of him as she could. He heard her sharp intake of breath as their kiss deepened, restraint vanishing. He drew her fully against him, a moan of pleasure and need escaping as he fought for air, his senses running wild, soaking up everything, the chirping of the birds, the soughing of the breeze, the hum of distant traffic, the scent of grass and flowers, all of it a detailed backdrop to the play of his tongue against hers, the light, hot kisses he trailed along her jaw.

"Ah, Mollie." He kissed her once more on the mouth, fiercely, before he pulled back, straightened. "A good thing for curious neighbors, wouldn't you say?"

"I suppose." She caught her breath, reeling. "I don't think either of us can make a case for neutrality right now."

"I expect not."

"You'll wait for me to lock the gates?"

He nodded. He wouldn't be spending the night with her. Under the circumstances, a spine-melting kiss was as much as he could expect for tonight. "'Night, Mollie."

She smiled, the stiffness of anger and self-doubt gone, a genuine openness in their place. He liked her unguarded, relaxed, not trying to pretend she wasn't still attracted to him. "Good night, Jeremiah." The smile faded, just for an instant, and she said quietly, "And I have forgiven you. And myself."

She was through the gates, and as they shut, Jeremiah wondered if a little part of her wasn't telling herself that next time, she should hope for the pack of wild dogs instead of a man who'd already broken her heart once.

10

⌘

Mollie had spread over her kitchen table everything that had ever been said about Chet Farnsworth from his first interview on joining NASA to a review in the Fort Lauderdale *Sun-Sentinel* of his Sunday performance. She felt sane, professional, able to concentrate on her work. Last night's lunacy was behind her.

But when her phone rang, she jumped and stared at it, heart racing, as if it were possessed by evil spirits. Yesterday's threatening call still reverberated. Her job, however, required her to be on the phone. She couldn't let one cretin deter her.

She took a breath, picked it up, and said her name.

"Can't you screen your calls?" Jeremiah asked without preamble.

"Not if I expect to stay in business." She thought she sounded remarkably steady given the rush of stress chemicals pouring through her bloodstream. "What's up?"

"I'm calling to check in."

"Where are you?"

He didn't answer at once. "Worth Avenue. I'm parked in front of a fancy children's clothing store. There's a mannequin in the window of a girl in a frilly dress. She looks like Little Bo Peep."

Mollie smiled. "I know the shop." Worth Avenue was Palm Beach's answer to Rodeo Drive. "Is your friend Croc with you?"

"Croc isn't my friend, and I don't know where he is. I never know, which is one of the hazards of my association with him. After last night, I'm afraid he's become a loose cannon. But it wouldn't be easy reining him in."

"That must be unnerving for you." Not to mention for her.

"Aggravating is more like it. Tell me about your day, Mollie. What do you have going?"

"I need to run an errand this morning—on Worth Avenue, as a matter of fact."

"We could meet for coffee."

She settled back in her chair at the kitchen table, calmer. "Don't you have a real story you should be working on?"

"I've got a few leads I could chase down, but right now I'm still officially between stories. I can focus on you." His voice was low, the twangy drawl not too obvious. "Don't you feel lucky?"

"Uh-huh. Sure. Since you waltzed back into my life, I've been attacked, threatened, suspected of being a thief, and driven to letting you and your mysterious friend Croc sneak around while I ate dinner."

"You've also been kissed quite thoroughly."

"Jeremiah, you are incorrigible."

"So people keep telling me, although not because I find myself kissing just anyone in a parking garage." He paused. "We should have gone upstairs last night."

She inhaled sharply, a hot jolt of awareness coursing through her. "You're in an awfully cheeky mood this morning."

"Comes from lack of sleep. What're you doing after Worth Avenue?"

He would not be distracted from the point of his call, which was to keep tabs on her. "I have a luncheon at the Paulette Mansion. A security expert is speaking to one of the local women's societies—"

"George Marcotte. How fortuitous. I'll be there myself."

"You will?" She frowned. "Why?"

"Gut instinct. Plus I've lined up a quick interview with Marcotte. I want to hear his take on our cat burglar."

"You just made that up."

He laughed. "For a publicist, you have a suspicious mind."

"That's because I know you."

"You're getting there." The sexy undertone was unmistakable. "Reconsider coffee."

He started to hang up, but Mollie said, "I talked to Leonardo this morning. I asked him if he had any enemies who might be targeting me to get to him. You know, that's what this could be about. Someone setting me up for the robberies or just capitalizing on them as a way of getting at Leonardo."

"What did he say?" Jeremiah asked, serious now.

She could almost feel his mind opening, taking in a new scenario.

"He has enemies—the usual jealousies and lost loves and whatnot—but he can't think of anyone who would take their animosity toward him out on me, and certainly not in such a byzantine approach."

"Did he say byzantine?"

"Yes, why not?"

"I don't think my father and I have ever used *byzantine* with each other, even when I studied Constantinople in the sixth grade. Okay. Never mind. Go on."

She sighed. "His enemies, he said, were more likely to take a direct approach or just sue him." She suddenly felt self-conscious, especially when Jeremiah went quiet on her. "Anyway, I just wanted to let you know. Consider every angle, right?"

"Yes. Thanks for telling me. I'll give it some thought and see you at the luncheon."

She hung up feeling prickly-skinned, as if she'd said something wrong, something that had spooked Jeremiah or sent him spinning off in a whole new direction. She could imagine him sitting in his truck, frowning, his reporter's mind at work. When she finally headed off to Worth Avenue, she found herself looking for him. All the parking spots in front of the children's store were taken, none with a beat-up brown truck. She ended up taking one farther down the street. She fed the meter, wondering if Jeremiah was watching her from a shop window.

Her errand took her to a small, eclectic music shop on one of the famous Worth Avenue vias—the shaded alleyways and patios Addison Mizner had set behind the buildings that fronted the street. Vines of fuchsia bougainvillea and ivy cascaded from the wrought-iron balconies of pastel-colored buildings, and there were window boxes and urns of bright flowers, decorative trees, stone fountains, and benches. Mollie breathed in the heavenly scents and sights, only half-pretending she wasn't keeping an eye out for Jeremiah or his skinny cohort.

"You can relax," she told herself. "It's just another day on the job."

She returned to her car without incident. Perhaps Jeremiah had already gone to the luncheon, she thought with a palpable sense of anticipation. Don't analyze it, she told herself. Just go with it.

The luncheon was being held in a 1920s mansion that had been purchased and restored by a group of south Florida women executives. They'd turned it into an exclusive retreat, with elegant rooms available for public functions, especially those of particular interest to women. Mollie made her way back to the spacious, airy screened porch, where she immediately recognized Griffen's touch in the mango-colored tablecloths and napkins in an array of vibrant colors. Each of the tables had its own small, perfect orchid in the center. Griffen herself was whirling around getting lunch pulled together, but caught Mollie's eye long enough to give her a cautionary look. Which could only mean Jeremiah had arrived.

Mollie turned, and there he was, casually dressed, a contrast to most of the women drifting in, a mix of professionals and volunteers. Mollie herself had opted for a navy suit, not particularly creative, but it made her feel more brass-tacks and in control.

Jeremiah was studying her with a seriousness that,

given the tone of their earlier conversation, she didn't expect. "Is something wrong? Don't tell me the thief's already struck—"

He shook his head. His slate blue shirt brought out all the colors in his eyes, but emphasized the grays. "Your call to Leonardo got me thinking. It hadn't even occurred to me before—" He inhaled, glancing around them for eavesdroppers. "Mollie, it's possible I'm the one who's brought all this down on you. You weren't even aware of a jewel thief until after you saw me at the Greenaway."

"But I was already the common denominator—"

"There are two ways of looking at that. One, it's a coincidence that the thief is capitalizing on after the fact. Two, he deliberately chose events you attended. Either way, he could be using you to get to me." His intensity charged the air between them. "It's no more farfetched than considering Leonardo's enemies."

"Then the thief would have to know about our past relationship," Mollie said, trying to get her brain around the complexities of what he was suggesting.

"That's not an absolute necessity. Again, he could be improvising as he goes along. He's luring me onto the story—"

"Through Croc?"

"Yes. Then you get involved, and he ups the ante." Mollie frowned. "This would mean you have an enemy."

"Darlin'," he said dryly, "I have dozens of enemies. I report on crime and corruption in a major American city."

She nodded, trying not to acknowledge the unsteadiness in her knees. She was aware of women circulating on the porch, glasses clinking, warm laughter, flamingos walking on the sprawling, manicured lawn. It was a perfect day. Warm, sunny, just enough of a breeze.

Jeremiah smiled gently, but his eyes were still intense. "This is still just speculation. I'm just thinking we might be wise to steer clear of each other for the time being. The last thing I'd want is to put you in danger."

"I hate this," she said, her throat tight.

Diantha Atwood and Bobbi Tiernay brought George Marcotte over, introducing him. He was in his mid-thirties, a beefy tree-trunk of a man with shaggy, tawny hair and a friendly manner. He wore an expertly tailored suit, although Mollie expected he would have preferred shorts and a T-shirt.

"We were just discussing the jewel thief," Bobbi Tiernay said. "Mr. Marcotte has agreed to address simple, common-sense ways we can protect ourselves without overreacting."

Marcotte turned to Mollie. "For the most part, this thief has been non-violent. You were smart not to put up a fight or go after him, Ms. Lavender."

She shrugged. "It's not like I had time to think."

"Which can make recovering from such an incident more difficult. Your mind fills with what might have been, how your fate can turn on the head of a pin." He was articulate, speaking as a man who'd been in her shoes. "But you trusted your instincts. That's good. Mr. Tabak," he said, shifting to Jeremiah. "Have you learned anything you can share with us?"

"Nope. It was only a coincidence I was there on Friday when Mollie was attacked."

"But you're investigating this story for the *Tribune*," Diantha Atwood said.

"Actually, I'm not."

"No?" She smiled, coolly polite. "Come now, you don't expect us to believe that."

Jeremiah regarded her neutrally, but Mollie knew his rude switch had been flipped. He seemed to check himself at the last minute and said only, "That's not my concern."

Diantha Atwood's cheeks colored. She wasn't one to back down to a reporter. "Then why are you here today?"

"Same reason I was there on Friday. I was invited."

"By whom, may I ask?"

He winked, the southern charmer replacing the cold, intense reporter. "Sorry, Mrs. Atwood, I never divulge my sources."

It was a line and they all knew it, but Diantha Atwood laughed. Several other women joined them, and she and her daughter and Marcotte spun off into the crowd. There was a sprinkling of men, mostly decades older than Jeremiah or the speaker, both of whom would have stuck out in any crowd. Mollie leaned toward him. "*Were* you invited?"

"As a matter of fact, yes, which I find curious at the moment. Oops. There's your friend Griffen. Ah, yes, if eyes could shoot daggers . . ." He grinned, his earlier seriousness having abated. "Or darts, as the case may be. Griffen's protective of you, I think."

"I'm new in town, and I don't know all the players. She does. She likes to help me negotiate the rapids of Palm Beach society. Um—if we're to steer clear of each other, I guess we'd better start. Shall I contact you if anything else happens that might be connected with the thief?"

"Yes, but if anything else happens, we won't be steering clear of each other, sweet pea. I'll be on you like a burr."

"A burr, huh?" She tilted her head back, eyeing him, remembering the feel of his mouth on hers not ten years ago now, but just yesterday. "That's not very sexy."

He laughed. "That's the spirit. I like it a lot better when you're not so pale."

He wheeled off into the crowd, and Mollie, left to her own devices, found a glass of wine and her table. She was seated with an accounts executive from Tiernay & Jones, who wanted to know all about how Mollie was faring out on her own. Marcotte's speech was intelligent and even humorous, but she could feel all eyes on her when he mentioned the Gold Coast cat burglar. None of his other victims, apparently, were present.

Even before the applause died down, Jeremiah, Mollie noticed, made his exit. He'd been seated at George Marcotte's table and probably had used up whatever capacity he had for social chitchat, after, of course, picking the security expert's brain to his satisfaction. Whatever his relationship to her and the jewel thief story, Mollie had no illusions that this wasn't a focused, driven man, no matter what he was doing.

As the luncheon guests dispersed, she found Griffen and offered to help clean up. "No, no, you go on," she said, whisking about in amiable efficiency, dark curls tamely pulled back. "You've got your own work to do. I'll just load everything into my van and hose it down when I get home.''

"Well, lunch was wonderful."

She smiled. "Thanks. And everyone said so, right?"

"But of course."

"I noticed Tabak," she said, noncommittal. "You two didn't sit at the same table. Last night didn't go well?"

"Griffen—"

But an attractive, well-dressed older woman interrupted them, frowning. "Excuse me, ladies, have you by any chance found a watch? I seem to have misplaced mine. I slipped it off in the ladies' lounge while I put on cream for a skin condition . . ." She sighed, her brow furrowing. "Something distracted me, and I forgot it. When I went back, it was gone. I was hoping someone found it."

"No, I'm sorry, Mrs. Baldwin," Griffen said, "I haven't seen it. Do you know my friend Mollie Lavender? Mollie, this is Lucy Baldwin." Mollie recognized the name of one of the wealthiest year-round residents of Palm Beach, a devoted promoter of the island. "Let me take another look in the ladies' lounge, just in case."

Griffen was so gentle and nonthreatening that Lucy Baldwin took no offense. She brightened somewhat. "Thank you, dear, I'd appreciate that."

While Griffen rechecked the bathroom, Mollie tried to engage Mrs. Baldwin in small talk. One of Griffen's helpers was scooping up the mango-colored table cloths. Virtually all of the luncheon guests had departed, and George Marcotte, who might or might not be interested in Lucy Baldwin's missing watch, had also left.

"How long has it been since you took off your watch?" Mollie asked, her hands shaking. Mrs. Baldwin seemed calm, although possibly she hadn't yet considered her watch could have been stolen rather than simply misplaced.

"Forty minutes, perhaps a bit less, I would say. I didn't remember it until I got to my car and glanced at my wrist to see the time. I hate to think I lost it. It was a gift from my late husband the Christmas before he died." Her eyes misted, and she sipped her water. "I hope I'm not becoming forgetful."

"I can't imagine that."

"Do you think it could have been that thief?" she asked, her voice just above a whisper.

"I don't know. Let's see if Griffen finds anything."

But she returned empty-handed. "I'm sorry. I didn't see it."

"Well," Lucy Baldwin said with a small inhale. "I suppose it's gone. Perhaps I accidentally threw it into the trash—"

"I checked the trash," Griffen said.

"This is rather upsetting, isn't it? I know it's only a watch . . . but the sentimental value . . . I suppose it's not important . . ."

Mollie touched the older woman's arm. "It *is* important, Mrs. Baldwin."

Something clicked, and she straightened, said, "You're the one who was robbed at Diantha Atwood's party the other night. I apologize if I've stirred up any disturbing memories for you."

"Please, don't worry about me, Mrs. Baldwin. I just

182

want to help you find your watch and make sure it wasn't this thief the police are after."

She blanched, and Griffen sent one of her helpers for the manager, who, after a brief search, decided it prudent to contact the police, just in case their clever, opportunistic thief had struck again.

"I quite understand," Lucy Baldwin said, looking as if she wished she hadn't mentioned her missing watch.

Griffen quietly resumed her cleanup, and Mollie hung around until the police came. Trying not to be obvious about listening in, she heard enough to realize they weren't convinced her watch had been stolen—and that it didn't exactly move their needle if it had been. They suggested Mrs. Baldwin first go home and make sure it wasn't there and that she'd actually worn it.

She was offended. "I wear that watch whenever I go out."

"Retrace your steps, Mrs. Baldwin," the officer said diplomatically. "Then give us a call if you still can't find it."

"Of course," she said coolly.

With word out of a jewel thief on the loose, Mollie expected the police had received numerous calls of potential robberies and not all would pan out. Obviously straining to keep her dignity intact, Lucy Baldwin retreated, and the police followed her out.

Griffen gave a low whistle and whispered to Mollie, "We'll never know if she finds her watch or not."

"She's a proud woman, isn't she?"

"And that cop just made her feel like an ass. With her status in town, she's not going to risk having people think she's gotten daffy. Bet she has that guy's ass in a sling by nightfall. You know those dignified rich old ladies. You don't want to cross 'em.''

Mollie laughed. "Maybe she *did* forget where she took off her watch.''

Griffen shrugged, starting out through the mansion with a big bowl of leftover salad. "It's possible. It's also possible our cat burglar has struck again.''

"Don't you think he'd want us to know he'd struck?''

"Not necessarily. He—or she—might get a secret thrill out of hitting a fancy lunch with a security expert up there telling everyone how to avoid getting robbed. Ballsy of him, if you ask me. But I don't know that he's in it for attention.''

"Good point. Really, we don't know much of anything, do we? At least he didn't attack Mrs. Baldwin.''

And here she was, Mollie thought, once again at the scene of the crime.

"You're getting into this, aren't you? Hanging out with Jeremiah Tabak, playing girl detective.''

"I'd like to see this guy caught, that's all.''

"Well, you're starting to scare me,'' Griffen said, grinning, and was off to her van.

Mollie headed out to the parking lot herself. She needed to get back for a scheduled meeting with Chet Farnsworth, and as she settled in behind the wheel of Leonardo's car and opened the windows, breathing in the warm, beautiful air, she couldn't wait to dive back into her work. She'd made the right decision ten years ago to abandon the flute, and she'd made the right decision six months ago to take the plunge and put out her own shingle. This jewel thief business was just a fly in an otherwise very fine ointment.

A mile along Ocean Drive, she glanced in her rearview mirror and saw an ancient red VW Rabbit three cars back. The infamous Croc. Mollie couldn't make out his features with any reliability, but who else could it be? The car immediately behind her turned into a seaside resort hotel. After another half-mile, the second car pulled into a marina. The red car drew up behind her bumper. The reflection kept her from seeing who was behind the wheel, not that she had any doubts.

What did this guy think he was doing?

She took an unexpected left off Ocean Drive.

The red car didn't follow.

"Well, there, you see?" she said aloud. "Maybe you're just getting a tad paranoid."

But two blocks from Leonardo's, back on her main route, the VW fell in behind her. She eased off the gas and squinted in her rearview mirror, trying to get a better look at the driver. A man. Sunglasses. Longish hair of a medium color. Thin. Definitely Jeremiah's informant.

She punched the button to open the security gates. What if he followed her in? Rammed her from behind? Pulled out a gun and shot her? Just because he was Jeremiah's friend didn't mean he was *her* friend.

But the red car drove on past her and disappeared around the curve.

She managed to get into the driveway, the gates shutting behind her, before slumping against the wheel, out of breath and immediately furious. She had half a mind to hit 95, track down Jeremiah, and tell him to keep his friend away from her. But Chet's Jeep pulled up, she hit the button to open the gates, and he climbed out for his expected meeting.

He frowned at her. "Jesus, have you been out chasing ghosts or what? Come on. Let's get you upstairs and fetch you a glass of water or something."

"I'm sure I look worse than I feel—"

"What happened?" Chet demanded, his military training clicking into gear.

"Nothing. That's just the thing. This car followed me from my luncheon—"

"Color, make, license plate?"

"It was red, an older two-door VW of some kind— a Rabbit, I think. I don't know cars that well. And I didn't think to get the license plate when he sped past me. I was just so relieved he was gone."

"Understood." He walked to the end of the driveway and peered through the gates up and down the street. "He's gone now. Do you want me to call the police?"

"No! Good heavens, Chet, the guy probably wasn't following me at all. I'm just jumpy after this weekend."

He turned and grunted at her. "These robberies are getting to you."

"There was another one today, at least potentially."

Before he let her explain, he insisted on getting her upstairs and a glass of heavily sweetened iced coffee into her hand. Then he listened to her tale of Lucy Baldwin at the luncheon. "You know," she added, "I've been present at every event that's been held up. Every one. I don't know if anyone else has—"

"The thief," Chet said.

"Yes. That's right." She nodded dully. "I wonder if anyone else—the police, whoever—will start thinking of me as . . . I don't know, a suspect. I mean, am I on someone's list?"

"Jeremiah Tabak's," Chet said. "Guys like that *always* have an agenda. You're his. He's onto this common denominator thing. Mark my words."

"I'm just rattled," Mollie said carefully. "I'll be fine in a minute."

Chet sat at the breakfast bar and spoke to her in crisp, straightforward terms. "Here's what you do. You work the problem. You don't get sidetracked. You don't feel sorry for yourself. You focus on what you need to do, and you do it. Fears and speculation are just distractions."

Mollie drank some of her iced coffee. She'd be perked up in no time. Not only was it strong, it was thick. Chet must have added a half cup of sugar. "You're right, Chet. Thanks." She smiled. "I guess I should be glad you're not getting all protective and telling me to hide under your bed."

"Hiding doesn't solve the problem."

"If there *is* a problem," she put in.

"Well," Chet said gruffly, "it's my bet this thief didn't follow you home in a rusted, banged-up red VW that sticks out like a sore thumb in this neck of the woods."

Mollie considered his point. "You're probably right. Whoever it was is long gone by now, and you didn't come here to discuss my problems. Shall we get to work?"

Chet beamed at her. "That's the spirit."

11

〰

Jeremiah fetched a cup of coffee and a hot dog from the cafeteria and ate in his truck on his way home after two minutes at his desk to check messages. There was one from Frank, his cop friend up in Palm Beach, demanding to know what he'd been doing at the luncheon today. Damned cops. Spies everywhere. Jeremiah deleted the message. First he'd lived through the long, miserable night, then he'd lived through the long, miserable day. He'd lost all perspective and objectivity. *He* was becoming a damned loose cannon.

He'd borrowed a friend's BMW for the day and trekked up to the Gold Coast just because his instincts had sounded the alarm and he didn't like leaving Mollie up there on her own. The BMW wasn't his stupidest idea of the past twenty-four hours, but close. He wanted to be inconspicuous, and he didn't want Mollie jumping in the front seat with him, pissed, distracting, thinking she had a right to every synapse that fired off in his brain.

He headed back to South Beach, where he growled at the old guys on the porch, who ignored him, and changed for a run on the beach. He'd torture himself with exercise instead of thoughts of Mollie and her troubles and his role in them. He'd seen the police arrive at the mansion. He'd called the paper and got the skinny. Old lady loses watch. Maybe the work of the Gold Coast cat burglar. Maybe just an old lady losing a watch.

In the thick of things again, Miss Mollie was.

He walked over to the water and ran on the hard-packed sand on the edge of the outgoing tide, pounding hard, pushing himself. But the thoughts persisted, surging up every time he managed to bank them down. Had he brought this trouble down on Mollie himself? It was convoluted thinking, but he remembered Croc's comment that up in Palm Beach, convoluted was the norm.

When he finally couldn't run another step, his lungs burning, his legs aching, Jeremiah forced out another half-mile, then splashed into the ocean. He dove deep, feeling the sweat and the fatigue and the tension slide out of him.

Afterwards, he sat on the sand and dried himself in the warm sun, like a big old sea lion. Maybe he should just give it up and head into the Everglades and go fishing with his father. What good could come from his continued involvement with a string of Gold Coast robberies? And if Croc was involved, if Mollie was involved, he could be risking his reputation.

Croc materialized out of nowhere and dropped down onto the sand two feet away. He had on jeans, a denim shirt, and sneakers, as if it were fifty degrees out instead of nearly eighty. "Nice afternoon to run yourself to death, eh?"

"Perfect. How'd you find me?"

"I came by your place and saw you head out in your shorts, figured I'd give you time to run off the demons. You succeed?"

Jeremiah stared out at the glistening, turquoise water. "No."

"Miss Mollie, Miss Mollie. Well, she's pretty and smart, but I don't trust her. Our thief had another attack of light fingers today. Lucy Baldwin lost a diamond Rolex in the ladies' room. The police aren't too sure if she *thinks* she was wearing it or if it was our guy. But I don't see Lucy Baldwin as a forgetful, spooked old lady." He stretched out his skinny legs in the sand. "Nah. I don't buy it."

Recognizing the name of one of Palm Beach's most respected, wealthiest year-round widows, Jeremiah frowned at Croc. "How do you know this stuff? Were you there?"

Croc squinted, his face crinkling up. "Yep. So were you. I saw you in your Beemer. Why didn't you stick around?"

"There didn't seem to be any need."

"I guess Lucy Baldwin losing a watch isn't up there in excitement with Mollie Lavender getting a necklace snatched right off her neck." Croc kept his eyes on the water, which was calm, no big swells moving in, and he added, "I followed her."

"Mrs. Baldwin? Why—"

"Miss Mollie."

"Jesus, Croc." Jeremiah cursed himself. He should have spotted Croc—if anyone would stick out in Palm

Beach, he would—but he'd never seen him. "What were you trying to accomplish?"

He shrugged. "I don't know, it just seemed like something to do. I figured you lacked the appropriate objectivity. Anyway, she made me on the way home. I'm surprised she hasn't shown up on your doorstep to blame you."

"You're lucky she didn't call the damned police. I would have. I'd have your ass in the slammer. Ever occur to you that you might have scared the hell out of her?"

"Trust me," Croc said, confident, "this lady's no damsel in distress."

Jeremiah was silent. Seagulls whined and wheeled overhead, and he could hear the laughter of beachgoers in the distance. His stretch of beach was quiet, just him in his wet running shorts, Croc in his jeans.

Croc yawned and fidgeted simultaneously. "You have to admit, it's a tad incredible that she's been at the scene of every robbery. *And* she's the only victim who's been physically assaulted. Awfully convenient, if you ask me. Nice way to take suspicion off yourself."

"Hell, you're even more cynical than I am."

"Ain't no one more cynical than you, Tabak." He grinned. "You're just not thinking with your head these days. If Miss Mollie isn't the thief herself, maybe it's a client or someone who works for her, or someone who's using her to gain access. Maybe she's being set up. Maybe she's got enemies we can't even begin to fathom. The possible scenarios abound."

"And maybe we're barking up the wrong tree altogether."

Jeremiah got to his feet, brushed the sand off wet shorts and legs, gripped with a tension he didn't want to fully understand. He knew it had everything to do with Mollie. He'd done stories more dangerous and complex than this one, but this time, he couldn't stand back and observe with clarity and neutrality. He was involved.

"You can lay off this story, Croc. You're going to land up in jail if you don't watch it."

Croc remained in the sand, angled a look up at Jeremiah. "You're falling for her, aren't you?"

Jeremiah ignored him. "Go for a swim. The water's nice."

When he arrived back at his building, Mollie was sitting out front with the guys. She'd changed from her business clothes to slim khakis and a white shirt that, he hoped, made her look paler than she actually was. Otherwise he'd probably have to head back to the beach and drown Croc.

"I stopped by the paper," she said, "but you weren't there. I found your street on the map."

Albert, the ex-mobster, settled back against his half-shredded lounge chair. He was plump and had a full head of snow-white hair. "Bennie and I was just showing her some of our wares." Indeed, they'd arranged a display of whittled animals on their table. Flamingos, parrots, toucans, alligators. "Sal's gone in for lemonade." Salvatore Ramie was a defrocked priest. Albert wiped sawdust from his knife blade with his thumb. "You want to stay for lemonade, Jeremiah? Or you want we should send Sal up with the pitcher?"

"Sal doesn't have to—"

"Sal won't mind," Bennie said. He was bony and

short, almost totally bald, his fingers still callused from decades of tailoring.

Mollie smiled at the two old men, both obviously taken in by her blonde good looks and easy charm. "I'd love some lemonade. If you're sure your friend won't mind bringing it upstairs, I really need to talk to Mr. Tabak."

"Sure." Albert grinned, dark, smart eyes flashing between her and Jeremiah. "You and *Mr*. Tabak go on up and talk."

Jeremiah led her inside and up the two flights to his apartment. Their rundown Art Deco building had potential, but it didn't approach Leonardo Pascarelli's sprawling house. Mollie seemed not even to notice. She said behind him, "I know you want us to steer clear of each other, but—"

He glanced back at her. "But the thief might have hit the luncheon today, and you were there."

She nodded grimly, and said nothing.

As he unlocked the door, she said, "Those men admire you."

"I add a little spice to their lives, that's all. A Miami investigative reporter in the building. Gives them something to talk about."

"That's not all. They think you're straight up. Ethical. Sal says you're a bleeding heart down deep—"

"Sal? He's an ex-priest. He got kicked out for punching out a cardinal or something. He should talk bleeding hearts."

He pushed open his door, motioned for her to go first. He did not ask if she could smell his critters, but he breathed in deep as he crossed the threshold. The cages of reptiles gave off no odor he could detect.

Mollie didn't wrinkle up her nose, just gave the place a quick, efficient scan, taking in the functional, spare furnishings. He had a hell of a stereo system and a great TV, one whole wall of books, a computer, a good leather reading chair with a decent floor lamp. White walls. No view.

She wandered into the kitchen, and he heard her gasp, then breathe out again. He came up behind her. She glanced back at him. "I didn't expect snakes and lizards." Her small smile helped her to look less pale. "Although I don't know why."

"Just one lizard, one turtle, one snake."

"Do they have names?"

"No."

She ventured over to the table and peered at the cages, keeping her distance, as if she weren't convinced they were properly latched. "How can you have pets with no names?"

"I guess I don't really think of them as pets. It's not like having a dog who knows its name. These guys're your basic reptiles."

"The turtle's kind of cute."

The doorbell rang. Jeremiah said, "That would be Sal with the lemonade."

Mollie followed him back to the living room, and he let Sal in with his tray holding a lemonade pitcher, two tall glasses filled with ice, and a vase with a single sprig of coral bougainvillea. "The flower was Bennie's idea." He set the tray on the trunk Jeremiah used as a coffee table. Sal was remarkably spry for a man coming up on ninety. He was, supposedly, an Old Testament scholar, and he'd become a fine whittler.

"Thanks, Sal," Jeremiah said. "I feel like I ought to tip you or something."

Sal winked. "Just stop by tomorrow morning and give the boys all the details." He turned, gave Mollie a solemn little bow. "Nice meeting you, Miss Lavender."

Jeremiah locked up after him and turned back to Mollie. "Worst house, best location."

"They're charming."

"Don't let them fool you. They've all lived long, full lives. Here, you drink lemonade," he said, starting down the hall. "I'll take a shower. I jumped in the ocean after my run and now I'm all salty."

He made the shower fast and cold. He hadn't brought any clean clothes into the bathroom with him and had to wrap a towel around his waist and trek into his bedroom. If Mollie was peeping around corners, he didn't see her. Just as well. Her presence was distracting enough without actually knowing for sure she was angling to see him in his skivvies. He pulled on chinos and a T-shirt, towel-dried his hair, and rejoined her.

She was sitting on his reading chair, lemonade in hand, knees together, ankles tucked to the side. No question. She'd seen him sneak from the bathroom. He suppressed a grin and poured himself a glass of lemonade.

She cleared her throat. Some of her earlier paleness returned. "So, how did you find out about Lucy Baldwin?"

"I have my sources."

"Croc," she said with certainty. "Well, the police aren't ready to say it was our thief. Could have been your garden-variety, strike-while-the-iron's-hot thief, not our guy. A lot of people could have slipped into the ladies' room, seen the watch, tucked it in their pocket, and slipped out again."

Jeremiah sat on the couch, taking a long swallow of the lemonade. It was too sweet for his taste. A hint from Sal, maybe, to lighten up. "Croc said he followed you home."

"Yes." A coolness came into her so-blue eyes. "You didn't put him up to it?"

He shook his head. "No."

"Does he always keep such close tabs on your stories?"

"No, never. I wouldn't allow it. He knows I'm not officially on this thing, and he feels some ownership of it because he brought it to me."

"I see." She drank more of her lemonade, her eyes not on him. "Tell me about this Croc character. How does he know I've been present at all the incidents? Be straight with me, Jeremiah."

He took another swallow of lemonade. "I don't know how he made you as a common denominator. He won't tell me."

She remained calm. "Then he's unpredictable."

"Unpredictable, yes, but I suspect he's just playing James Bond. I told him to stay away from you. Now. Tell me about Leonardo. What are you going to do when your year at his place is up?"

"What does that have to do—"

"Indulge me, Mollie."

"I don't know what I'll do. I hope I'll have enough saved for a condo, maybe a little house. I don't think

I want to stay in Palm Beach. I'd like to move a bit farther south, to Boca or even Fort Lauderdale."

"As far south as Miami?"

"There'd have to be a good reason."

Jeremiah glanced at his bare-bones furnishings, his reptile cages in the next room. Dangerous thinking. Very dangerous. He shifted back to the subject at hand. Work. It had always pushed back the dangerous thoughts. "You won't miss Leonardo's place? All that space, the pool, the hired help."

She sat back, relaxing slightly. "I've been living in the lap of luxury. It's been fun. But I can always pop in for a visit. Leonardo's one of the most generous people I've ever known. My parents have a standing invitation to come down, but they're always so busy and involved with their work—and they'd probably barely notice their surroundings if they did come. That kind of stuff's wasted on them."

"They don't swim?"

"Mother does laps for exercise. Swimming's purely utilitarian for her. She'd love to see Leonardo, of course." Mollie paused, narrowed her eyes on Jeremiah, suddenly suspicious. "You don't think I'd start stealing because I'm worried about having to give up my Leonardo Pascarelli lifestyle, do you? You know, I'm not so different from my parents that I even want that much opulence. It wouldn't occur—"

"Mollie, I don't suspect you."

She inhaled, the blue of her clear eyes deepening with irritation. "But you're neutral," she said stiffly. "You won't say categorically that I couldn't possibly be the thief. You won't take my side. You're incapable of taking anyone's side. That's why you're a reporter. You can remain apart, aloof, uninvolved."

"I strive for balance and objectivity, yes." His tone was steady, but he was already on his feet, already moving toward her. "It's a goal, not necessarily something that comes easily or is even always possible. In this case, it's not."

And he removed her lemonade glass from her stiff fingers, set it on the floor, and drew her up to her feet. A flush of color, of anticipation, had risen in her pale cheeks. He touched her mouth. "Mollie, Mollie." He tasted her lips. "Do you think I can be neutral where you're concerned?" He tasted them again, felt the spark of her response. "Objective? Balanced?"

"I don't know."

"Really?"

And he kissed her, long and hard and deep. If she'd drawn back, if she'd even hesitated, he would have come to his senses. But she didn't, and he let his hands drift down her back, the curve of her hips. He let himself experience the full impact of their kiss on him, on her. She tucked her arms tentatively around him, and he could see she'd shut her eyes, probably trying to convince herself this was a memory of a past encounter, not a real moment in the present.

"Open your eyes, Mollie," he whispered, "don't try to pretend this is a memory."

She looked at him, her mouth close to his, her eyes half-opened. She raised one hand and brushed it along his jaw. "It'll be a memory soon enough, won't it?"

"It's not one now."

"I have to be realistic. As much as I want this . . ." She kissed him lightly, her hand drifting down his shoulder, and it was all he could do to stand there and listen to her. She drew back slightly. "I know it won't last."

"Because it didn't last time?"

"You went into it last time wanting a weeklong diversion. I went into it . . ." She breathed, maintaining her calm. "I went into it not knowing what I wanted. Now, I'm not so inexperienced. I know myself better. And I know you."

He eased his fingers into her hair, caressed the back of her neck, where she was warm and not so tense. "Maybe we're here now because what we had ten years ago did last."

His mouth found hers again, and their bodies melded, nothing held back as they tasted, touched, rekindled a desire like no other he'd ever known. It boiled through him like a hot river, and he knew at some point, soon, it would rage out of control, break down all his dams of resistance. Then where would they be? In the past again. Succumbing to instinct and desire instead of using their heads. Even as his palms skimmed over her soft breasts, as he explored her mouth, he knew he would have to exercise self-discipline now if he didn't want to lose her forever. Physically, she was ready. Emotionally, she didn't trust him. More important, she didn't trust herself to trust him.

Slowly, with a control he'd lacked ten years ago, he slid her back down onto her chair and stood back from her. Boiling still. Not simmering. Not even close to simmering. "I know a nice, quiet Cuban restaurant a few blocks from here. Inexpensive. Good food. It's not much on atmosphere, but if we stay here . . ." He smiled, shrugged. "I'm afraid my picture'll go back up on your dartboard."

She licked her lips, adjusted her shirt, cleared her throat. It was no use, and he suspected she knew it. Nothing she did could make him forget her response to their kiss, her body pressing wildly against his. "That sounds fine. And I don't suppose you need Bennie and Albert and Sal to start thinking we're going out together, which we're not."

"No. Absolutely not. I only kiss women I have no interest in going out with."

"That was—" She searched for the right word. "—inevitable."

"Inevitable?"

"We've had to get it out of our systems once and for all." Her eyes fastened on him, as if she needed to make herself take a good, hard look at him. "So we'd know there are no sparks left."

"No sparks."

"Jeremiah, if you keep repeating everything I say like I'm not making any sense . . ."

"Sorry, sweet pea, but you're not. You know as well as I do that if we don't get the hell out of here within the next ten minutes, we're going to end up in the sack together. Then we'll see about sparks and what's really inevitable."

His frankness had her swallowing, and, he could tell, swallowing hard. Which only meant he was dead on.

"I love being right." He scooped up the lemonade glasses, set them on the tray, and started for the kitchen. "However, I shouldn't have said that. I lured you into something you didn't want ten years ago—"

"No, you didn't. It's what I wanted to believe, but

you didn't. I knew what I was getting into when I went to dinner with you that first time. Jeremiah, I'm just as responsible for what happened between us then as you are. Yes, I was confused and twenty, but I wasn't stupid. I understood very clearly what kind of man you are."

He grinned. He couldn't help himself. "What kind of man I am? Mollie, Mollie. I'm a nice Florida boy out of the Everglades who investigates crime and corruption for a living."

"It's more than a living for you." She rose, her legs looking remarkably steady under her. Jeremiah's own felt like Gumby's on a bad day. The run, the self-restraint. Mollie tilted her chin up at him, dignified, pushing back any urge to delve into personal matters. "I didn't come here to discuss our relationship. I want you to warn this Croc character that if I catch him tailing me again, I'll phone the police."

Jeremiah set the tray on the kitchen table. "The message has already been delivered."

"Why don't you suspect him of being the jewel thief?"

"Who says I don't?"

She inhaled sharply, rigid, not moving, an unsteady mix of outrage and heat in her eyes, her mouth. Sparks. Definite sparks. It was like holding a magnifying glass over a dried leaf and waiting for it to burst into flames. He figured he had less than five minutes to get her out the door. She fisted one hand and pushed it into his chest, not hitting him so much as holding him in place.

"Jeremiah, I have a right to know *everything* you

know about this story. You're not compromising your ethics. It's not as if you're going to write it."

"Mollie. Let's go eat. We'll talk."

His calm seemed only to inflame her further. "I don't think this thief is about you—or even me."

"Mollie."

"We must be missing something—some clue—"

"Mollie."

She paused, frowned. "What?"

"Our ten minutes are almost up."

The restaurant was small, simple, and within easy walking distance of Jeremiah's building. The good, inexpensive Cuban food reminded her of the lunches and dinners they'd had together ten years ago. Their waiter brought her cup of black bean soup, and Mollie, feeling more in control of herself, spooned into it as she cast Jeremiah a dubious look. "You were bluffing. You wouldn't really have dragged me off to bed."

He smiled, amusement crinkling the corners of his eyes, reminding her he was no longer twenty-six. "I don't think I'd have had to do any dragging."

"It's because of our past." She tried her soup, which was thick and spicy and steaming hot. She was being pragmatic. With Jeremiah Tabak, pragmatism was the only sensible approach. "If we hadn't already slept together, you wouldn't be tempted."

An eyebrow quirked. He'd ordered a margarita, no soup. "Mollie, that's the most twisted logic—"

"No, it makes perfect sense. One, I'm not your type. I'm a publicist. You're a hard-news journalist. I live and work in Palm Beach. You work for a tough, urban newspaper, and you live with Bennie and Albert and Sal."

"I don't live *with* them. We simply share the same building."

"Because you don't care where you live. It's immaterial. Jeremiah, I grew up with people like you."

"Are you comparing me to your parents?" He laughed, giving a mock shudder. "I need another margarita."

"You've never even met my parents."

"They're violinists. Flakes."

"The point is," she said, refusing to be distracted, "that you and I have and want different things out of life. I listened to *Carmina Burana* on the way down here. I looked at your CD collection while you were in the shower. Rock, blues, jazz. All stuff I like, but no classical, which I love, which I used to *live*."

He frowned. "How can you live classical music?"

She threw up her hands. "There. I rest my case."

"Mollie, you have no case."

"I do. The reason you and I would have ended up in bed together is because of some kind of hormonal memory or something. Probably some chemical. A throwback to our week together. You know, it was so fast and furious that—" No, best not to go down that road. She grabbed the pepper shaker. "I'm sure it's chemical."

"Right."

She felt warm and tried to blame the soup. "Well, that was the first reason why we wouldn't have ended up in bed if we already hadn't. The second reason is business. You're more experienced than you were ten years ago. You wouldn't sleep with me now because it's too risky. It'd look bad. You've a reputation to maintain."

"Mollie." He leaned across the table, the candle-light bringing out even more colors in his eyes. A fiery yellow, a gleam of black. "I don't give a rat's ass about my precious reputation. I do what I do because I think it's right. Ten years ago, I thought it was right to sleep with you. Twenty minutes ago, I didn't. Twenty hours from now . . ." He shrugged. "Who knows?"

She swallowed, her throat dry. "What about me?"

"You'll have your say."

Just as she did ten years ago. She'd been caught up in her righteous anger over his duplicity for so long that she'd neatly forgotten how solicitous he'd been about making sure she knew what she was doing, wanted it. It was that same peculiar sense of honor that had compelled him, a week later, to tell her he'd used her to get his first front-page story when he hadn't. He'd tried to spare her regrets that he simply didn't realize he had no power to spare.

The waiter brought their meals, and Mollie inhaled the delicious smells of the fried plantains, yellow rice, and grilled lime chicken. Jeremiah ordered another margarita. She asked for more water and seized the opportunity to make a smooth transition out of a sub-ject she'd stupidly brought up. "Tell me about this Croc character and why he's above suspicion and I'm not."

"I never said he was above suspicion." Jeremiah sipped his margarita, his expression all business, the professional journalist at work. "I go where the facts lead me. I've known Croc for about two years. He thinks of himself as my secret weapon."

"But you didn't put him up to following me," Mollie said.

"No, that was his brilliant idea."

"Because *he* suspects me."

"Croc suspects everyone. It's his nature. He doesn't have much faith in people."

"He must in you."

Jeremiah set down his margarita, suddenly looking troubled, distracted. "That doesn't give me a great deal of comfort, you know."

Mollie considered his words. "You don't want to feel responsible for him."

"I'm *not* responsible for him. What Croc does, Croc does on his own."

"But if he's living vicariously through you—"

"He's not. He just brings me what he hears."

"What's his real name?"

"He says it's Blake Wilder. I don't know if it is or isn't. I don't even know where he lives."

Mollie started on her food, which was hot, spicy, and perfect for her mood. She felt that Jeremiah's relationship with his young source was more complicated than he was willing to admit. She wanted to press him, but when Jeremiah commented on the food, she took the hint and let the subject shift to innocuous things. Favorite restaurants, the weather, movies they'd recently seen, books they'd recently read. Mollie found him insightful, thoughtful, less black-and-white in his outlook than she would have expected. A man of many different facets was Jeremiah Tabak. She'd had such a straightforward, uncomplicated view of him for so long that getting used to him as a complex, real, live, breathing man wasn't easy.

He paid for dinner. He insisted, because if they hadn't had to leave on short notice he'd have cooked for her. Mollie didn't remind him that she'd never expected to stay for dinner at all.

She relished the warm evening air on the walk back to his apartment, enjoyed the bustle of the crowded streets, imagined how different a late February night in Boston would be. A year ago, she'd have worked late, maybe gone out for dinner with friends, or to a concert with her parents or sister. There had been no steady man in her life. Jeremiah Tabak was a distant, if still very real, memory.

There wasn't a steady man now, she reminded herself, glancing at Jeremiah as he strode beside her, preoccupied with his own thoughts. She had no illusions. He was driven and utterly focused on one thing: investigating the Gold Coast thefts. Just because he couldn't do the story didn't mean it didn't absorb him. The physical part of their relationship was just an extension of that focus and drive. If it became a distraction, something apart from the story, it would end. The story determined everything. And when it ended, so would his interest in her. As much as he might want to believe she was his reason for being on the jewel thief story, she wasn't. *He* was the reason. His need to know things, his need to unravel and solve and figure out and just know.

When they arrived back at his building, the guys were all still outside, Bennie smoking a fat, putrid-smelling cigar. "Old habit," he said. "My wife never let me smoke inside."

Jeremiah turned to Mollie, his eyes flat now, lost in the shadows, his voice low. "I'll walk you to your car."

She shook her head. "There's no need. It's right there." She pointed across and down the street. She smiled. "Thank you for dinner. I enjoyed myself." She drew in a breath, so aware of him standing close, silent. "Of course, it was business."

" 'Course. I'll deduct dinner from my taxes." He winked, smiling. "You can sit out here with the guys for a while, if you want. Good night, Mollie."

She felt three pairs of old-man eyes on her. "Good night, Jeremiah."

He headed inside, and Mollie frowned, wondering what had possessed her to drive to South Beach in the first place. Sal, the ex-priest, settled back in his rickety chair and said thoughtfully, "He's afraid to want something he doesn't have because he might lose it."

"Nah," Albert said, "he's just got to be jerked up by the balls and forced to pay attention to what's important. Reporters, you know?"

Bennie shook his head. "Jeremiah's an honorable man. He wants to do what's right. He's not going to press himself on a woman if he doesn't think it's right."

"Jesus," Sal said, "you're making the lady blush."

Albert grinned at Mollie. "It's not like we have this conversation every week with a woman."

"He hasn't been right lately," Bennie said. "You can tell by his whittling. You see that?" He picked up a carved piece of something that looked vaguely like a palm tree. "He can whittle better than that. He was just hacking. His mind was somewhere else."

Meaning, presumably, Mollie thought, on her. But she expected it was more likely on the jewel thief story and her potential role in it, Croc's behavior, his own next move. Jeremiah would love a story he could chew on, that would occupy him fully.

"Go on upstairs." Albert gave her an encouraging nod. "We have coffee and bagels down here at eight every morning. You can come sit with us and tell us how things worked out."

"You're a dirty old man, Albert," Bennie told him, his putrid cigar tucked between thumb and forefinger.

Sal shrugged off both their comments and turned to Mollie. "Jeremiah needs more for company than reptiles and us old men. That much we know. I'm just not sure he knows it—or is willing to take the risk of hurting himself, and you, to admit it."

He seemed so sincere, so certain. Finally, Mollie nodded and without a word went back inside and upstairs to Jeremiah's apartment. What happened next, she thought, happened. But she wasn't ready to climb back into Leonardo's car and drive north.

12

Mollie knocked on Jeremiah's door with a calm that surprised her. She had no intention of changing her mind. He opened up, tilted his head back, his eyes half-closed, his expression unreadable. She thought she saw a twitch of humor but couldn't be sure. "Forget something?" he asked.

She shook her head. "I've been talking to the guys downstairs."

"Ah, the council of wise old men."

She smiled, noticing that he hadn't moved from the doorway. "They observed your abrupt departure with interest."

"They observe everything I do with interest. I suppose they had opinions on my motives?"

"Of course. They believe you're being honorable or you're scared—or a mixture of both—except for the one old guy who thinks you just need to be jerked up short."

"That would be Albert, and I'm sure he was more colorful in his choice of words. He thinks I have a one-track mind about my work and need a two-by-four upside the head every now and then to get my attention." He shrugged, the amusement reaching his eyes now. "Which could be true."

"What about the honor and fear factor?"

"I try to do what I think is right. I don't know if that's being honorable. As for fear—" He smiled, leaning in close to her. "I'm not afraid of you, Mollie."

She folded her arms on her chest in an effort to be cool, collected. "Does that mean I'm invited in?"

He stepped back from the door, motioning her inside with a mock bow and a sweep of his arm. Mollie eased past him. His apartment was silent and still, no television or CD playing, no reptiles stirring in their cages. As stripped down as Jeremiah's tastes were, she felt comfortable. She remembered waltzing around the pink bedroom in Leonardo's house, picking out her dress for the ball, caught up in the luxury and temptation of diamonds and rubies and beautiful clothes, all fun, but, somehow, not as real as standing in Jeremiah's apartment with his books, CDs, videos, newspapers, magazines, simple furnishings, lizard, turtle, and snake.

"As much as I hate to admit it," he said behind her, "I understand where Bennie, Albert, and Sal were coming from tonight. We've gotten to know each other, sitting out whittling, eating bagels in the morning, smoking an occasional cigar. They don't know about you and our week together, but they know about me. The work I do, my commitment to it—and

my determination not to inflict myself on a relationship that can't last."

Mollie turned to him, emotion and desire knotting
her insides. A seriousness seemed to have enveloped
him, darkening his eyes, bringing out the harsh angles
of his face. But she didn't regret her decision to walk
back up to his apartment. "Jeremiah, right now I'm
not worried about what can last and what can't last.
I'm not here about anything except tonight."

"I don't want to hurt you again."

"That's the risk we take, isn't it?"

"Maybe it is." He moved to her, toe to toe, and
curved an arm around her waist, his mouth finding
hers as he whispered, "I'm awfully glad I didn't have
to follow you up to Palm Beach tonight."

"Would you have spied on me?"

"Darlin', I'd have found some way inside your
gates."

He slipped his hands under her shirt and opened
his palms against her warm, bare skin, sending waves
of sensation through her as their mouths came together again, and she said between kisses, "I brought
a change of clothes, just in case. They're down in
the car."

His eyes flashed, sending more tremors through her
with their blatant desire. "What about my plan for us
to steer clear of each other?"

She drew her arms around him, felt the strong muscles of his back. "Did you think even for a half-second
that would work?"

"It seemed like a good idea." Again, the seriousness
descended. "Mollie, if I've brought trouble down on
your head—"

"It's okay, Jeremiah." She kissed him softly, easing herself against his chest. "I'm not twenty anymore."

"No," he said, smoothing his hands up her back, triggering memories that she thought she'd suppressed forever, "but I wouldn't be surprised if you still sit on a musical note towel and listen to opera on the beach. Mollie, Mollie . . . I've never known anyone like you."

She laughed, the rest of her quaking with a yearning that reached her soul. "I haven't had a lot of Jeremiah Tabaks walking around in my life."

"We don't have to figure out our lives tonight."

And he swept her into his arms and down the short hall to his bedroom, where the blinds were pulled against the dark night and the furnishings just as utilitarian as the rest of his apartment. It was as if ten years of pent-up desire suddenly was released. His mouth found hers again and again, her mind numbing with the sensation that he was drinking in all of her with their kisses.

"Don't close your eyes," he said, "stay with me now. I don't want you to pretend this is a memory. See me as I am now, Mollie. Love me as I am now."

"And you'll do the same?"

"I am. I have been."

And he kissed her, slowly this time, savoring, tasting, easing any last tension from her body. Soon, every muscle was warm, loose, vibrating with a desire that had been a part of her for so long, dormant, waiting for the day it would explode again.

"Jeremiah . . ." She breathed, focused for a moment on the stillness around them. "I didn't think I'd ever let myself want you again." She smiled, kissing him. "And it had nothing to do with honor."

"If I could undo . . ."

"Don't go there. I had to figure me out before I could figure us out. But what I've realized—" She inhaled at a jolt of desire that rocked her to her very soul. "I've realized that the figuring out isn't ever really finished. Change is inevitable. We just can't leave behind the wrong things."

"Mollie."

"Hm."

"We can talk now or we can make love now."

She smiled. "It's that one-track mind of yours, isn't it?"

She lay back on his bed, and he came with her, peeling her shirt over her head and casting it off onto the floor. His eyes locked with hers as he skimmed his palms up over the curve of her hips, leaving hot pools of lava in their wake. She could feel his arousal pushing against his pants, against her, inhaled sharply just at the thought of him bursting free.

His palms suddenly slid over her breasts, and she dug her hands into his sides, eased them up over his sleek, hard muscles. He lowered his head, slowly, her breasts swelling even as she imagined his mouth on them, and then with excruciating care and patience, he took one nipple between his lips, tugged gently, followed with his tongue, and finally his teeth, until she was bubbling hot, molten, tearing her hands up and down his back. He didn't speed up, she didn't divert him from his task. He eased off her shorts and underpants, using mouth and tongue and teeth to make her delirious with wanting and take her to the very edge of exploding.

"Now," she said, amazed at the urgency she was

feeling, the strangled sound of her own voice, "please, don't wait."

He drew back, tugged off his clothes, threw them every which way, and fell on her, all restraint gone, his patience as exhausted as her own. She had no chance to explore him, to move across his body with hand and tongue. "Stay with me," he murmured, settling heavily between her legs. "Don't close your eyes, don't lose me." He plunged into her, moaning softly as he seemed to savor the feel of their bodies intertwined. "We're here, together, now."

There were no more words after that, no possibility of speech or thought. When the explosion came, it was more than Mollie could have imagined, not just erupting out of her, but into her, into him, its heat and ferocity fusing them together. She was aware of nothing beyond him, herself, the moment. Warm, her muscles liquid now, she felt him scooping her onto her pillows, holding her as he drew the covers up over them both.

She cuddled up against him, but even as she was drifting off, her body refusing to stay awake any longer, she knew that it would be a long time yet before he would sleep. At his core, she realized, Jeremiah was a man who needed—was compelled by the force of his nature—to think beyond the moment. He would have to ponder what they'd done and all its ramifications, and how and if and whether what they had together should last.

Jeremiah didn't fall asleep until well after midnight, but he was up again at dawn, restless, prowling his apartment as if he were in a cage himself. He peeked in on Mollie, asleep in his bed, her pale hair spilling across his hunter green sheets, only her bare creamy shoulders exposed. He saw their clothes tossed all over the floor. He saw the cotton blanket she'd kicked off in the night.

Mollie Lavender, in his bed, in his apartment. In his life, he thought, once more.

And in trouble. For certain. He just couldn't fit the pieces together yet and see the clear picture of what, how, who all was involved.

The memory of their lovemaking flooded over him as he stood in the doorway. It was a gully-wash of sensations, memories, emotions that rocked him back on his heels.

Yet he didn't have it in him to regret a single second of their night together. If he was going to have regrets, he wouldn't have opened his door to her in the first place.

"The woman deserves her sleep," he muttered, chastising himself for the quick, inevitable urge to rouse her and make love to her again, over and over until the sun was high and hot in the sky. It was, he thought, that way between the two of them. It had been ten years ago, and it was again now.

Some things didn't change.

With a strangled groan, he grabbed up a pair of shorts and a shirt and headed for the bathroom. After a torturous burst of ice-cold water in the shower, he went downstairs to whittle with Sal, who was always up at dawn. The ex-priest had his ubiquitous Thermos of coffee and a Miami mug with flamingoes on it. Without so much as a good morning, he filled the Thermos top and handed it over.

"I've got troubles, Sal," Jeremiah said, sipping the hot, surprisingly good coffee.

"Only dead people don't have troubles, Tabak."

"Words of wisdom from a former priest?"

"Nah, from an old man. But I guess forty years in the clergy, a few things are bound to get through. Whittle awhile. Dawn's a good time of day to reflect, not to make decisions."

Jeremiah took out his jackknife and chose a hunk of wood, and he might have been nine, listening to his daddy's careful instructions, his mother hovering in the background, fretting about him cutting off a finger. There was no hurrying the wood, his daddy would say. You just stay with it.

The air was still, the light had a lavender cast to it, and the two men whittled awhile, saying nothing. Jeremiah felt his demons push back to the edges of his consciousness, at bay if not less threatening.

The blade of his knife slipped, nicked him between the knuckles of his left thumb. He saw the cut before he felt the pain.

"Cut yourself?" Sal asked, calm.

"Yes, dammit." Blood spurted from the clean slit. *"Hell."*

"That's the world you're swearing at, not that little old piece of wood."

"I'm not swearing at the goddamned wood, I'm swearing at the cut."

"You want me to get Bennie up? He's got a first aid kit you wouldn't believe. Let me tell you, that man—he's ready for the apocalypse."

Jeremiah put pressure on his thumb. "Sal, I'm bleeding here."

"I can see that. Here, take my handkerchief."

It was stark white, pressed, neatly folded, immaculate. Jeremiah shook it open with his uninjured hand and wrapped it around his bleeding thumb. He pulled it tight, knotted it. "I owe you a handkerchief."

"The question is, what do you owe yourself?"

Jeremiah stared at him. "Sal."

The old man smiled, embarrassed. "Sorry, it's habit. I try to find lessons where sometimes there's no lesson to be found."

"Or a simple one, like you shouldn't whittle before you've had your morning coffee." Or, he thought darkly, when you'd rather be up with the pale-haired woman asleep in your bed.

"Think it needs stitches?" Sal asked.

"No."

It was pounding now. Jeremiah applied pressure, cursing himself and Mollie both. If she'd just gone home, he wouldn't have had to whittle at dawn. He could be asleep, not tortured by the contradictions, desires, miseries, joys, and fears of falling for her all over again.

Then again, if he hadn't made love to her last night, he could have been down here anyway and cut off his whole damned hand. Whether upstairs or behind Leonardo Pascarelli's gates, Mollie was in his life, and the frustrations of that abounded.

And also, he thought, the possibilities.

Sal handed him his coffee; Jeremiah sipped, grimacing at the pulsing pain. The cut wasn't that deep. It would hurt and bleed like hell for a while, but it'd be fine.

"You ever think about getting married, Sal?" Jeremiah asked.

"When I was in the priesthood?"

"Whenever."

Sal sat back, hands folded serenely on his middle. Jeremiah suspected Salvatore Ramie had academic degrees going up one arm and down the other. Bennie and Albert said his apartment was overflowing with books; they worried about them being a fire hazard. But now that he was a civilian, Sal liked to pretend he was just one of the guys, not a man who'd studied esoteric theological and philosophical subjects. He breathed in and out slowly, contemplating Jeremiah's question.

Finally, he said, "I thought about marriage all the time."

"That's not what I asked."

"I know it isn't. I thought about marriage in terms of an institution. As for myself and marriage . . ." He paused again, as if Jeremiah had asked him to define the meaning of life. "There was never any one woman, either before I became a priest or after I was unceremoniously booted out of the priesthood. But sometimes I'd imagine if there was a woman, if I did get married, and of course, it was all hypothetical because there wasn't and I wouldn't. So what did it mean? It meant I could fantasize about perfection. About everything I would want in a woman, a marriage. I could set the highest standards."

"Because it wasn't real."

"Mm. And I kept it from ever becoming real."

"Well, you were a priest."

"It was more than that," Sal said. "I performed

hundreds of weddings over forty years. And there's one thing I think I learned." He shifted to Jeremiah, his old eyes pinched but clear. "The one who gets you is the one who makes you forget you ever had standards, who makes you forget you ever desired anything as dull and ridiculous as perfection."

Jeremiah frowned, trying to figure out if Sal was making any sense or just pontificating.

The old man sat back. "You see? A time of day for reflection."

"I'm going to go up and find a Band-Aid."

"You do that."

First he went out to Mollie's car and found the tote bag of clothes she'd insisted she'd brought along. He felt no pang of guilt whatsoever at having had the passing thought that the clothes-in-the-car line could have been a strategic lie on her part, a way to convince him that returning to his apartment last night hadn't simply been an impulsive act.

Which, of course, it had been, change of clothes in Leonardo's Jaguar or not.

He managed not to run into any other elderly gentlemen with theories on romance before reaching his apartment, where he washed off his cut in the kitchen sink and bandaged it up as best he could. The throbbing had stopped. The bleeding hadn't. Now he just felt like a damned klutz. He fixed a pot of coffee and sat at the table with his critters, all of whom had the sense to be asleep at six o'clock in the morning.

The telephone rang, jolting him out of his self-absorption. Sal with more revelations on the mysteries of romantic love? His father, perhaps, with an invitation to go fishing?

He snatched up the kitchen extension. "Tabak."

"Tabak, it's Frank Sunderland. You awake?"

Jeremiah ran a hand through his short hair. Frank Sunderland was his cop friend up in Palm Beach, and he wouldn't call this early—or any time—without reason. "Yeah, I'm awake. What's up?"

"I'm at Good Samaritan Hospital in West Palm. They've got a kid here—says his name's Blake Wilder. He had the hell beat out of him last night."

"Jesus, Frank, he's a friend of mine." Saying Croc was a friend was simpler than trying to explain the complexities of what he was to a cop or even, Jeremiah thought, to himself. "What happened? Is he okay?"

"He'll live, but he's not okay. Busted ribs, broken nose, broken jaw, cuts, bruises. Doctors are working on him. You'd have to talk to them to get the details. A couple of beachcombers happened to spot him. Another hour, he'd have drowned in the tide, maybe even been swept out to sea. We figure the guys who beat him up got spooked before they could finish the job."

"Kill him, you mean?"

"Yeah, Tabak. Kill him."

His stomach lurched. He got shakily to his feet. Mollie, he noticed, had stumbled into the kitchen. She was wearing one of his shirts, her hair tangled, the color drained out of her face. He said, "I'm on my way."

"Listen, Tabak, this kid—he gave your name and his name and that's it. You know anyone else I should contact?"

"No."

"Well, that's too bad, because it gets worse."

Jeremiah went still. "Tell me, Frank."

"We found the diamond-and-ruby necklace that got yanked off Mollie Lavender the other night in his back pocket. Way I look at it, we've got three choices. One, the guys who beat him up didn't know it was there. Two, they didn't have time to steal it. Or, three, they planted it on him. None of which I like, I have to say." Frank inhaled, reining in his own irritation. "If I find out you haven't been straight with me, we're going to have a reckoning, Tabak. I'll see you in a couple hours."

Jeremiah hung up and turned to Mollie, and his stomach ached and burned and his head spun. She inhaled, staying calm, at least on the surface. "What happened?"

He told her. Succinctly, accurately, his word-for-word reporter's memory for conversations, his professionalism, clicking into gear. He left out nothing, not even the part about her necklace in Croc's back pocket.

"We'll take the Jaguar," she said without preamble, digging the clothes out of her tote bag and pulling them on. Underwear, pants, shirt. She started back to his bedroom, presumably for her shoes. "It'll be faster."

Jeremiah shook his head and followed her back. "No. I'll take my truck, and you can stay here."

She snorted. "Forget it. I'd just end up passing you on the highway and beating you to the hospital, which would drive you crazy." She sat on the edge of the tousled bed to slip on her sandals, but stopped suddenly, blue eyes on him, suspicious. "Or are you going to steal my keys?"

"I'm not a Neanderthal, Mollie."

"Good." She grinned, but her color didn't improve. "Then let's roll." She shot to her feet, and as she passed him in the doorway, her expression softened. "At least they got to him in time, Jeremiah. He's not dead."

He inhaled sharply. "I haven't gotten hold of him yet."

They took the stairs fast and bolted outside, sunlight spilling out across the city. Sal had gone in, leaving the wood he was carving on his chair. Jeremiah felt as if his chest were being squeezed. He could no longer feel the pain of his cut.

Traffic on I-95 North was light. Mollie, steady behind the wheel, hit the left lane and drove fast. One after another the questions and doubts pounded, crowded Jeremiah's thinking. One after another, he shoved them aside. Answers would come later. Now, he had to see to Croc.

"There's a first aid kit in the glove compartment," Mollie said. "You can change the bandage on your thumb. You cut it whittling?"

He gave a curt nod.

Her quick smile didn't reach her eyes. "Your concentration must be off."

By the time they arrived at the hospital, Croc had been admitted to a regular room. They went on up, running into Frank Sunderland in the corridor. He was a tall, stringy, serious officer of the law, and he didn't look happy. "Whoa, you two," he said. "Tabak, I want everything you have on this kid."

The door to Croc's room was shut. Jeremiah stiffened, refused to let his impatience get the better of him. He told Frank, "I've known Croc about two years. He brings me the occasional tip. Half the time it's nothing. The other half, maybe. He does odd jobs, nothing steady. I don't know where he's working now. I've never known where he lives. I don't know anything about his past." He gave out the facts shotgun style, and kept his opinions to himself. Mollie, he noticed, was staying close, listening to every word. "He says his name is Blake Wilder."

" 'Says' being the operative word," Frank said. "As far as we can tell, it's a phony name. We're running his prints."

"I'm not surprised. I always had the feeling Blake Wilder was something he'd pulled off a tombstone or out of a Hardy Boys book. Croc lives in a fantasy world half the time, Frank. Spies, fairies, elves, conspiracies. He listens at keyholes. He's not a man of action. I don't see him as a jewel thief."

Frank sighed irritably, his dark, smart eyes flashing. "Yeah, well, maybe if you'd told me about him sooner—"

"There was nothing to tell. Still isn't."

"Damned reporters. What about this jewel thief story? It's not your thing, Tabak. What're you doing sniffing around in it?"

Jeremiah debated a moment, his instincts on alert anytime a cop was asking the questions and he wasn't. "Croc put me onto it."

"How?"

"Asked me to look into it." In Jeremiah's opinion, there was no need to bring up Croc's Mollie-Lavender-as-common-denominator theory. "He believed there was a single thief at work even before the police did."

Frank frowned, suspicious. "How come?"

"He refused to say. I've been at his throat about holding back on me right from the beginning. Frank, I don't have anything. If I did—" He tightened his hands into his fists. "Damn it, maybe that kid wouldn't be in there—"

"All right, all right. Go see him. You want to hire him a lawyer?"

"Give me a minute. By the way," he said, touching Mollie's arm, "this is Mollie Lavender."

Frank looked grim. "I figured. Go ahead, Miss Lavender. We can talk after."

Jeremiah pushed open the door to the double room. The first bed was unoccupied. The second bed, along the window, held a bandaged, bruised, miserable-looking Croc. He barely made a rumple in the bed covers. Most of his head was bandaged—his neck, his right arm, both hands. His eyes and nose had swelled up, his mouth was cut and stitched, his jaw was wired shut. He was hooked up to an IV.

An attractive, fiftyish nurse was fiddling with his IV line. "How is he?" Jeremiah asked.

"He's dozing at the moment. He's been very restless, agitated, and he's in a great deal of pain. His medication is helping."

"Will he need surgery?"

"I don't believe so, but you'd have to speak to his doctor. Right now the best thing we can do is to let him rest."

"He's been worked over pretty good," Jeremiah said, more to himself than to either Mollie or the nurse. Rage clouded his eyes. Croc, he thought. Jesus. But he needed to stay focused, think, make the right moves now, before it was too late.

"Yes, I'm afraid whoever did this to him—" The nurse shuddered. "I don't want to think about it."

Mollie, pale and breathing shallowly, said nothing.

"If there's a change, you can let me know? I'll leave numbers where I can be reached. I'll be back later." He walked to Croc's bed, leaned over his battered, bruised, skinny body. His chest ached from tension. Who the hell could do this to another human being? But it was the same question he'd been asking since he'd reported on his first mugging eighteen years ago, just a kid himself. He touched Croc's bony wrist. "You hang in there, buddy."

Outside in the corridor, he gave Frank his various numbers: the paper, his apartment, his cell phone. Mollie supplied her work and home numbers, and Frank said to her, "I wonder if you can come down to the station and ID this necklace." She knew that compliance with his request wasn't as optional as he tried to make it sound.

"I'd be glad to," she said politely, "but I'm driving Jeremiah—"

Frank interrupted. "I can drive you over and then drop you back at your place."

"Sure, okay." She fished out the keys to the Jaguar and handed them to Jeremiah; she was staying calm, doing what had to be done in the thick of a crisis. "Leonardo also has a Jeep. I'll use it, and you can bring his car back later."

Frank, Jeremiah noticed, resisted comment. "You'll be okay?" Jeremiah asked Mollie.

She smiled weakly, the sight of Croc, who'd had her pissed off to the point of speechlessness less than twenty-four hours ago, taking its toll. "I'll be fine. Once I'm done with the police, I'll go back to Leonardo's and try to get some work done." In other words, Jeremiah would know where to find her. "You'll be in touch?"

He nodded, even as he felt himself pulling back, fighting for distance, not because he regretted last night but because he owed Croc, aka whoever. "I'll be in touch."

"So will I, Tabak," Frank growled, and he escorted Mollie out.

13

≈

Griffen Welles and Deegan Tiernay arrived at Leonardo's five minutes after Frank Sunderland had dropped Mollie off. She hadn't even had a chance to scoot upstairs yet. All she wanted to do was dive into the pool and swim until she couldn't think coherently, then sleep in the shade. But when Deegan said, "Mollie, was that the *police?*" she rallied.

"Come upstairs, you two," she said. "I have a tale to tell."

She put on coffee and boiled an egg and told them about Jeremiah, Croc, herself as common denominator. She told them about seeing Jeremiah at the Greenaway, knowing him ten years ago, having his picture on her dartboard. Her voice sounded detached and clinical, yet her insides felt frayed. Coffee and food helped.

"Jesus, Mollie," Griffen breathed. "I had no idea."

Deegan paced, pounding a fist into a palm. "The police think this Croc guy's the jewel thief?"

"They're not sure. I just identified the necklace they found on him. It's definitely Leonardo's cursed diamond-and-ruby necklace. But whether it was a coincidental mugging and the attacker just missed it, or it was some kind of setup—" She shrugged, feeling drained, confused, on overdrive. "I don't know."

"This sucks," Deegan muttered. "Look, I need to get out of here awhile. I'll talk to you both later."

He shot outside, and Griffen unfolded herself from a bar stool, walked to the door, peered out, and turned back to Mollie. "I wonder what that's all about."

"Something I said? He hasn't liked Jeremiah—"

"What's to like? The guy's a rough customer, even if you've fallen for him like the proverbial ton of bricks." When Mollie started to protest, Griffen held up a hand, silencing her. "Do not argue with one who knows. Well, I suppose where one romance dies, another pops up somewhere in the universe to take its place."

"You and Deegan?"

She flopped back onto her stool. "The last few days especially . . ." She frowned at Mollie's egg. "You're eating that dry?"

"I put pepper on it."

"A hard-boiled egg with pepper. Mollie, that gives me the willies."

She smiled. "Tell me about Deegan."

"He's been remote lately." Her eyes shifted, and she picked at a red-polished nail. Today's sundress was a shock of red and purple flowers. Her dark curls hung down her back. "Usually he's so much fun, sarcastic, witty, just a great guy, you know? I never expected our relationship to last, but I'm sorrier than I thought I'd to be now that it's falling apart."

"I'm sorry, Griffen."

"Yeah, yeah. What about you and Jeremiah Tabak? Any hope there?" She squinted at Mollie, then laughed. "My God, you're blushing! We must be talking fast and furious then, huh?"

Mollie bit into her egg and toast, noticing Griffen's involuntary shudder of disapproval, as if she couldn't help herself. "I just came from the hospital. It doesn't seem right to be fretting about my love life right now."

"It's human nature, Mollie. Don't beat yourself up over it. Some of us know the real thing when we see it, and we find it right out of the chute. Others of us—" She sighed, obviously meaning herself. "Others of us either don't know it or just have to keep trying. If I find the right guy before I'm forty, I'll be happy. Heck, after I'm forty."

"Ever the optimist, right, Griffen?"

She grinned. "You got it. So, does Tabak think his buddy Croc is the jewel thief?"

"I don't know, we haven't talked outside the presence of the police."

"But you doubt it," Griffen said.

"Maybe . . . I'm trying to keep an open mind." Her egg finished, she rinsed her hands in the sink. Her mind was racing, impulsivity rearing its head. She looked around at her friend. "Griffen, why don't I have a party?"

"A party? Mollie, what the hell—"

"Tomorrow night. Are you free? I can hire you to cater. We'll make it spontaneous and fun, real informal. It's supposed to be nice weather. We can have it out by the pool."

Griffen was eyeing her dubiously. "What, are you trying to set a trap for the real jewel thief?"

"I would if I could—if he's not already in the hospital with his jaw broken. No, I just want to assert some control over my life. A spontaneous cocktail party could be my statement about the attack on me the other night, my relationship with Leonardo, my intentions here in south Florida. I'm my own person, and I make my own decisions."

"And you won't be driven off by a nasty phone call and a nasty thief."

She nodded. "Right."

Griffen mused a moment, the sunlight streaming in through the kitchen window, the curtains billowing in a pleasant breeze. "It could be a fun, gutsy thing to do. I expect it doesn't hurt to assert your independence with a guy like Jeremiah Tabak, either." She clapped her hands together, grinning. "I'm getting to like this nutty idea better and better."

"Is tomorrow night too soon?"

"Of course, but that's what makes it perfect. It won't conflict with any of the big parties this week, and Leonardo doesn't do parties, so people are already curious about this place. We can capitalize on that. And, of course, they're yakking about you a mile a minute, and now we've got this jewel thief in the hospital and a sexy investigative reporter . . ." She drummed the counter with her red nails, musing. "Oh, this definitely could work!"

"People will come?"

"*Everyone* will come." She slid smoothly to her feet,

tucked thick curls behind her ear. "I'll put together a menu and guest list and stop back by this afternoon. We'll have to move on this thing if we're going to pull it off. Deegan can help—I'll see if I can track him down. Guess it's a good thing we came in separate cars."

After Griffen left, Mollie wandered aimlessly around the apartment before she came to grips with what she had to do. Take a shower, get dressed, put out any fires that needed putting out in her office, and check back in at the hospital. Maybe the police would have more information. Maybe Jeremiah would. Either way, hanging around inside Leonardo's gates would only drive her crazy.

Jeremiah drove out to the stretch of relatively isolated beach and marsh where Croc was found, then to the police station to see the necklace and talk to the officers first on the scene, not that they had much to offer. Croc still wasn't in any condition to give a statement, but he'd managed, apparently, to indicate that he hadn't recognized his attacker and couldn't provide a detailed description. The police had no reason to believe there was more than one attacker.

Mollie had already gone home. Frank had driven her himself, and he was still steamed at Jeremiah. "You're holding back on me, aren't you, Tabak?"

Jeremiah debated, then gave him the rest. "Mollie Lavender is what got me into this thing." He tried to sound detached, professional. "Croc found out she's been at every event we know the thief hit."

"How'd he know?"

"How does he know anything? He must have been

snooping around, had access to guest lists—I don't know. He wouldn't tell me."

Frank appraised him with cop skepticism. "It's a bitch having that kind of missing link. What about you and this Lavender woman?"

"What about us?"

"You came up from Miami in the same car."

"That we did."

The conversation ended there because Frank had all he needed without Jeremiah explaining the nitty-gritty of his and Mollie's relationship. Hell, he didn't know it himself. He'd fallen for her ten years ago, and he was falling for her again. Simple.

"Any luck on running down Croc's real name?" Jeremiah asked.

"No, but when we find out, we'll track you down right away, Tabak, and let you know, especially seeing how forthcoming you've been with us."

"Hey, I made Mollie call you about her threatening phone call."

Frank just scowled, and Jeremiah, who prided himself on knowing when a well was dry, headed back to the hospital. He barely noticed the crush of snowbirds out enjoying the perfect winter day, just drove the winding, pretty streets of Palm Beach with his mind focused on the task at hand. Croc, jewels, Mollie. The lies Croc had told him, the dozen different ways Mollie might fit into them. He didn't speculate, didn't let his thoughts get ahead of him, just articulated the questions and the facts with cold precision.

He was walking past the information desk when he heard a hoarse, familiar voice. "Tabak—thank God." He turned, and there was Helen Samuel in a pink ladies-who-lunch suit that made her look like a wizened Loretta Young. He wasn't sure, but he didn't think he'd ever seen her outside of the *Miami Tribune* building, maybe not even in the parking lot. She grinned at him. "They won't let me smoke in here. Nazis. Two more minutes and I'm having a seizure."

"What're you going to do when you get sick, Helen?"

"I'm never getting sick. I'm going to fall over dead at my goddamned computer, you wait and see. If I don't, drag my ass out of the hospital, sit me at my desk, and put a bullet in my head. Okay? You'll do that for me?"

He frowned at her. "You have been without nicotine too long."

She waved a dismissive hand. "Look, I heard about Weasel getting beat up—"

"Croc."

"What?"

"His nickname's Croc, not Weasel."

"Oh. I knew it was some disgusting animal. Well, I figured maybe there's a connection—maybe not, either—but you could look into it—" She made a face. "Damnit, I'm not making any sense. What's one goddamned cigarette? You think the building'd blow?"

Fatigue gnawed at Jeremiah. "Look into what, Helen?"

She straightened, focusing. "Michael and Bobbi Tiernay have two sons. This is widely known but not widely discussed. Deegan, the younger son, is at school down here, interning for your Mollie Lavender as a thumb in his old man's eye—or maybe his mother's, or his grandmother's, or the whole damned family's.

It's hard to say because they're the stiff-upper-lip type, and because they know how to do spin control better than most. The older son is Kermit. He's twenty-two. He flunked out of Harvard after his freshman year. He went in as a top student, but he flipped out after he got his first C, then couldn't pull it together, and next thing, he's back home in Palm Beach."

"Jesus, Helen, you think—"

She silenced him with a look. "So his family tells him to sink or swim. It's some weird, warped tough-love thing, I guess. Anyway, he takes off, disappears, there are rumors of substance abuse and general rebelliousness. They figure he's in Colorado or someplace and go on with their lives, making it clear they do not wish to discuss their number one son."

Jeremiah couldn't speak. He stared at Helen, knowing she wouldn't have dragged herself to a West Palm Beach hospital to give him rumors and innuendo. What she had was solid or she'd have kept it to herself. She certainly wouldn't have gone without a cigarette for this long.

Croc was Michael and Bobbi Tiernay's son?

"I've got his high school graduation picture somewhere." She dug in a handbag, circa 1980, and produced a black-and-white photo cut out of a high school yearbook or newspaper. "He went to private school. Apparently he was quite the egghead."

It was Croc. Younger, cleaner, meatier, more optimistic, less world-weary. He probably hadn't slathered his french fries in ketchup in those days, or bussed tables and detailed cars for a living.

Then Helen said, "I think he came into his Atwood

trust fund when he turned twenty-one. Nothing the family could do about it."

"That would be a lot of money?"

Helen grinned. "For an *investigative* reporter, you can be so naive about some things. Yeah, it's a god-damned lot of money. I don't know, Tabak," she said, going philosophical on him, "where love and support and respect stop and enabling begins—well, I never had kids. Thank God, because I'd have messed it up."

"Why?"

"The job. You know it as well as I do." She shook off the attack of introspection. "Okay, so I've given you what I've got. I wished I'd put it together sooner, but there it is."

"It was there for me to see, too. I just needed to do the legwork."

"Yeah, well, the kid's a friend, right?"

Jeremiah stared at her.

She sighed, nodding with understanding. "Happens to the best of us, Tabak. I've got some snooping I might as well do while I'm up here. A society colum-nist never sleeps. Plus, I need a freaking cigarette or I'm going to start foaming at the mouth."

"Thanks for the tip, Helen," Jeremiah said, his voice flat, his senses dulled.

"No problem. Get your head around this one, Tabak. That little shit's been lying to you from the get-go. You know, this is going to leak out. The long-lost Kermit Tiernay, heir to the Atwood fortune, son of Michael and Bobbi. You'd better decide where you want to be standing when the poo-poo hits the fan."

She strutted out, and Jeremiah made his way blindly to the elevators. If Croc could turn out to be a rich ne'er-do-well, he supposed he could end up a Helen Samuel in another thirty years. He shuddered at the thought.

Frank Sunderland caught up with him at the elevators. "We've got an ID on your buddy Croc," he said, out of breath.

"Kermit Tiernay."

Frank scowled. "One day, I'm going to scoop you. The younger brother's up there with him now, and Miss Lavender. She called from the hospital." The elevator dinged, and they got on. Frank smiled thinly. "I like her. She tells me stuff."

"She's a publicist, not a journalist."

"Exactly."

Two minutes later they were in Croc's room. Frank stood back, reluctantly, and let Jeremiah approach the bed. A pale, subdued Deegan Tiernay stood over his injured older brother. Croc—Kermit Tiernay—was conscious, dazed, swollen, and beat to hell, but his blue eyes were trained on Deegan. When he saw Jeremiah and Frank, Deegan went visibly rigid, his emotions held in check.

Mollie, however, was easy to read. She glared at Jeremiah and pounced. "Damnit, you could have told me."

"I didn't know."

His words didn't register. "Your pal Croc and Deegan are *brothers*. You had to know."

Jeremiah remained steady, despite the gnawing pain in his gut. "Well, I didn't."

Mollie still didn't give up. "But you've known him for two years—"

"As Croc, a street kid, this crazy guy who brought

me information and liked too much ketchup on his fries." He shifted to Croc, felt a molten mix of emotions hurtling through him. "I could toss you and that bed out the damned window. Just as well you can't talk. You'd probably try spinning me another tale. And I'd probably swallow it."

Kermit Tiernay was too swollen and bruised to provide a readable expression, and he couldn't speak with his jaw wired shut and his lips stitched.

Jeremiah bit off a sigh. "How're you feeling?"

Croc nodded slightly, an acknowledgment that he was alive but that was about it.

"You hang in there, okay? Trust me, I'm not going anywhere." He turned to Deegan, was aware of Mollie fidgeting to his right, ready to jump out of her skin. "When's the last time you saw your brother?"

"Last Tuesday." His voice was steady, straightforward. "I helped him get hold of guest lists from several parties. Between Griffen and a few other contacts, it wasn't difficult."

"Did you know why he wanted them?"

"Not at first."

"When?"

"After the Greenaway robbery. I just assumed he was playing private eye."

So had Jeremiah. Now, he wasn't ready to make any assumptions until all the facts were in. A hard lesson learned. "How long have you two been in touch?"

"The past two weeks."

"Not before?"

Deegan shook his head and glanced back at Frank, who stood quietly by the empty bed, taking it all in.

Jeremiah kept pushing. "He sought you out?"

"Yes. He asked me not to tell anyone, and I didn't."

"Then your parents don't know, your grandmother, Griffen Welles, Mollie—"

"Obviously *I* didn't know," Mollie put in.

Jeremiah glanced at her, knowing she was scared and upset, and he pushed back the memory of her sleek body last night. He said nothing, shifting back to Deegan, who shook his head. "Nobody knew."

Satisfied, Jeremiah turned back to Croc. He pushed back the conflicting emotions, the anger at himself and concentrated on what he had to do. "One finger up for yes, two for no. You can do it?"

One finger went up.

"Do you want me to find you a lawyer?" Jeremiah asked.

Two fingers.

"You know the police are here right now, listening in?"

One finger.

"Croc," Jeremiah said, leaning over the hospital bed and the battered body of a young man he considered—he could no longer deny it—a friend. "Is someone setting you up?" He raised one finger, and Jeremiah asked, "Do you know who?"

This time, Croc managed a shake of the head before his eyes, already heavy, closed and he drifted off.

"I'll tell Mother and Father." Deegan Tiernay's voice shook; the cockiness of the young man who'd tossed his girlfriend in the pool the other night gone. "They need to know."

Not *want* to know, Jeremiah noticed. "They haven't heard from him?"

"Not since they kicked him out. It's been over two years." He pushed a shaky hand through his hair. "They won't like it that I've been in touch with him, but they'll understand—I had no choice—"

"Good heavens," Mollie said, "I would hope they understand. Of course you had no choice. He's your brother."

He smiled wanly at Mollie, without condescension. "I wish it were that simple."

"Your brother's in trouble," Jeremiah said, "but we don't have the full story yet. We need to reserve judgment."

"Innocent until proven guilty? That's not how it works in my family." But he sucked in a breath before he said too much and turned back to Mollie. "After I talk to them, I'll head back to Leonardo's and clear out my stuff—"

"Why? I'm throwing a party tomorrow night. I need your help."

"But I—"

"But you what? You didn't tell me you were in contact with your brother?"

"Mollie, he's a suspect in the attack on you on Friday. He might have made the threatening call on Monday—"

"First things first, Deegan." Her voice was strong, clear, confident. "Will you tell Griffen, too, or shall I?"

"I'll tell her," he said, and retreated, with Frank Sunderland spinning on his toes and following him out.

Mollie touched Jeremiah's hand. "I'm sorry I jumped on you."

"I probably would have done the same in your place."

"Do you want to hang in here awhile?"

He nodded, watching Croc sleep. "I can't believe the little bastard's a damned millionaire. Helen Samuel says his Atwood trust is worth a fortune."

"He's tapped into it?"

"We don't know." He winced at the *we*. "Damn, I can't believe I've collaborated on a story with her."

Mollie smiled. "You two are a lot alike."

"Don't you start, too. That's what she keeps telling me. You walked into a hell of a scene, didn't you?"

"Deegan was sobbing. The cop guarding Croc called your friend Frank." She was silent a moment, her clear gaze on the broken body in the neat, clean bed. "What do you suppose drove him onto the streets?"

"I don't know, but he got into Harvard. After that, things seemed to fall apart. Maybe the parents can tell us."

"Do you think they will?" she asked.

Jeremiah took in a breath. "I'll find out, one way or the other."

She curved a hand around the back of his neck, slid her fingers into his hair, and kissed him lightly. "Yes, you will, and not because you're a reporter." She dropped her hand, smiled warmly. "You're also his friend."

"Mollie." His voice quaked, but he ignored the knot of fear in his throat. "If the attack on Croc wasn't a coincidence—if he was set up—then someone's trying to cover their own tracks."

She nodded, still steady, although he could see that she'd followed his thinking, perhaps had already reached the same conclusion. "I'm the common denominator, and we still don't know what it means, if anything. And I was attacked and threatened—" She swallowed visibly, but maintained her composure. "If Croc isn't the jewel thief, or if the police don't accept him as the jewel thief, I could be in danger."

"You could be in danger, period."

"Well. I guess next time I speak to Leonardo, I'll tell him he's not paranoid after all for having such an elaborate security system."

"You'll be there?"

"Waiting for you," she said, and left him alone with Croc, aka Blake Wilder, aka Kermit Tiernay.

Jeremiah leaned over the kid's sleeping body. "Where the hell your folks get a name like Kermit? No wonder you went off the deep end."

He pulled up a chair and sat, wondering if Kermit Tienay's parents would show up.

14

〰

"**Y**our brother's a derelict and a jewel thief?" Griffen repeated for at least the third time, her stunned rage upon hearing news of Kermit Tiernay no surprise to Mollie. She, Griffen, and Deegan were at Leonardo's pool, sitting in the shade, oblivious to the bright, hot afternoon sun. Griffen sputtered, still furious. "And you didn't *tell* me?"

"I didn't know for sure," Deegan said, remarkably calm under the circumstances. "I only suspected."

Mollie watched a chameleon scurry into the grass. "We still don't *know* your brother's the thief."

Neither reacted to her comment. Griffen, straddling a lounge chair, her sundress billowing in front of her, was still beside herself. "This explains why you've been acting so weird. You should have called the police, Deegan. They could have picked him up before he did any more damage."

"Call them with what? I didn't even know where to

find him." He was on his feet, pacing, the only sign he was affected by the morning's events. "I did the best I could with what I had."

Griffen wasn't mollified. "Well, maybe someone did him a favor by beating the crap out of him. This thing was escalating. I'm glad it's over."

Deegan paused a moment, his gaze resting on his lover. "As Mollie said, we don't know that Kermit is guilty."

"It's the most obvious, easiest explanation. So, it's probably the *right* explanation. That's how things work in the real world, even in Palm Beach. Conspiracies are for the movies. Most criminals are idiots. Your brother's an idiot who got mugged by an idiot." She leaned back and hoisted up her knees, her bare feet on the chair in front of her. She squinted up at Deegan. "Simple."

He sighed, threw up his hands, and grinned suddenly, turning to Mollie. "Don't you love it when she's on a tear?"

"Go to hell," Griffen told him.

Mollie shook her head. "I'm not saying a word."

But all the fight had gone out of Griffen. "So, how'd Mum and Dad take the news their number one's son's back in town?"

Deegan's grin faded. "About like you'd expect."

"Ah. Flared nostrils and no comment."

He managed a thin smile. "Pretty much. They were deciding whether to see him in the hospital when I left."

Mollie resisted a knee-jerk negative reaction. She didn't know what had occurred between Croc and his parents. Maybe they, too, had done the best they could with what they had and had simply tried to save a nineteen-year-old son bent on self-destruction. On the other hand, she couldn't imagine her parents kicking her out and not seeing her for over two years. They weren't always tuned in the way other parents she knew were, practicing what their friends sometimes called "healthy neglect." Discipline was never much more than a knitted brow, and she and her sister had had more freedom early on than most of their friends. But they knew they had their parents' unconditional love. They took it for granted, as, Mollie thought now, children should. But they instinctively appreciated and never abused that love. It just wouldn't have occurred to them to do so.

Such was not the case, it seemed, in the Tiernay household.

"What did Kermit do to get tossed out?" Griffen asked.

"He embarrassed the family." Deegan's tone was neutral, even a trace of sarcasm impossible to detect. "He flunked out of Harvard for no reason anyone could understand. He just chose not to do the work. Then he had the gall to ask for a year off to sort things out and work odd jobs. My parents said he could go to school or get out."

" 'Get out' as in 'you're on your own but we love you and want to keep in touch' or 'get out' as in—"

"As in 'we disown you.' "

She grimaced. "Ouch."

"Was he abusing drugs or alcohol?" Mollie asked.

"He got drunk maybe twice that I can remember, but that wasn't it. He didn't have his act together at nineteen, and my parents decided the only way he would ever get it together was if they severed all ties. They truly thought they were doing the right thing."

Griffen snorted in disgust. "There has to be more. Was he lighting cats on fire, screwing the household help? You don't just toss a kid out and sever all ties because he wants to wash cars for a year. I mean, why not give him the year?"

"Kermit has always had a vivid imagination," Deegan said. "He's sensitive, maybe too sensitive. He went against the grain."

"Yeah, well, now he's snatching brooches out of people's pockets." Griffen shook her head, just not getting it, and turned to Mollie. "How's this sitting with Tabak?"

"I'm not sure. I haven't talked to him without a cop around since he's seen Croc . . . Kermit."

"Well." Griffen shook her head, as if trying to shake off the tensions of the past hour. "We've got a party to plan—unless you want to cancel."

Mollie thought a moment, then shook her head. "No, let's do it. We won't invite the world, and we'll keep it low-key. If the police have their thief, there's no need to worry about him striking again, and it'll prove that whatever ax he had to grind with me, I wasn't intimidated. And if they don't have their thief—" She settled back, breathed in the warm, scented air. "Then maybe he *will* strike again."

"And we can catch him in the act," Griffen said.

Mollie eyed her young intern. "If you don't want to be involved—"

"No. It's okay. In fact, it's perfect. My parents would approve, carrying on in the face of adversity and all that, and Kermit . . . Croc . . ." He faltered, his only display of emotion. "I think he'd understand, too."

"Good." Griffen sat up and dug in her big leather bag for a clipboard and her laptop. "Then let's get to work."

Jeremiah found Mollie on her back in the pool, her toes pointed, her head tilted back, blonde hair floating out around her. Not sure how to work the gate release in the Jaguar, not wanting to scare the hell out of her, he'd called from the driveway, and she'd opened up. She must have scooted right back into the pool. He could see the portable phone on her chair, which was covered, he noticed with a tug of amusement, with a towel covered with the busts of various composers. He recognized Beethoven's scowl.

"Any news to report?" she asked, barely moving in the still, azure water.

"I'm just back from my apartment. I checked in with the guys and asked them to look after my critters. All considered, reptiles are low maintenance. Albert started to regale me with tales of eating snake in the jungles of southeast Asia."

"Think he has designs on yours?"

"He assured me not."

She went very still. "And Croc?"

"Kermit Tiernay is making steady progress. He should be able to make a limited statement to the police tomorrow. It's not easy to talk with your jaw wired shut, and he's still swollen, which doesn't help."

"Nothing more from the police?"

"Nothing."

"Any word on when Croc will be released from the hospital?"

"Maybe tomorrow."

"Then what?"

"I don't know." He bit off the words, not angry at the question or anyone, just frustrated with his fruitless days, his own worries. He hated worrying. Better just to gather information, jot it in his notebook, chew on it, and write it up. "I don't even know if he has a place of his own. He needs an attorney . . . *damn*!"

Mollie dropped her feet and stood in the pool, the water up to her neck. The burn from her necklace was healing fast, some of its redness already gone. She swirled her arms through the water, studying him. "Croc hasn't asked for your help?"

"No."

Jeremiah dropped into a chair in the sun and watched her splash backwards, kicking her feet up in front of her, not swimming so much as playing in the water, stretching, perhaps easing out some of her own tension. He could feel it coiled in him. A long, hard day that had yielded more questions than answers.

But there was, he thought, something very sexy about being fully clothed around a woman in a swimsuit. Hers was turquoise, the color of the water, and thus made her look even less clothed.

She flipped over onto her stomach and swam over to the edge of the pool, hoisting up her forearms. Water dripped down her face, and her hair was slicked back, making her eyes seem even more bottomless, the lashes ever blacker. "So, have you reached any conclusions about the attack on Croc?"

"I don't have enough information yet."

"But you have theories," she said.

"Theories are the easy part." He knew he sounded short and grumpy, didn't care. Of course, she didn't seem to care, either. "It could have been a random attack. It could have been an attack by a professional. It could have been an attack by an amateur. It could have been intended to kill him, scare the hell out of him, scare the hell out of someone else, mislead him, mislead someone else."

"These someone elses. Meaning who?"

"You, me, the police, the real jewel thief if it's not Croc."

"The real jewel thief? How would an attack on Croc mislead the real jewel thief?"

Jeremiah shot to his feet, unable to sit still. "I don't know. My point is, we can speculate endlessly and end up right back where we are, knowing next to nothing."

She stretched out her arms, still hanging onto the edge of the pool, and eased her behind up as she did a slow frog-kick that struck him as intensely erotic. But she was preoccupied with her sleuthing. She didn't think like a cop or a journalist. She wasn't bound by their professionalism, their cynicism, their ethics, and she was seldom impartial or removed from her emotions. Yet it would be a mistake, Jeremiah knew, to underestimate the keenness of her mind, her ability to see nuances and layers that others might miss. She was, he remembered, a woman who could unravel the intricacies of a symphony and zero in on the essence, the appeal, of a particular client.

Still, right now, he had to admit he was more interested in that wet, slim body. He watched her, feeling the heat of the afternoon, of his own body.

"Speculating," he told her, "will make you crazy. You have to force yourself not to go beyond the facts." He moved to the edge of the pool, squatted down in front of her. "And the facts still have you in the thick of things. I just can't figure out how or why."

"Because Croc is Kermit Tiernay, my intern's older brother."

"That's one reason. You're also still the only known common denominator, the only victim of violence, the only person who's received a threatening call."

She dipped her chin under water, studying him. "I'm just a publicist who happened to be in the wrong place at the wrong time."

"I hope so," he said.

Her eyes widened in irritation. "Are you still keeping an open mind about me? You think it's possible I'm lying?"

He frowned. "Mollie, I simply said I hope you've just been in the wrong place at the wrong time. You can take that at face value."

"Then you don't suspect me," she said stubbornly.

He scooped up a handful of water and flicked it playfully into her face. "Go up and get dressed. If I go up with you, we might not make it back down here until morning. I promised Croc I'd be back this evening." He eased to his feet, felt the day's dramas all the way to his bones. "I still can't get my head around the little bastard being a rich kid."

"You took him on his own terms. Maybe that's all he wanted from you."

"Maybe."

She climbed out of the pool and grabbed her composers' towel, so caught up in her own thoughts she didn't notice him watching her. Her wet suit clung to her curves, her flat stomach. Water glistened on her arms and legs. She slung the towel over her shoulders. "I'll be down in ten minutes, tops."

She made it in seven. She had on a little sheath of a sundress, in dark blue, and sandals, her legs bare, her hair pulled back and still damp. She'd dabbed on pale lipstick and a touch of mascara, and Jeremiah couldn't imagine what had possessed him to put this woman on a plane to Boston ten years ago. Except that if he hadn't, there'd be no hope for them now. She'd needed those ten years. Probably so had he. And that still said nothing about the next ten years.

They took the Jaguar to the hospital, and Mollie, saying she was tired from her swim, let him drive. "You just want to see if I can really handle this thing," he said, grinning at her.

"Not true. If that truck of yours doesn't intimidate you, nothing will."

On their way, she told him about her "spontaneous" cocktail party tomorrow night. She, Deegan, and Griffen had worked on it that afternoon. "Deegan didn't stay—he went back to the hospital to see his brother."

"You're baiting him," Jeremiah said.

She glanced sideways at him, mystified. "Who, Deegan?"'

"The thief. If he's still out there, this 'spontaneous' party is a way of baiting him."

She sat back, miffed. "So what if it is?"

He shrugged. "So what is right. Let's just not be disingenuous."

"I.e., don't lie to you."

"I.e., don't bullshit me. And don't bullshit your-self."

"You do feel free to speak your mind, don't you?"

"Always, Mollie," he said without remorse. "Not just with you."

"Must be from growing up in a swamp. I mean, if you're surrounded by poisonous snakes and alligators and big ugly bugs, you learn pretty quick to tell it like it is." She glanced over at him, the glint of the devil in her eyes. "Am I right?"

He smiled. "From a certain point of view."

When they arrived at the hospital, he was surprised to find it wasn't crawling with reporters. Word was out about the police finding Leonardo Pascarelli's necklace on "Blake Wilder," but not that Blake Wil-der was Michael and Bobbi Tiernay's long-missing older son, Kermit. Helen Samuel was either being re-markably discreet or not tipping her hand. Knowing her, Jeremiah suspected the latter.

Croc was looking marginally better, definitely more alert. His father, still in his business suit, was at his son's bedside and when he glanced at Jeremiah and Mollie, tears shone in his eyes. The resemblance be-tween father and son was there, in the way their eyes crinkled, in the lines of their jaws. Jeremiah just hadn't seen it when he'd met Michael Tiernay at his mother-in-law's cocktail party.

"We can wait outside," Jeremiah said.

"No—no, it's all right." Michael smiled tentatively. "You've been a better friend to Kermit in the past two years than I have. Please, stay. I . . . well, there's no excuse. If I'd wanted to find my son, I could have found him."

Croc moved the arm with the IV in it. His lips were swollen and cracked, but he managed to say through his wired jaw, "Forget it."

"Kermit, whatever you need—a place to stay, an attorney, anything—you let me know. *You* tell *me*." His voice faltered, and he blinked back tears. "I'm in it for the long haul this time, son. It won't be so easy to get rid of me."

"Dad . . ." Croc spoke haltingly, barely able to get the words out. "Thanks."

Mollie took a step forward. "What about his mother?"

"She got as far as the elevator before she had to turn back," Michael Tiernay said without looking around at her. "It's difficult . . . I don't know if you can understand, or I can explain. We were afraid he was dead. We would believe it one day, and then decide it couldn't be true the next."

"He never got in touch with you?"

"No. We'd made it clear we didn't want him to unless it was on our terms. We thought—" He broke off, a proud man fighting for composure. "We thought we were doing the right thing. Helping him become independent."

"Mr. Tiernay," Mollie said gently, "I'm not in a position to judge you."

"You should judge me, Mollie. We cut our son out of our lives. We insisted our friends and family do the same and cut him out of their lives. He was a troubled nineteen-year-old boy, difficult, hypersensitive, recalcitrant, failing at everything he did, refusing to live by our rules and standards. We didn't see another choice."

"What would have been another choice?"

Such a simple question, Jeremiah thought. Michael Tiernay gave a bitter laugh. "Love him."

"But you didn't stop loving him—"

He shook his head. "I don't mean love as a feeling. I mean love as something we do. And we stopped. If he had been engaged in criminal activity, drinking and doing drugs, perhaps our alternatives would have been starker. But he wasn't. He was simply . . ." He smiled meekly, turning back to his son. "He was simply a pain in the ass."

Mollie was frowning, not fully understanding.

Michael Tiernay touched his son's hand. "I'll let you visit with your friends. I'll be right out in the hall. It's a clean slate, Kermit. In my eyes, we're starting fresh."

"Croc."

"What?"

"You can call me Croc."

His father laughed softly, his pain almost palpable. "Then Croc it is." He turned to Jeremiah and Mollie. "Please, take your time. I'm not going anywhere."

"The police know anything more?" Jeremiah asked him.

"Not yet." His gaze went steely, and Jeremiah could see his pride, the core of a man who'd built Tiernay & Jones into a formidable force in international communications. "But it doesn't matter what they find out. I'm here to stay."

He left the room in long, determined strides, and Jeremiah glowered at Croc. "Blake Wilder. You lying little shit."

Croc gave him a crooked, miserable grin and flipped him a bird.

Jeremiah laughed. "I guess if I had a name like Kermit, I might head to fantasy land myself."

"I'm named after my grandfather," Croc said slowly, laboriously, "not the frog."

"Kermit Atwood," Mollie supplied. "Diantha's husband."

"Well." Jeremiah straightened, felt the emotional and physical agony Croc must be feeling. "You're here. You're alive. And your father's at your bedside eating some crow. You going to forgive him?"

"Already did."

"Were your parents authoritarian? Did they beat you, make you toe the line?"

But Croc sank deeper into his pillows, drifting in and out, his pain medication, fatigue, and injuries taking their toll.

"We were disengaged," Michael Tiernay said from the doorway. He walked into the room and adjusted the blanket over his son as if he were still a small, innocent boy, not a young man with a policeman outside his hospital door. "He would do anything to get our attention. And did. Positive, negative—it didn't matter what kind of attention he got. When we finally did focus on him, we decided he wasn't worth our effort and kicked him out."

Jeremiah stared at him. "Aren't you being a little hard on yourself?"

"No, I'm not. That's why my wife couldn't come up here, not because of what Kermit—of what *Croc* might have done, but because of what we'd done. He was still so young at nineteen. He needed us to love him—not without rules and standards, but unconditionally."

That wasn't how Jeremiah and his father had operated, not even in the dark, pain-filled years after his mother had died. When they had problems, they'd go off in the swamp together with a jackknife and matches. After a few days, everything would sort itself out.

Michael Tiernay gently stroked his son's ratty hair. "He had everything. Boarding school, the best camps, trips to Europe, everything electronic a boy could want, his own private suite at home. Harvard. But he wasn't a part of our lives, and he knew it." He looked back at Jeremiah abruptly, as if he'd tried to contradict him. "We're not bad people. In fact, we're very good people. We loved him in our own way."

"Mr. Tiernay, Croc never discussed his past with me."

Tiernay might not even have heard him. "It's not the money, you know."

Jeremiah nodded. That much he did know.

"The money just made it easier for us to think we were doing everything for our son when what we'd done was nothing."

"What about Deegan?" Mollie asked.

Tiernay shifted to her, as if he'd forgotten she was there. "Deegan's always been different. You don't have children, but they come . . . I don't know, they come with their own personalities. Kermit was always sensitive, creative, intuitive. Deegan's more action-oriented, more direct, not at all introspective. That made him easier for reserved parents like Bobbi and myself to raise."

She smiled, her naturalness not unexpected but infectious. "Croc would have done well in my family.

Things were always chaotic, there was never enough money, and my parents and sister are the quintessential flaky musicians. I guess they'd have had fits with a kid like Deegan, though."

Tiernay seemed to relax at her warmth and clarity. "Perhaps we all just have to play the cards we're dealt. You've been good to him, Mr. Tabak. I gather he looks up to you."

"Mr. Tiernay, I'm responsible for him being here. If I'd taken his warnings more seriously, worked harder—"

But Michael Tiernay was shaking his head. "I've known Kermit—Croc—all his life, and he has a mind of his own, which he's willing to use. Which he's *desperate* to use. He wants, and deserves, to take responsibility for his own decisions. It wasn't his decision to abandon us. It was our decision to abandon him. In any case, unless he's changed drastically—and my wife and I had nineteen years of trying to change him— it's my guess he would only be annoyed if you tried to take the blame for his condition."

"You're probably right. Will your wife be in later?"

"I don't know. I'm not sure it's fair to ask of her what she can't give." A tear traced its way down his handsome face, but he made no move to brush it away, seemed unembarrassed. "Whoever did this to him . . ."

"I'm going to find out," Jeremiah said, meaning it.

"Yes. I believe you will. Thank you for being his friend."

Jeremiah stared at the battered, broken body in the hospital bed and had to fight back a tear or two of his own. No matter how many times he saw young men shot, knifed, beaten, drugged, and drunk, he had this same twisting pain in his stomach, this same overwhelming sense of loss and waste. When he didn't, he promised himself he'd quit. Control and objectivity were one thing. A loss of compassion was something else entirely.

"That's a two-way street, Mr. Tiernay. Your son's been a friend to me as well."

15

They picked up sandwiches in a little shop that had Griffen's stamp of approval and ate them on the deck above Leonardo's lush backyard. Roasted vegetables on flatbread for Mollie, plain old roast beef for Jeremiah. She'd filched a bottle of pinot noir from her godfather's wine closet, knowing he would not only have approved but insisted, and poured two glasses. Jeremiah held his in one hand, his fingers so rigid she thought he might shatter the glass. She understood. He wasn't irritated or unnerved or anything that she might have been in a similar position.

It wasn't his mood, she realized, fascinated, but his mind at work.

Jeremiah Tabak was doing what Jeremiah Tabak did, which was sort his way through facts, bits and pieces of information, scenes, comments, vignettes, anything and everything that came his way, then sit back and process them into a coherent whole.

Mollie suspected that the coherent whole wasn't materializing. He could speculate, perhaps, and come up with a variety of possible wholes, but he would avoid getting too far ahead of his precious facts.

She also suspected—no, she thought, she *knew*—that he wasn't really quite out on the deck with her. He couldn't smell the greenery and flowers in the warm evening air, couldn't hear the cry of the seagulls, the hum of traffic, the not-too-distant wash of the tide. He was in his story that he would never write. An occasional sip of wine was all that told her he hadn't gone catatonic.

But this altered state, of course, was familiar to her. She'd grown up with people who would stare off into space—not over crime and corruption, perhaps, but over music. A difficult phrase, an elusive cadenza, a new interpretation of a favorite sonata. These were the things that would occupy her parents and sister, her godfather, and take them mentally out of the room. She'd had these experiences herself, particularly when she was playing flute, but also, although less often, when she was brainstorming on behalf of a client. Definitely, however, her mind didn't have the same tendency to wander as her parents' did.

And Jeremiah would disagree that his mind was wandering at all. He would say he was concentrating. Deliberately focusing. And maybe he was, but she didn't believe it was strictly a matter of control or choice on his part. He was a reporter, she realized now, because of the way his mind worked, the way he took in the world around him, not the other way around.

She pictured Croc's battered face, his skinny, beaten

body, his father in tears at his bedside. Gut-wrenching. Appalling. Who would do that to a defenseless human being? And *especially* miss a diamond-and-ruby necklace in his back pocket in the process? She didn't buy the theory that the attacker had been interrupted before he could find it, or before he could get Croc's body to wash out to sea. He'd wanted Croc found with the necklace on him, if not necessarily found alive.

Which, she acknowledged and accepted, was getting herself way ahead of the facts.

Jeremiah shifted, his jaw set hard, and with an abruptness that made her jump, he polished off the rest of his wine in a gulp. Then the tension went out of his body, and he rolled up out of his chair and stalked into the kitchen. She heard him rinse his glass in the sink and set it on the drainboard.

He was back here in Leonardo's guest quarters with her, tuned in to his surroundings.

Mollie followed him inside, her own wine half drunk. She slid onto a stool at the breakfast bar, the counter between them as he stood staring out the window. The crickets had started. She knew he would stay tonight. He'd arranged for the elderly men in his building to take care of his animals, and he'd need to stay close to Croc. He'd left her number with the police. But he'd said nothing about staying, and given his preoccupation, she hadn't brought it up.

He pulled his gaze from the window and turned to her, his eyes a swirl of color, none of the grays and golds and blues distinct. "Your deep, dark secret's out, sweet pea."

"Yes, I know. We're the subject of intense and lurid gossip."

"Sorry?"

"Nope. I can get a lot of mileage from having had a mad, weeklong affair with a dark and dangerous Miami reporter. It'll make me seem more mysterious." She grinned at him, wondering if he thought she was serious. "I wouldn't just want to be Leonardo Pascarelli's goody-two-shoes goddaughter."

"You think we're having another mad, weeklong affair," he said, a palpable seriousness descending over him.

She shrugged, refusing to let his dark mood affect her. "I left my crystal ball in Boston."

"Mollie . . ."

"Don't, Jeremiah. Being honest with me is honorable in and of itself. It allows me to make informed choices. You're not in the frame of mind to make promises, and I'm not in one to receive them. You've taken a hit today." She eased off the stool, her knees unsteady. "Absorb it first. Then we'll figure out what next week will bring."

"When you were twenty, you couldn't wait to get to next week."

She laughed. "Nothing like turning thirty to change that. I'm not into hurrying time these days. I'm off to the shower. I still smell like chlorine. If you want, you can throw some darts. I find it relaxing." She grinned over her shoulder at him as she started down the hall. "Although less so since I took down your picture. It's tucked in the Yellow Pages if you want to throw a few darts between your own eyes and beat yourself up a little, at least metaphorically."

He didn't respond, and she could feel his eyes on her, their intensity making her shudder with awareness on every level, physical, emotional, mental. With Jeremiah, there was no hiding, no pretending, no eluding. From herself, from him.

She darted down the hall and into her bedroom, her body telling her in a thousand different ways that she'd made love to Jeremiah Tabak last night. Her nightmare. Her one dark and dangerous man. Except, after seeing him with his battered young friend, he'd seemed less dark, less dangerous, less volatile and remote and determined never to connect with another human being.

"You're getting way ahead of the facts," she warned herself sarcastically and flung open a drawer, staring at her nightgown selection. They came in degrees of utilitarian, some with feminine touches, none with sexy overtones. Well. There was no assurance Jeremiah would even see her in her nightgown. She chose one that was full-length, white cotton, and not too utilitarian, then slipped into the shower, welcoming the stream of hot water on her tensed muscles, the smell of citrus soap and chamomile shampoo. She shut her eyes, forgetting the past, postponing the future, just focusing on the present, her shower, her body.

She toweled off and decided to blow-dry her hair just enough to keep it from becoming a rat's nest overnight. It was not, she told herself, a delaying tactic. When she returned to her bedroom, she slipped a terry-cloth robe over her nightgown before venturing back to the kitchen and the rest of her wine.

She could hear the rhythmic tossing of darts in the den. She sipped a bit more of her wine and stood in the semidark kitchen, listening. Throwing darts was an effective release, she thought, after a twenty-four-hour period in which you'd been to bed with a woman who'd once, fervently, wished you a long stay in hell and then found a friend in the hospital. Those were enough, without the added complications of a jewel thief, a missing heir, questions from the police, and a journalistic reputation on the line.

When she went into the den, she wasn't really surprised to see that Jeremiah had pulled out the sofa bed.

"I'll get sheets," she said without preamble.

A dart thwocked home. A bull's-eye. Others, she saw, had gone wide. "Mollie." His eyes pinned her as surely as any dart. His dark mood hadn't lifted; if anything, it had intensified. "I want you to know I don't regret last night. And it wasn't a fluke."

"I understand."

"But I don't know if I can be what you need."

"I don't want you to be what I need." She walked around the sofa bed and stood in front of him, close, seeing every tensed muscle, every line, every speck of gray in his cropped, dark hair. She imagined that straight line of a mouth on hers, sliding over her body, bringing her to a kind of ecstasy she'd never known with anyone else. "Just be honest with me, Jeremiah, and be who you are. That's all anyone has a right to ask."

The straight mouth twitched, almost imperceptibly. "That's all?"

"Well, who you are is sexy and not exactly celibate and—" She smiled, raising her eyebrows at him. "Do I really need to get sheets?"

"I have amazing self-restraint, you know."

"About some things, I'm sure."

"But not about you." His voice lowered, and he closed the small distance between them. "Not ten years ago, not now."

He swept his arms around her and caught her with a kiss that rocked her back on her feet. She nearly fell onto the unmade sofa bed. His mouth and hands were suddenly all over her, hungrily devouring any self-restraint she might have had. She exulted in the feel of him, turned her body loose, boldly slipping a hand down his chest, past the waistband of his pants, testing his arousal, teasing him with delicate flicks of her fingertips. Playing with fire.

She wriggled out of her robe. It dropped to the floor. Her nipples were outlined against the translucent fabric of her nightgown. He gave a soft moan, opened his mouth to hers, already lifting her nightgown up to her hips, cupping her bottom with his palms.

And he stopped. It was her turn to moan. "Jeremiah . . ."

He eased her down onto the bed, and she fell back against the cool mattress, her nightgown up around her hips. Slowly, languorously, proving he could make this last as long as he wanted, he slid his fingers between her legs, found where she was wet and hot, and did a little delicate flicking of his own. Even when her breath was coming in gasps and she was grabbing at his back, he didn't pull back. Instead, he followed with his tongue.

He pushed her nightgown up with one hand while the other kneaded the warm, firm flesh of her bottom, while his mouth continued to plunder. She made short work of getting her nightgown off, tossing it aside.

She heard him unzip his pants. "Yes, now, *now*."

In one swift movement, he was free, driving into her, lifting her hips up on him, her legs squeezing him as she responded wildly, everything fast now, furious, total delirium setting in.

Hours later, or seconds, she was clinging to him, limp, spent, aware of a cool breeze floating through the windows and her mind drifting.

A decade ago, they'd made love like that. No wonder she hadn't forgotten.

"You're cold," he said, his voice ragged.

"That's because you still have your shirt on and I don't have anything on."

He smiled. "I noticed."

"So," she said, still breathless, yet every muscle loose, warm, "do I fetch the sheets or do you think maybe we can dare sleep together? I mean, at twenty I could do this ten times in a night. But now . . ." She grinned at him, running one finger along his jaw. "I don't know, once or twice more might not kill me."

He popped up off the sofa bed, laughing. "Innocent flute player, my ass. You were a wanton woman ten years ago, and you're one now. I'm going to take a shower and rebandage my poor cut thumb. Then, darlin'," he said with a wink, "we'll see who's not twenty anymore."

The night brought out the smell and the sounds of the south Florida coast, and as Jeremiah sat on Mollie's deck, he breathed them all in. They were a part of his soul, he thought, the way they never could be of hers. He had his feet up on the rail, his mind focused, not wandering as he sipped a martini. He'd been surprised to find the makings in Mollie's cupboard. Probably her godfather's doing.

They'd made love again, slowly, tenderly, in her sprawling bed, and he'd had the feeling she was absorbing every nuance in case it would be another ten years before they had another chance.

Maybe it would be.

The breeze shifted, carrying a touch of the Everglades to the posh streets of Palm Beach. Jeremiah had another sip of his martini, and he had to accept there was no way he could pretend he was out on the dock at his father's outpost, looking at the stars.

He was in freaking Palm Beach, as Helen Samuel would say.

Mollie had fashioned a nice life for herself here. He had wandered around her office and sensed that her relationship with her clients, while professional, had a personal quality that was uniquely hers. She would dive in headfirst and risk really understanding them as human beings, not simply chess pieces, means to an end. She wasn't just an opportunist after money and success. There was a stark integrity to her that required courage, confidence, commitment.

He squeezed his eyes shut, and he could see his mother puttering around the yard while his father was out on the lake. He could feel the comfort of knowing they would be together forever, his mother and father. Even as a boy, he'd known that what Reuben and Jenny Tabak had was special and unusual.

When she was dying, she'd told her husband and son, "We need to learn to go on without each other, you without me, me without you."

His father's grief was quiet and complete. Yet, eventually, Jeremiah had come to see that Reuben Tabak *had* learned to go on without the love of his life. He was content, he said. He felt he was lucky to have had that kind of relationship at all. He had no regrets, no bitterness.

"I'll never get over her, son. It'd scare me to death if I thought I would. That doesn't mean I'm some pitiful old fool, it just means that nothing's ever going to take away what your mother and I had, no matter what I do from here."

But he never remarried. He wouldn't. He'd had the one great love of his life, and that was all for him.

Jeremiah headed back inside, rinsed his glass, and walked down the short hall to Mollie's room. He stood in the doorway, listening to her rhythmic breathing. His throat was tight, his body coiled with a tension that seemed to grip his soul, too. He didn't know what the hell he was feeling, even what he was thinking. Had his father known what he'd had before he lost it?

Slowly, not making a sound, he peeled off his shorts and shirt and slipped under the light covers. Mollie rolled over, throwing one arm over him as naturally as if they'd been sleeping together for years. He kissed her hair, and he closed his eyes, not giving a damn if he slept again tonight.

Jeremiah rolled out of bed to the melodic sounds of a flute concerto and the smell of coffee. Mollie's side of the bed was empty, cool to the touch, which meant she'd been up for a while. He found his shorts on the floor, slipped them on, and took a quick shower. Last night had settled things for him. He knew exactly where he stood. He would find the truth about

Croc, the jewel thief, Mollie's role in whatever was going on. And he'd find it, he thought, not because he was a reporter, but because he was involved. Croc was his friend, and Mollie was—

He flipped off the shower. Mollie was whatever she was.

She was dressed for business, hair shining and pulled back, coffee mug and a bright yellow file folder on the table in front of her. "You've got ten minutes before Griffen and Deegan get here."

"I should make the sofa bed look slept in?"

"You should get dressed. They won't know what to do finding a half-clothed man in my apartment." She smiled over the rim of her mug. "Not that you'd be easy to hide. And as you pointed out last night, my deep, dark secret's out anyway."

"Regrets?"

"None."

She watched him pour coffee. He didn't hurry. It wasn't as if he was indecent. He sipped the hot, strong coffee, then set his mug on the counter. "You're sure? Two nights in a row, Mollie."

"I'm aware of that." She grinned at him. "You're no dream, Tabak, but I suppose you're no nightmare, either. You're just . . . here."

"So I am."

"Trust me, okay? Even if you prove to be an utter snake in the grass and slither off after we've settled who's behind what regarding Croc and the jewel thief, I will not for one single, solitary second regret the past two nights."

"Will you wish me time in a fiery hell?"

Her bottomless eyes sparked with sudden, irreverent humor. "An eternity."

By the time Griffen and Deegan arrived to pull together the cocktail party that evening, Jeremiah was fully dressed and at the table, drinking his second cup of coffee. Mollie didn't explain his presence. Her friend and intern took their raised eyebrows into her living room office.

"You see, Jeremiah," Mollie whispered in his ear, "I'm not what most people would regard as your type. Publicist, flutist, goddaughter of a world-famous tenor. You're a reporter who keeps reptiles on his kitchen table."

"You have your oddities, sweet pea."

She winked, enjoying herself. "You're one of them. Off to the hospital?"

He nodded. "And I'll check in at the paper. Helen Samuel's going to want a full report."

"You're invited tonight, of course."

"Ah. I'll check my calendar."

"I've seen your desk, Jeremiah. You don't keep a calendar."

He shrugged, finished off the last of his coffee, and got to his feet. "My life's not that complicated."

"It's not *planned*. It's plenty complicated."

Before he left, he popped into the living room, already a whir of activity. Deegan glanced at Jeremiah and seemed to read his mind. "I checked in on my brother this morning. He's doing well, all considered. His doctors think he can be released today."

"Isn't that soon?"

He shrugged. He was dressed casually, expensively, a contrast to his older brother's ragged, threadbare clothes and general scraggliness. "Hospitals don't like to keep you hanging around these days. He doesn't need surgery, and he's off intravenous."

"Where will he go?"

Deegan's expression was unreadable. "My parents were still arguing that question this morning. My father wants him home. Mother doesn't. She's suggesting they put him up in an apartment and hire a home nurse until he's back on his feet."

"Then what?"

"Up to him. She's not a monster—she's just trying to establish proper boundaries."

"And your father?"

He swallowed, cutting his eyes around at Griffen, who was listening to every word even though her ear was stuck to a telephone. He said, "He doesn't think this is the time to worry about boundaries. First, get him well, then find out what happened to him, *then*, if necessary, kick him back out into the streets."

"What about his Atwood trust fund?" Jeremiah asked. "Doesn't he have money of his own?"

The blue eyes leveled on Jeremiah, steady, just a tad surly. "I wouldn't know. And if you're wondering, I want my brother home, too."

Jeremiah grinned at him. "I was."

"But my father's concerned with appearances—how this will affect his reputation—and I'm not."

Griffen hung up the phone before he could clear out. "That was George Marcotte," she said with a twinge of amazement. "Granny Atwood and Momma Tiernay have hired him for us for tonight. Under the circumstances, they think we should have a private security guard or two, and Marcotte's firm will provide them or he'll be here himself."

"Then they don't believe the police have their man?" Jeremiah asked sharply.

"Beats me." She lifted her thin shoulders in an exaggerated shrug, her dark curls framing her face, lessening the tugs of tension at the corners of her eyes and mouth. "I just figure they're worried about Mollie's bad luck and their boy Deegan."

"Well, it can't hurt to take extra precautions."

She smiled, rallying. "Guess not."

"Then Gran and Mother are coming tonight?" Deegan asked.

"They say they are. But I would think it will depend on your brother and his condition, if the police learn any more today. He'll probably be able to talk to the police today."

Deegan grinned at her. "Griffen, Griffen, it'll depend on what else is on their calendar and whether making a show of support of me is in their best interests. They'll want to be seen in public and still the wagging tongues." He shrugged. "That's reality, not criticism. They have their survival techniques, just as a kid on the streets does."

"Come on," she said, "it's not as if you're in any danger of following in big brother's footsteps. I don't know how you can stand to be so cynical."

"Okay, I'm wrong. They don't care about their reputation and the gossip. They'll show tonight because they want to see Leonardo Pascarelli's house."

Griffen laughed in mock horror. "*Deegan.*"

Mollie entered the room, her presence enough to end the conversation. Griffen started dialing a number, and Deegan sat at the computer. Jeremiah, thinking that he wouldn't like to be a fly on the wall when these two were alone, blew Mollie a clandestine kiss, just to see her fume and blush at the same time, and departed.

Croc was being visited by Frank Sunderland, a lawyer, and his father when Jeremiah arrived at the hospital. He didn't hang around. He headed back to Miami in the sleek black Jaguar, appreciating its maneuvering ability on the road even if it didn't intimidate people as much as his truck did. In a beat-up, rusted old truck, you found that drivers in fancy cars gave way. Not so in a Jaguar.

He checked in with Helen Samuel, back at her desk, cigarette smoking on her ashtray, another smoking on her lower lip. "Christ," she croaked. "I'm in the goddamned boiling pot with you. The brass told me to get them on the horn the minute I saw you. They're probably getting a million calls right now. Half the building's on the lookout. Spies everywhere, Tabak."

He was unconcerned. "Anything more on the Tiernays?"

She eyed him through half-closed eyes. "About once or twice every five years or so I regret not having kids. This isn't one of those times. I'd have no doubts I'd have screwed mine up as badly as the Tiernays have screwed up theirs. Kermit, at least. The younger one—Deegan—seems okay, except he's got a girlfriend ten years older than he is and he's interning for your blonde instead of for his father."

"That's not in the same league as what Croc's alleged to have done."

"Alleged? I love you hard-news types."

"Helen . . ."

"Well, it's not as if it's easy to get anyone to talk about the Tiernays, parents or kids. Most think Kermit needed his ass kicked, if not tossed into the gutter. After two years on the streets, they figure, yeah, he could go the cat burglar route, have a little fun, stick it to his old pals up on the Gold Coast."

"Not to mention his parents."

"Yeah. Not to mention. The grandmother—Diantha Atwood—always had a soft spot for Kerm, but she's not saying a word, not interfering. Momma's a cold-fish socialite, but that could be style, not substance. And Dad's a respected, hard-nosed businessman who spent a lot of time on the road and in the office when his kids were little. There are," she said, blowing smoke out her mouth and nose, "no innocents here."

"But no secret lives, nothing we can latch onto to explain why a twenty-two-year-old kid had the shit beaten out of him the night before last?"

"If you want that explained," Helen said, peering at him with a gravity he seldom witnessed in her, "you're probably going to have to look at his world, not his parents' world. Their world provided the victims, Jeremiah. Marcie Amerson, Lucy Baldwin, even Mollie Lavender. His world, I suspect, provided the goons."

Jeremiah frowned at her. "You see why you're a society columnist, Helen? You deal in gossip and supposition. If you deal in facts, you'll see that I have to look wherever I'll find the answers. His world, their world, the goddamned moon. Right now, it makes no difference to me."

He was halfway to the door before she'd blown enough air out of her lungs to answer his insult. "Kiss my ass, Tabak," she yelled. "I hope they seal off the building before you slither out of here."

He winked at her, which further incensed her, and was down the corridor and out to the parking garage before his bosses could grab him by the short hairs and ask him what in hell he thought he was doing, up to his ears in a big story and not one word of it on the pages of the *Miami Tribune*.

Spies everywhere, indeed. After she cooled off, Jeremiah would tell Helen he appreciated her warning.

There was something to be said for driving a vehicle not his own at such times. He waved to the guard at the garage, who recognized him too late, leaped out of his little cubicle of a building, and chased after him, on the alert for an errant reporter.

But by then, Leonardo Pascarelli's little black Jaguar was well on its way to the on-ramp of 95 North.

16

Mollie chose a dressy suit from her own closet and joined Deegan, Griffen, and Griffen's small part-time staff on the terrace. Leonardo's house and grounds were immaculate, designed for parties, and Griffen, with enviable calm, had whisked in food and drink, tossing brightly colored cloths over folding tables to make instant hors d'oeuvres tables and wine bars. She'd rearranged Leonardo's pots, added more of her own, did up strings of dried flowers, and somehow, with very little apparent effort, made the terrace look festive.

George Marcotte's security guard had posted himself at the gates, which he'd agreed to leave open for arriving guests. Mollie was unaccustomed to having security guards lurking. The guard was big and beefy and intimidating enough that if Mollie were a thief, she'd stay away from Leonardo Pascarelli's house tonight.

The weather was perfect, warm and calm under a cloudless sky. A night for spontaneity and friends, she thought, feeling optimistic.

Jeremiah had called from the hospital. Croc was being released, still no charges filed against him. His parents had compromised, agreeing to let him stay in their guest house until he recuperated. Mollie wondered if Bobbi Tiernay really felt she knew her son after more than two years. She couldn't imagine becoming that alienated from her own family. Why hadn't Croc just stewed awhile, then gone home? Was that ever an option?

She found herself articulating her thoughts to Griffen, who was, she said, enjoying the lull before the storm. Guests hadn't yet started to arrive. Griffen was uncorking wine bottles. "I've known kids like Kermit Tiernay my whole life," she said, looking tired but not unduly so. "The poor little rich kid who'd practically commit murder to get his parents to acknowledge his existence. Or her. I don't know if it's worse with girls or not. People feel sympathy for poor kids with neglectful parents, but not rich kids, because they've got all the trimmings. The camps, the private schools, the lessons. But they still want the nights home watching TV or playing cards with their mums and dads. That's only normal."

"You're not describing yourself, are you?" Mollie couldn't contain her shock at the depth of Griffen's emotion; she seemed personally outraged. "Is that what your upbringing was like?"

"Mine? No, no. I've got a great relationship with my parents." She seemed a bit irritated, even offended, at

Mollie's misinterpretation. "Not all us rich kids are fucked up, you know."

"Deegan doesn't seem to have suffered his brother's fate."

"No." She uncorked a bottle of cabernet sauvignon, calmer. "Some people are just naturally more resilient, I think. But imagine, Mollie. You're the child of rich, selfish parents who think they adore you. I mean, they really believe they adore you. They believe you can do no wrong. That you're perfect."

"That would be a hard way to live. Nobody's perfect. Everybody makes mistakes."

She set the wine bottle down, a slight tremble to her long, thin hands. "Yes, exactly. So you have these adoring parents, and they never ask you to do anything hard in your life. In fact, they make sure you never do anything hard, which makes you wonder if they really *do* believe in you—if all that adoration is just an excuse for them to ignore you. If you're perfect, you don't need attention. If you can do no wrong, you don't need attention. If you never have to do anything hard, you don't need attention. They get to congratulate themselves for the wonderful life they've given you."

"And you end up perpetuating the illusion that you're perfect, because that's what's expected of you."

"But you grow up craving your parents' attention, only you're cocky and you're fun to be around and you've never, ever had to face the consequences of your actions."

"That would be tough," Mollie said carefully, wondering if Griffen was trying to tell her more than was on the surface, but she could hear Jeremiah warning her against speculating. "At some point, you *will* make a mistake. You'll shatter the illusion."

"It'd take a lot to shatter that kind of illusion."

Mollie felt a chill despite the warm temperature. "I suppose you could also grow up and realize your parents are what they are and there's no changing them."

"Yeah. I suppose. But how many people accept their parents' shortcomings before they've acted out against them?" She grinned suddenly, but there was no humor, no pleasure, in her dark eyes. "God, I'm sounding like a therapist. Not to worry. I'm just a Palm Beach girl who knows how to cook."

"Griffen, are we talking about Deegan here? Or are you getting theoretical? Where is he, anyway?"

"He's out front meeting guests." She grabbed another bottle of wine, shoved in the corkscrew. "If I give everyone food poisoning, I guess I can always become a shrink. Here comes Chet Farnsworth. The guests must be arriving. I'd better concentrate or I *will* poison the guests." She spun around, her cheeks rosy with exertion, a touch of embarrassment. But she was being evasive, and Mollie knew it. "Look, what I said—forget it, okay? It's bullshit. I've been working too hard. It's my busy season, and I just . . . I've just been thinking too much, I guess. You won't mention this conversation to Tabak, will you? Reporters. You know what hounds they are. And he was born suspicious. God knows what he'll read into this, and then he'll have to know."

"I understand, Griffen. I don't need to tell anyone about our conversation, unless you know something that the police—"

"No!" She paled, horrified. "No, of course not. God. I'd better get to work or there go both our reputations."

She breezed off into the kitchen of the main house, which was brightly lit, almost looking lived in. Mollie greeted Chet and his wife, still feeling vaguely uneasy. But she pushed back her questions and concentrated on her guests and her party.

"You're okay?" Chet asked, concerned. He was a man who missed nothing, a good thing, Mollie supposed, in both an astronaut and a pianist.

"Just a little nervous. I've never done this kind of party."

"Relax. It'll be fun." He winked at her. "If things start dragging, I'll pull everybody inside and play the piano. Pascarelli has one, I assume?"

"A grand piano in the front room. He likes to play it and sing drinking songs with his friends."

Chet laughed. "I think I'm going to like this guy when I finally meet him."

He and his wife drifted off to the hors d'oeuvres and wine, and Mollie moved to greet the Tiernays and Diantha Atwood as they came down the brick walk. They were simply but elegantly dressed, and only if one were looking—and Mollie was—would one see the strain of the past forty-eight hours. What a horrible way, she thought, to have a long-lost son reenter their lives.

Before she could welcome them, Deegan materialized behind his parents and grandmother with, incongruously, Jeremiah at his side. Mollie's breath caught. Jeremiah wore a dark, casual suit that fit his frame perfectly, emphasized the breadth of his shoulders, the length of his legs.

Mollie smiled, "Welcome—thank you for coming."

"Our pleasure," Bobbi Tiernay said, taking her hand briefly. "What a wonderful setting, Mollie. Deegan told us you'd considered canceling after what happened. I'm so glad you didn't. We brought Kermit home late this afternoon."

No mention of shoving him in the guest house. "Are the police any closer to finding out who attacked him?"

"No," Michael Tiernay said, his wife visibly uncomfortable beside him, "and I'm afraid Kermit's not able to be of much help. The attack happened fast, and it was dark."

Diantha Atwood smiled politely. "There's so much confusion right now. We're just delighted to have an evening free to meet some of the people Deegan has been working with. I see Chet Farnsworth." And she subtly moved in his direction, her daughter and son-in-law following her lead.

Deegan, looking sheepish, said with just a hint of sarcasm, "Gran's the expert at coping with the socially awkward moment."

Mollie grimaced. "I should learn to keep my big mouth shut."

"You're just direct," he said. "Be glad. If you'll excuse me, I'll go give Griffen a hand."

"By all means."

Mollie turned to Jeremiah, who, she knew, had been watching and listening with interest, if not objectivity. "Anything new?"

He shook his head. "Croc has no idea how the

necklace ended up in his back pocket. None. Zip. Or so he says. I think he has *ideas*—Croc always has ideas—but I've been on his case for two years about sticking to the facts."

"What's his mood like?"

"Contemplative. When he has something to say, he'll say it. That's one thing, anyway, he and his Kermit Tiernay alter ego have in common."

Mollie could sense Jeremiah's confusion, his sense of betrayal mixed in with his loyalty, his affection, for a troubled young man. "Have you had a chance to speak with him alone, or are his parents always hovering?"

He smiled thinly. "Trust me, Mollie, the Tiernays don't hover. Michael's trying, and maybe in her own way so is Bobbi. But, Jesus, could you be here tonight? Sure, they want to support Deegan, but he's right—they're also running up the flag, demonstrating that their older son might be a suspected jewel thief, but they're from strong stock, they'll carry on."

"Where would you be if you were in their shoes?" Mollie asked.

"We'd all be with Croc." His eyes darkened, lost in the shifting shadows of the pool lights, Griffen's candles. Mollie could feel his somber mood. "The parents, the grandmother, the brother. I'd have told him his publicist boss could throw a cocktail party without him."

"Which I did tell him."

"I know you did. I'm not criticizing them, him, you. Look, you've got guests," he said. "See to them. Have fun tonight."

She sighed, felt a little breathless, asked abruptly, "Do you think the real jewel thief will show?"

He went still. "Mollie . . ."

"It's not Croc. You know it's not. And it's not me."

It was as if a mask had dropped over his face. "This isn't the time. I think your mutt owner has just arrived." His smile didn't reach his eyes. "I'll go mingle."

She watched him saunter off to the wine bar, couldn't stop herself from imagining more parties, all different kinds of parties, with him at her side. His was a commanding presence, mitigated by his dark good looks and easy humor. Like herself, he was accustomed to going it alone, forging his own way, yet he was also surprisingly good with people, at ease with them, tolerant if opinionated.

He wandered among the crowd, saying little, and she could see that a Palm Beach cocktail party just wasn't his thing, that where he was most comfortable, most himself, was when he was working a story. And that knowledge slammed her fantasies up against the hard wall of reality. Resolving mysteries, unraveling intricacies. *Those* were what made Jeremiah Tabak get up in the morning. And once he had things sorted out in his mind, resolved and unraveled, finished, he was on to his next mystery, his next set of intricacies.

And no matter how good his intentions, how much he believed he wanted to be with her now, his attention span for her just might not extend beyond figuring out who'd ripped the necklace off her neck Friday night, and why, and how all the pieces fit together.

He joined her at the wine bar. "You're looking restless," he said.

She managed a smile. "I was just thinking the same about you."

"I *am* restless. Have you noticed Griffen and Deegan? They seem to be on the skids to me. I'm wondering if they know more than they're saying."

"Me, too." She inhaled, thoughts and images swarming over her, snippets of conversations flooding her brain. "Jeremiah—"

He stiffened. "What is it?"

"I haven't thought of this before, but it's been sifting around since I talked to Griffen a little while ago. It's possible—they could be another common denominator."

"Griffen and Deegan?"

She nodded. "I'm not positive. She said something to me earlier, and it's been eating at me . . ." She paused, pushing through her uncertainties about him, about what she was saying. "I could never testify to it—and maybe it's just the wine and the stresses of the past few days—but I wouldn't be surprised if they made some kind of appearance at every event the thief hit. They might just stop in for a few minutes, like they did on Friday, or Griffen would be catering—"

"Like the luncheon yesterday."

Mollie nodded. Guests were floating around, but not within earshot. "I'm not suggesting they're involved, just that with Croc turning out to be Kermit Tiernay, maybe we need to look at this thing from a different angle."

"Croc might have known they were common denominators, too, and just not told me. He could have suspected his brother, his brother's girlfriend, his brother's boss, or any combination of the three of you. He asked me to check you out first, maybe hoping you'd be the thief, and you were acting alone, and his worst suspicions about his brother weren't true. He didn't know about our past."

"But once I was eliminated as a serious suspect, he had to take a good, hard look at his brother."

"And it got him beaten up and left for dead."

"Deegan couldn't have—"

Jeremiah cut her off. "We're speculating, Mollie, and I hate it because it usually ends up making me miss something important. But there's nothing wrong with keeping an open mind and entertaining all the possibilities."

"Then you're saying it's possible—just possible—that Deegan had his brother beaten up—or did it himself—to throw suspicion off himself."

"Only the police aren't biting," Jeremiah said thoughtfully, "at least not yet. Frank Sunderland's instincts are telling him the necklace was a plant."

"Griffen?" Mollie suggested, her heart pounding, blood rushing to her head.

"Possibly. Maybe she's the thief and Deegan's protecting her. Or they're in it together. I'll go talk to Croc."

"Now, you mean?"

"Sure. You've got a crowd here, a security guard. It's a good time. And if Croc will level with me, maybe we can end this thing tonight. It's a distraction," he said, "from things I'd rather be thinking about. And doing."

She felt a welcome rush of heat. "Tell Croc I forgive him for thinking I was a jewel thief."

Jeremiah grinned, the light suddenly catching his eyes. "You think he'll care?"

After he'd gone, Deegan joined her on the terrace. "I see Tabak just left."

"Oh—yes, he promised your brother he'd stop in."

"Mollie, are you okay?"

"I'm fine." She hated herself for what she was thinking. That her intern could be a thief capable of beating up his own brother, that her best friend could be in on it. She gave him a phony smile. "Looks as if you, Griffen, and I are pulling off a pleasant party. Shall we see to our guests?"

Jeremiah made the fifteen-minute drive to the Tiernays' elegant oceanside home in ten minutes. There was a security system, but no fence, no gates. He felt a little strange driving a Jaguar up the long, curving driveway of a very expensive, beautifully landscaped home. As if he could belong here if only he tried.

And this was Croc's home, he thought, gritting his teeth.

He parked in the driveway, hurried up the brick walk to the front door, and rang the doorbell. A uniformed maid answered and sent him around back to the guest house, which was easily three times the size of the glorified shack where he grew up. The door was open, the maid had said. He knocked and went in.

Croc was installed in a cheerful blue and white

room with an incredible view of the water. His swelling had gone down even further, which made talking somewhat easier. He was sitting up in bed with a basketball game on a small television. His posh surroundings seemed to have no effect, positive or negative.

"Hey, Tabak." His words were slurred, but intelligible.

"How're you doing? Settling in okay?"

He nodded. "For now."

"Doesn't look as if your parents want to crowd you. If you're going to go back to living out of a box, that's what you'll do."

He shrugged, saying nothing.

"You'll sort it out, Croc. Hell, a year from now maybe you'll be a suit at Tiernay & Jones. You never know."

Croc's brow furrowed, and he hurled a pillow at Jeremiah, missing by yards, groaning in pain as he sank back against his pillows.

Jeremiah grinned. "You won't be playing shortstop in the majors, that's for sure. You're young, Croc. You've got time to screw up your life and put it back together again." He walked over to the windows and looked out at the horizon, sky and sea meeting in a haze. Twilight. Calm. He thought of Mollie and her party and her worries. "Provided you don't get yourself killed."

"I came too close this time."

"Yes, you did."

Croc made a slurping sound, trying to keep spit from running down his chin. "You'd have blamed yourself?"

"And whoever beat the hell out of you."

Jeremiah sighed, feeling his fatigue, the frustration of his role in this mess. As a journalist, he knew where he stood: his job was to get the story and report it. But this time, he wasn't acting as a journalist. He didn't have a prescribed set of rules to follow. He was involved.

He walked over to the edge of Croc's bed, his body barely visible under the blue-and-white striped coverlet. "Croc, you didn't steal Mollie's necklace."

It wasn't a question, but Kermit Tiernay said, "Nope."

"But you know something," Jeremiah said.

Croc turned his attention back to the television.

"I've had most of today to think because my best source on this thing has his jaw wired shut and can't yak at me the way he usually does about conspiracies, fantasies, goblins, and ghosts." His stab at humor failed, his voice registering all the tension and urgency he was feeling. "Left to my own devices, I've come to the tentative conclusion that we're dealing with more than one person. One is willing to use violence. One isn't."

Croc's eyes never left the television, but he pulled his scrawny arms out from under the covers and said, "The thief and whoever hired the thug."

"I'm thinking coverup," Jeremiah said. "Someone wanted to pin this thing on you to keep the real thief from being caught. In order to frame you, he had to steal the necklace from Mollie. He did it in the most expedient way he could, possibly because he doesn't blend in with the Palm Beach crowd as easily as the real thief." He paused. "Are you following me?"

Croc lifted his gaze to him and said nothing.

Jeremiah smiled, without humor. "You're not following me—you led me here. Mr. Harvard." He felt his body go stiff, willed himself to stay centered. "The thief steals. He likes the element of risk and danger. He doesn't attack. This second person wants to mislead the police, you, me, Mollie. Mislead, cover up, and scare off."

"Protect." Croc winced, hissing as he breathed through his wired teeth. "Mislead the police."

Croc's words were almost unintelligible, but Jeremiah got their meaning. He breathed in, thinking.

"The thief . . ." Croc adjusted his position, groaning almost inwardly from the pain. "Ribs."

"I know, Croc. You don't need this aggravation."

He waved a bony, bruised hand in dismissal. His eyes, a muddier green than usual, grew serious. "The thief . . . daring and stupid . . ."

"Like you were at nineteen?"

He nodded without comment, but Jeremiah knew he, too, was thinking about his younger brother. His face screwing up in pain, he threw back the covers and kicked his legs over the side of the bed.

"Croc, what the hell are you doing?"

"Mollie's party. I gotta go."

Jeremiah felt a sudden chill. "Why? What do you know?"

His bony feet landed on the floor, and he reeled, steadied himself, held a crooked arm over his wrapped ribs. He had on shorts and a polo shirt, both new. "Let's go, Tabak." Drool dribbled down his chin. "No time."

"Croc, this is insane. You're hurt. You'll never

make it to the damned car. *I* won't make it before the maid calls the police and accuses me of kidnapping."

"Let her."

"Croc . . ."

The eyes leveled on Jeremiah, the imaginative, hyperbolic Kermit Tiernay replaced by a young man of great focus and clarity. "Tabak, Mollie's next."

He held his breath. "You can tell me on the way."

Mollie's first Palm Beach cocktail party went off without a hitch, her guests departing promptly at eight, off to other dinners and parties. She and Griffen slumped on lounge chairs, Griffen moaning in relief before beginning the cleanup. "I don't know why I was so nervous," she said, kicking off her shoes. "You'd think it was my reputation on the line."

Deegan dropped onto a chair beside her. He looked handsome, calm, confident. Mollie wondered if she'd been an ass for suspecting him. He grinned at her and Griffen. "At least it went off without incident."

Griffen groaned. "Thank *God*."

"It makes me wonder if my brother really is . . . well, no, it doesn't. Kermit wouldn't have the energy or the ambition to steal."

"You think he's innocent?" Mollie asked.

"Yeah, I do."

Griffen, suddenly restless, flung herself to her feet. "I'd better start cleaning up or I'm likely just to strike a match and call it a night. Deegan, would you mind doing a survey of the house, give me an idea of what kind of mess I've got to face in there?"

"No problem."

He strode off to the well-lit house, and Mollie followed Griffen over to her makeshift wine bar. "Griffen, there's no rush—"

"Thanks, but we're all tired. I know I am."

Mollie hesitated. "About what you said earlier—"

Griffen swung around, her dark curls whipping into her face. "Will you forget what I said earlier? *Please?*" She sounded grouchy and tired more than distressed. "It didn't mean anything."

"But, Griffen, if you've got any ideas or insight about what's going on with the Tiernays and this jewel thief—"

"I don't. I'm sorry, Mollie. Look, I need to get busy. I'm dead on my feet."

Mollie relented, wondering if Griffen's obvious romantic problems with Deegan had affected her judgment and what she'd said *hadn't* meant anything. She'd rehashed her friend's words dozens of times while trying to enjoy her guests.

It would help if Jeremiah returned.

She retreated into the house to see about cleanup and Deegan. She felt a faint uneasiness at not quite knowing who was still behind Leonardo's gates, on the property with her. When she got everyone out, she planned to jump in the pool, clothes and all.

If Jeremiah was back, maybe not clothes and all.

She smiled, her body humming at the thought of him.

She gathered up paper cocktail napkins on the kitchen counters, no sign of Deegan in the sprawling kitchen.

Then she heard a noise coming from the media room. She stopped, motionless, and listened, her heart drumming.

A sob.

Someone was crying.

Moving quietly, she edged to the doorway and peered into the huge leather-and-wood room.

Deegan Tiernay sat in the middle of the floor, his arms wrapped around his knees, shaking, sobbing.

"Deegan?" Mollie rushed in. "Deegan, what's wrong? Are you hurt?"

He shook his head, and when she reached him, she saw tears streaming down his cheeks and chin, dripping onto his knees, all the cockiness and charm gone. His eyes were bloodshot, his nose was running. And she knew it had all gotten to him. He was twenty, and his brother had nearly been killed, and it was his fault.

"Deegan . . ."

"You know, don't you?" His voice was hoarse from crying; she could see him squeezing his knees together as hard as he could, as if that would somehow keep him from flying apart. "Griffen . . . Griffen's suspicious. I can tell. She's different . . . God, I can't believe . . ." He sank his face between his knees and sobbed uncontrollably, his back shaking.

Mollie touched his shoulders, felt the hot sweat and strong muscles through his shirt. "Deegan, you're young." She was surprised at the gentleness of her own voice, her lack of animosity toward him. He would have to account and make amends and pay for what he'd done, and he would have to get help. "You can't see the forest for the trees right now. If you call the police yourself . . ."

His head shot up, and he screamed, a numbing, wordless, fierce sound that seemed to come from his very soul. Finally, his shoulders slumping, he got control of himself. He sniffled. "Mollie, this isn't your problem. I never meant to make it your problem." His lower lip and chin trembled. "I'm so scared. Kermit . . . he can't take the fall for me."

"I know. I understand."

"No, no, you don't. I didn't . . . I could never have done that to my own brother. To you. I . . . you . . ." His voice croaked, tears and spit mixing together on his chin. "I was just having fun. Then everything went haywire."

She frowned. "You mean you didn't attack me or make the threatening call? Deegan—"

"Whoa, kid. Don't answer that."

They both looked up at the sound of the calm, unfamiliar male voice. The security expert. George Marcotte. His man must have let him in. He was a big, fit, muscular man whose size at the luncheon yesterday Mollie had found reassuring. Now she stared at him, confused, banking back the flutter of fear.

He addressed Deegan first. "Relax, kid. I'm not here to hurt anyone."

Mollie rose. "Mr. Marcotte—"

"Now, hold on, Miss Lavender. Just hold on." He seemed perfectly calm, as if he did this sort of thing every day. "I'm glad my guy kept your little party this evening crime-free. However, I have something I need to do. You can sit on the couch there and be quiet. Okay?"

As if she had a choice. Glancing at Deegan, whose face had gone pale beneath the red splotches, she dropped onto the couch in the middle of the room. Leonardo's media equipment—for viewing, recording, and listening—surrounded her.

Marcotte moved deeper into the room. He didn't swagger, didn't waste any energy on unnecessary displays of ego. Again he addressed Deegan. "Here's the deal, kid. The thefts stop."

"They already have—"

"Wait." He held up a hand, quieting Deegan. "Let me finish here. As I said, the thefts stop. If they've stopped already, that's good. Then I can stop beating up skinny kids and robbing pretty blondes to throw the police off your scent. I mean, it was a kick at first, and a man's got to make a living, but I take no pride in that kind of work."

Mollie came forward on the couch. "The police—"

"The police have shit. They're confused as hell. This whole thing will die a nice, quiet death if this spoiled little fuck here knocks it off and you and that reporter knock it off."

"Jeremiah and me? We haven't—"

"You have and you are. Look, I don't care. Really. I'm on a time clock, so to speak. I'm hired to get results, and results I get. My point is, if we all just figure out what's in our individual interest, we'll do okay here. If not, then this thing keeps going, and it keeps getting worse. That's hard on you. It's hard on me. You remember my speech, right? Expedience is the key here. You fight only to get away. And I'm offering you a way out."

Mollie suddenly felt chilled. "Mr. Marcotte, you don't understand Jeremiah Tabak. He isn't going to back off a story just because you want Deegan—"

"Not me, Miss Lavender. I don't give a shit about Deegan."

"All right. Then Jeremiah isn't going to back off

just because whoever hired you wants to keep Deegan from getting caught. My God. Why didn't you put the fear of God into him sooner?"

Marcotte shrugged his massive shoulders. "We thought he'd get scared off at the idea of some real muscle horning in on his territory."

"That was the attack on me."

"Yep. Didn't work. The little fuck swiped Lucy Baldwin's watch. Didn't work to try to put the fear of God in you, either, I might add. So, it was on to Plan B."

"Croc."

"He'll take the fall for the thefts. Deegan here will get with the program and shut up."

"And me?" she asked quietly.

"I'm thinking."

Deegan sniffled, but he'd stopped crying. He looked spent. Dropping his hands to the floor, he pushed himself up on his feet. A flash of the old cockiness asserted itself. "You can go to hell. So can whoever hired you. I'm calling the police and confessing. *You* can explain what you did."

"They'll lay everything on you. All the thefts, the call, the attack on your brother. That's the idea, you know. To put you between a rock and a hard place. If you confess, you get the whole ball of wax dumped in your lap because it's easier that way."

"You fucking son of a bitch—"

"Who hired you?" Mollie asked, breaking in before Deegan could try to jump the guy. "The Tiernays? They must have realized Deegan was in over his head and tried to stop him—"

Marcotte snorted. "You kidding? They don't have a clue what their little angel here's been up to."

Diantha Atwood came into the room from the opposite entrance. Regal and calm, she sighed at her grandson. "I thought this might work. I honestly thought it might. Obviously we'll have to try sterner measures."

Deegan gaped at his grandmother. "What are you talking about?"

"I had hoped we could leave this case unsolved. But I can see that even if you will listen to reason, Mollie and Jeremiah won't. So, we have to solve this case for them. Or for Jeremiah, at least."

"I said I'd confess—"

"No, no. That's not an option." She quietly removed her hand from behind her back and leveled a gun, not a big one but big enough, at George Marcotte. "We caught Mr. Marcotte here in the middle of robbing Mr. Pascarelli's house. He tried to fire on us, but I, in self-defense, shot him. We then discovered my favorite, most expensive bracelet in his pocket. He's our thief."

"You crazy old bat," Marcotte said. "What about Tabak and Lavender?"

"Let me worry about them. I believe you're what's called the fall guy, Mr. Marcotte. Everything will be credited to you." She kept her gun leveled at him. "Please don't despair, Deegan. It's no loss."

Mollie's tongue and lips had gone dry, her throat was so tight she could barely breathe. Deegan, motionless, continued to stare at his grandmother. "Gran, you can't do this. It's wrong. Jeremiah will be back any minute, and Mollie will tell the police exactly what she saw. She won't lie for you."

"But you will," Diantha Atwood said.

Which had to mean, Mollie thought, that she wouldn't need to lie. "You're going to kill me, aren't you? You'll say I got caught in the cross fire or that Marcotte killed me first and that's why you fired on him. Something."

"That's *stupid*." Marcotte glared at the older woman, showing no sign he was afraid. "Lady, you don't know what you're doing."

Diantha Atwood gave him a cold look. "I should remember, if I were you, who has to resort to beating up weaker people in order to survive in this world. Deegan, please leave the room. I don't want you to have to see the ugly reality of what your behavior has forced me to do."

"Gran . . ."

"Go, Deegan. Now."

He hesitated, panic and confusion clouding his face. His grandmother aimed her gun. Mollie had no idea if the woman knew how to shoot. Marcotte, she could see, had the same question. He moved. Deegan jumped, dove for his grandmother, yelled, "No!" as the gun went off.

Diantha Atwood screamed in horror. "Deegan! Deegan, my God, no!"

Mollie dropped beside him, saw the blood oozing from his right side. She grabbed a throw pillow off the couch and pressed it against the wound while his grandmother became hysterical. "It's okay, Deegan," she whispered as he grimaced, barely breathing, barely conscious. "I'll get you to a hospital. I'll take care of you. Just hang on."

In her peripheral vision, Mollie could see Marcotte moving fast, removing the gun from Diantha Atwood's flagging grip and backhanding her to the floor.

"You stupid bitch," he said, calm, cold, "you shot your own grandson."

At which point, Jeremiah charged into the room, Kermit Tiernay hobbling behind him, white-faced, taking in his bleeding brother and horrified grandmother.

Mollie made her voice work. "He's got a gun."

"I see," Jeremiah said.

But he didn't stop. He couldn't. Some dark force seemed to drive him forward, and Mollie shot to her feet, grabbing another throw pillow and whipping it at Marcotte. It was just enough to distract him for a fraction of a second. Jeremiah dove. The two men went down hard, Marcotte's superior size and experience no match for Jeremiah's fury. He gripped Marcotte's gun hand, keeping him from firing, pounding his knuckles into the floor, yelling, "Mollie, goddamnit, get the gun!"

Croc jumped down beside his brother, ignoring his grandmother as she tried to push him away. Kermit wasn't her favorite anymore.

Mollie scrambled to Jeremiah, pulled the gun from Marcotte's hand even as he got position on Jeremiah and threw him off. Both men sprang to their feet, coiled, ready to rip each other apart.

Hating the feel of the gun in her hands, Mollie leveled it. "Stop. *Stop!* Marcotte, I'm not a good shot, but you're one hell of a big target. Who knows what I'd hit. So cut your losses and . . . and just stop."

He did, breathing hard. "You're a bunch of crazy fucks. The money's not worth this crap. Damn, I don't know why—" He glared at Diantha Atwood. "You're going down with me, bitch."

Jeremiah turned to Mollie, and she gave him a quivering smile. "You're late."

"I'm never late," he said. "I was just in the nick of time."

The gun was shaking. *She* was shaking. "Deegan . . ."

Jeremiah moved toward her. "We need to call an ambulance and get the police here. I don't know where the phones are. Maybe if you give me the gun . . ."

She had it in a death grip. She couldn't seem to pry her fingers loose.

Marcotte watched it, the color going out of him. "Jesus Christ. Her finger's on the damned trigger."

"It's *stuck*."

"Tabak . . ."

"Mollie." His voice was soothing, as if he were making love to her. He eased beside her and touched her shoulder, a whisper of warmth. "I'll put my hand under the gun. You just relax and let go. Okay?"

She nodded.

One hand still on her shoulder, he placed the other one palm up under the butt of the gun. His skin felt so hot. No wonder she couldn't let go. Her fingers were icicles.

"Mollie, the phone. You need to call 911. Just let go, and I'll get rid of this thing. Come on, sweet pea. I'm here. We're here together."

Her fingers released.

Marcotte sagged. He sank against the wall.

Croc had his arms around his brother, his head in his lap, and if he was in any pain from his own injuries, he didn't show it. He kept the pillow pressed up hard against the wound. Deegan was unconscious. Diantha Atwood sobbed soundlessly, her slender body shaking violently. "Call an ambulance," she said hoarsely. "Please. Hurry. I was only trying to protect him. Things just got out of hand."

With a fresh wave of adrenaline kicking in, Mollie left Marcotte and Diantha Atwood to Jeremiah and raced into the kitchen. She gave the 911 dispatcher everything she had, told her she might want to get Frank Sunderland here, and in the back of her mind — far back, where she was still sane and led a normal life—she knew she'd have to tell her family and Leonardo about this one.

When she hung up, she stood in the dark, quiet kitchen. Jeremiah. There'd been nothing neutral or objective in the way he'd tackled the thug who'd beaten up his friend, who had a gun on her. She smiled, fighting back tears. He was maddening. Utterly maddening. And yet, once again, she couldn't imagine her life going on without him.

But it might have to.

The story had reached its conclusion, and as confident as she was that what they'd had in the past few days was real to him, she just couldn't be sure it would last.

Then she thought of Deegan Tiernay, bleeding in the next room, and Croc, and Diantha Atwood, and she picked up the phone to call Michael and Bobbi Tiernay.

But as she reached for the phone, it rang. She picked up the receiver. "Mollie Lavender."

"Mollie, m'girl, I knew you'd be there."

It was Leonardo, boisterous and exhausted. She felt the tears forming, spilling into her eyes. "Leonardo, it's what, three or four o'clock in the morning in Austria?"

"I couldn't sleep. I had to know. Tell me, m'darling, how was your party?"

17

The Palm Beach cat burglar was front-page material on virtually every newspaper in the country, including the *Miami Tribune*.

Helen Samuel wrote the story.

It was her first front-page story in her fifty-year career. She arrived on Jeremiah's doorstep to show him. He told her she got the front page because it was a slow news day. "Otherwise, it'd be buried inside."

"Ha! You're just jealous." She was out front with the boys, passing out cigarettes and copies of the *Trib* with her byline above the fold, as delighted with herself as Jeremiah had been at twenty-six. "We've got not one but two rich boys, we've got a doting rich grandma with a gun, we've got a hired thug, and we've got you, Tabak." That last she clearly loved. "A Pulitzer Prize–winning reporter tackling a two-hundred-twenty-pound security expert in Leonardo Pascarelli's media room. Damned good thing you were heroic or your reputation would be shit right now. You watch, it'll be a TV movie."

"Don't forget the publicist," he said.

"I'm not. She's the innocent, the ordinary person caught up in extraordinary circumstances with her unique set of clients. A jazz-playing Apollo astronaut. A mutt. Then there's the caterer."

"Griffen Welles."

She'd entered the kitchen to finish cleaning up and had found her boyfriend shot and bleeding, a battered Croc holding him, a white-faced best friend, and Jeremiah holding a gun on a near-catatonic elderly socialite and a well-known security expert. The police and ambulance were en route. And so were the Tiernays. Unwilling to leave his brother's side, Croc had asked for a portable phone and called them himself.

"It's a great story," Helen said with a satisfied sigh. Forty-eight hours after it was over, and she still hadn't let it go. "Of course, I knew it would be. That's why I kept giving you the dish and letting you do the running around. I'm too old for that shit."

Sal, Bennie, and Al passed around a book of matches and watched her, transfixed. Sal looked particularly smitten. Jeremiah just shook his head.

Helen grinned at him. "God, this feels good. The kids're going to be all right, you know. Deegan and Kermit. Their folks got with the program in the end. Momma was a little late on the upswing, but she's at the hospital round the clock, had Kermit moved into the main house. They're making the younger boy take responsibility for what he did, but they're right there with him."

"He got their attention," Jeremiah said.

"That he did. Atwood's only talking to her lawyers, but the way I see it, she was raised by disengaged parents, then raised her own daughter that way. The generational cascade at work. The triumph of form over substance." She flicked her half-smoked cigarette onto the porch and ground it out with her foot; the guys, Jeremiah knew, would do likewise. "You figure out what to do about your blonde?"

He rolled up on his feet. He'd spent last night at his apartment; he'd needed the space, Mollie had needed the space, and his reptiles needed to know he was still alive. Plus, Bennie, Al, and Sal had wanted details. They'd left a message on his voice mail—it was Sal who figured out how to use it—saying they were renting a car and driving up to Palm Beach if he didn't get down there. Over bagels and coffee and a little whittling on the porch that morning, Jeremiah gave them details, and they gave him advice. Unsolicited advice. It had to do with marriage, commitment, kids, and having a life. And a dog. Bennie thought he should get rid of the reptiles and get a dog. A beagle would be good.

Then Helen had arrived.

He regarded her with an affection that even a month ago he would have thought impossible. "Yes," he told her, "I most certainly know what to do about my blonde."

Mollie didn't know how they did it. Busy musicians all, her parents, her sister, and Leonardo all managed to arrive at the West Palm Beach Airport within an hour of each other. They brought their instruments, and tons of unnecessary clothes because they hadn't taken the time to think about what they really needed, and they wanted to hear everything, the whole story, all over again, from start to finish. It was a transparent show of support that Mollie appreciated.

They were out back, now, with Griffen Welles and Chet and a few other of her clients, all making sure she was okay, that she didn't feel alone and isolated in her new home. She'd wandered out front to get her bearings.

A battered brown truck rattled to a stop in front of Leonardo's driveway. Her heart skipped a beat when Jeremiah climbed out and sauntered around front, then leaned against the hood. "Going to let me in?"

"We had the security codes changed, just in case."

"Ah. Is this a hint?"

He knew it wasn't. His tone, his bearing, even his straight line of a mouth told her he knew exactly how hard she'd fallen for him this time. She opened the gates, and he left his truck where it was, just walked on in and slid his arms around her, kissed her.

Stopped cold.

"What the hell is that?"

Mollie listened a moment. " 'The Volga Boatmen,' I think."

"A recording?"

"Leonardo Pascarelli, Bart and Amy Lavender, Cecily Lavender, and Chet Farnsworth. I think Griffen might be singing, too."

He frowned. "Your family's here?"

"Uh-huh. They called en route. That's an improvement, you know. Usually they don't call at all."

"Flakes," he said.

She laughed. "They'll never change, you know. They are what they are."

His arms tightened around her. "We're fortunate, Mollie. Very fortunate. You have your crazy family, and I have my father. Croc and Deegan . . . I don't know. I wouldn't have wanted to grow up like that."

"How is Croc?"

"Last I saw, he was eating a plate of french fries with way too much ketchup out at his parents' pool. He'll be okay. He's got a lot to work out."

"And you'll be there helping him."

"He lied to me, and he's no prize. Harvard, a damned trust fund baby. But yeah, I'll be there." He stared out toward the backyard, the singing growing louder and more boisterous with every measure. "You know, I have a feeling that lot out there won't care if we keep a lizard on the kitchen table."

"We, huh?"

He grinned at her. "You want your own lizard? I'm of the what's-mine-is-yours school. If I get Leonardo Pascarelli and your daffy family, you get my lizard."

Her stomach fluttered, her head spun. It was the heat, the trauma of the past days, the proximity of this man she'd loved too hard, too long. Yet she didn't give away her turmoil of feelings. "What about your family?"

"My mother died when I was twelve. My father never remarried and never will. I used to see that as depressing, as an unwillingness to move on with his life, but now I don't. He's happy. He's grateful for the years they had."

"But his experience made you afraid to commit yourself to anyone."

"But I did anyway," he said, his mouth meeting hers briefly, a promise. "I love you, Mollie. I've loved you for a long, long time. I was just too stupid to see it until now. I'm like my father, Mollie. There's only one woman for me. When you know that, in your gut, and yet when you've seen life's unfairness—" He paused, and she could see him searching for the right words. "Ten years ago I just thought I was a romantic fool."

"You still are, Tabak, and you're the one for me." She kissed him softly. "You always have been."

"Even when you were telling me to rot in hell?"

"Even then."

He smiled. "Shall we go tell your family?"

"They won't be surprised."

"They see it coming, do they?"

"No. They're just never surprised. They'll just say, 'Oh, wonderful, then come, sit, and sing along with us.'"

"I can't sing."

"You can't?" She grinned, tucked her hand into his. "Now *that* will surprise them."